THE RAGE THAT FOLLOWS

NATHANIEL BADERTSCHER

Cover Art by Ameur Makhloufi

ISBN-13: 978-0-9991738-0-0

❀ Created with Vellum

CONTENTS

Dedication   v

1. The Face in the Woods   1
2. Last Day of Peace   15
3. The Story   31
4. Disappearance   64
5. The Search   80
6. Massacre   117
7. Pursuit   134
8. The Cavern   149
9. Murder   161
10. Final Ascent   189
11. The Burnt Lady   195
12. Rage   221

Author's Note   231

THE FACE IN THE WOODS

J oren Olensen crouched down behind a mossy tree, glanced carefully around it, and scanned the other side of the thundering river. Something tugged at his sleeve, and he turned to see Princess Agata's expectant face, mouth open and about to speak. Before she could, he quickly placed a finger on his lips, and she swallowed and let go of his tunic, her eyes wide. They had come a long way in the last three days, since the monster he was tracking had killed the king, and could not risk alerting the beast to their presence before they had an opportunity to strike.

Joren looked past the trees again and saw the horrible monstrosity on the near side of the river, crouching over a bloodied carcass. Crooked tusks rose from beneath its porcine snout, and its eyes surveyed the grasslands before it in a haze.

The volcano above them raged, spilling molten innards down its flanks. Joren knew it would not be long before the lava overran the fields, so, clenching his jaw, he stepped out from behind the tree. With the princess following close behind, he slunk as low as possible through the grass, using scattered rocks and old stumps to shield himself from the monster's view.

Something snapped behind him, and he whipped around to see Agata's tiny foot retreating from the twig it had just cracked in two. She turned guilty eyes up toward him as a screech ripped through the evening around them. He turned back just in time to see the beast charging, a giant cleaver held at the ready.

"Run, Agata!" Joren shouted, drawing his blade from its scabbard. He swung hard, and their weapons met with a mighty clash. The princess shrieked and ran, her stubby legs moving clumsily under her long dress. The beast squealed again as it leveled another blow at the warrior, but Joren leapt back, swinging his ancient blade in a desperate arc.

The sword shivered with a loud crack as he connected with his enemy's head. The monster staggered and looked up at him, and its eyes widened. "Ow," it whined, "too hard, Joren!"

"Sorry, Pedr!" Joren dropped his little stick as the world faded back into reality. He went quickly to his little brother and grabbed his head, rubbing vigorously where the blow had landed. Pedr squeezed his eyes shut, little tears escaping and running down his pink cheeks. "Any better?"

He shrugged Joren off and carefully prodded his scalp. "No," he grumbled. "Why am I always the one who gets whacked?"

Joren smirked. "Because I'm better than you."

"Well," Pedr said, glancing surreptitiously behind his older brother's back, "that's only because I haven't revealed my secret ally yet!"

"Oh really? And who might that be?"

Pedr leapt into an attack stance, pointed with a flourish, and bellowed, "Get him, Aggy!"

Before Joren could turn and look, their baby sister stumbled back out from behind a stump, giggling and shrieking, her over-sized head too busy looking down at her feet to see where she was going. Agata ran full into his leg and bounced back, falling on her bottom, while Pedr leapt forward with a flurry of slaps and half-hearted punches.

"Ouch, hey!" Joren laughed, using one arm to hold back his assailant and the other to reach down and mercilessly tickle Agata's belly. "Alright, I yield, I yield!" he hollered, and crouched into a ball to defend against Pedr's onslaught. After a moment, his little brother relented, whooping and leaping away to flex his arms in victory.

Joren bent and scooped up Agata, resting her on his hip. "I thought you were supposed to be on my side." Breathless, she shielded her belly from him.

The sun had just settled, turning the raging volcano above back into the snowy peak of the Ymr Mountains, and the cool air of early-summer evening coursed down into the valley.

"Boys!" their father's voice came from the pasture behind their steading. "Come, I need your help with the sheep!"

Together, they plodded back across the little stream. Darting past them, their shaggy sheepdog made to cut off a stray. Pedr chased after her, making battle noises and waving his stick over his head, while Joren carried his sister around the flock to their father. The big man leaned on his old crook as he ushered his sheep back into their little shelter for the night.

"Here, let me have her," he said, taking Agata, and pointed with his chin back toward the stream. "One of the lambs fell behind, there." He passed his crook to Joren. "Go fetch him, and bring Hala with you."

Joren shouldered the weighty staff and took off at a trot, calling the sheepdog to him. He could see the lamb at the stream's edge, strutting about on unpracticed legs. Hala fell in step and they hurried to retrieve him.

As they reached the spot, Hala circled around the little animal to urge him back toward the shelter. She stopped short, however, and turned to face the forest. Joren nabbed the lamb as he tried to escape, tucked him under his arm, and started back. When the sheepdog did not follow, he turned to see what had caught her attention. "What is it, Hala?"

She sniffed at the air and kept her eyes trained on the forest. The shadows between the trees were deepening rapidly, and the breeze shifted the darkness before him, bringing strange shapes to life.

Hala suddenly jumped and positioned herself between him and the trees, barking angrily. Joren took a step back, then another as the lamb squirmed in his arms. He inspected the shadows of the forest hastily, terrified of the wolves he was sure would burst out at any moment.

His eye caught a shape moving opposite the branches and shrubs that swayed in the wind and he stumbled. A small white face stood out from the shadows, gaunt and withered, twisted in fury. Its cracked lips moved deliberately, whispering words he could not hear.

His throat too tight to scream, Joren turned to run, but his foot caught on a stone and he tumbled to the ground. The lamb spilled out of his arms and took off toward the safety of the shelter. Joren's mind was white with fear as he scrambled back to his feet. Hala abruptly quieted and came up beside him, poking his leg with her nose. He clutched the crook desperately before him and looked to where the face had been. It was gone.

Struggling to compose himself, he reached down and laid his hand on Hala's head. She was calm again, which put him a little at ease. He hoped that meant the thing was gone, or better, that he had imagined it. After a long few moments of waiting and searching the trees, the horrible face did not reappear, so he turned away, and together they hurried back to the hall.

"Joren, you're ashen," his father remarked, stepping out of the shelter and closing the heavy gate behind him. "Is everything alright?"

Joren started to tell him about the face, but stopped before the first word escaped. He was eleven years old now, and young men did not go crying to their fathers about frightening shadows in the dark. Instead, he nodded and forced a smile, and his father handed Agata back to him in exchange for his old crook.

With the sheep bedded down and secured for the night, they made their way back around the long hall to the lantern–lit doorway. Joren could just hear the voices of his mother and siblings coming through the thick sod walls, and he took one more calming breath before heading inside.

His baby sister wriggled in his arms, so he let her down. Pedr stood by their mother near the fire pit and held his bowl in both hands, his head cranked back at the ceiling, gasping, "I'm so hungry!"

Their mother gave his hand a little smack and he straightened. She filled her children's bowls one by one with a hearty stew and they all sat at the table. Joren grabbed the big pile of scraps and placed them on the dry, dirt floor for Hala, then took Agata back up and placed her on his knee to help her eat. Usually it was his older sister Vandra's job, but after his fright, he took comfort in her hand holding his while she slurped her oatmeal and babbled happily.

"Joren, eat up before it cools," his mother urged. She turned to her husband. "How were my little shepherds today? Were they a help or a bother?"

Their father gulped down a mouthful of stew. "Oh, they were fine, love, not to worry. This one, though," he glared playfully down at Pedr, "he's more sheepdog than shepherd, running circles around the flock nearly better than Hala."

Joren laughed and looked over at Vandra, who was stirring her supper absently. Their father noticed her listlessness, too. "What's wrong, Van?" he asked, wiping his bristly black beard with the back of his hand. "Is supper not appealing tonight?"

Instead of answering, she took a reluctant bite.

"More, please!" Pedr requested, holding his empty bowl aloft. Their mother sighed and rose to fill it. "Wait, I can do it!" he cried, and swung his legs over the bench to race to the pot.

She held a commanding hand out toward him, stopping him in place. "If you think for a moment I'd let you anywhere near this fire, you're a madman. Sit." He obeyed with an unhappy grumble. "Vandra has been swooning over the boy who came up with Old Havar last autumn," she explained to her husband.

"Mama!" Vandra cried, her cheeks reddening. Their father threw his head back and let out a bark of laughter.

Joren thought back, trying to remember Old Havar's last trip. The old trader had brought goods to barter with their father before winter set in. He did not remember anything special about the man's grandson, other than the fact that he was annoying.

"Your father needs to know these things, Vandra," her mother said, returning to the table. "I was only a few years older than you when our fathers placed us together."

"Well, hold on now." Her husband held up his hand and coughed as he tried to regain his composure. "I intend on doing much better for Vandra than Havar's mewling little churl." Joren and Pedr both snorted. "No, one of those well-to-do farmers in the east, I think, or maybe even one of Chieftain Ranjarson's men, eh?"

Tears welled in Vandra's eyes and she stood without a word, ran to the loft ladder, and hurried up and out of sight.

Joren's father gave his wife a baffled look. "What did I say?"

"She's not interested in farmers or chiefs' men!" she replied, indignant. "She saw a boy her age for the first time in her life and she's dreaming about his handsome eyes. Just let her have that, Olen."

Joren's father put his hands up in surrender. "Of course, my lovely wife, I had no idea what was at stake here." His face was grave. "By the Slain, the mention of it will never cross my lips again!"

His wife rolled her eyes and they all finished their stew in silence, save Agata, who continued her wordless jabbering.

After supper, Joren and Pedr took Hala out to the shelter so she could keep watch over the sheep through the night. The warmth of hearth and home had all but erased the memory of Joren's earlier scare, and his mind was on other, happier things: galavanting as a knight in a strange land, exploring the world, saving mortal-kind from the monsters that roamed the earth.

They used the latrine, hurried back inside, and scrambled up the ladder to their beds in the loft. Vandra was curled up at the far end, facing away from them. He decided the smart thing would be to let her alone and so mimed to Pedr to be silent as well.

As he lay on his favorite fleece, Joren watched through the spaces in the loft floor as his mother took Agata to their parents' bed at the far end of the hall, and his father heaped ashes up over the blazing embers of the fire to keep them alive until the next day. As darkness settled, his mind still wandered the fantasy of his imagination, where there was no room for evil, disembodied faces.

～

Garret Rhys, sergeant of the Knights Seraphin, lowered himself with a wince, stretching out his sore legs and letting his toes warm by the fire. Camp had been set much more quickly that evening than previously; the cold rolling off the mountains had motivated the small group of soldiers to prepare things with a haste that had been lacking in the warmth of southern summer. He was glad to see the improvement, for the harsh climes of the Ymr Mountains — their destination — were known for their bitter treatment of travelers.

Around them, the green reaches of Fjalvard stretched out and dipped into a lush valley before swelling and climbing up to the mountains. The sun had just gone down, and the stars were beginning to twinkle through the twilight. The single tent they erected each night glowed with candlelight, where the detachment's captain and hospitaler worked together in setting down the events of the day in their log.

"Soup, Sergeant?" asked Grim, one of the conscripted fighters they often brought out on assignment.

Rhys took the wooden bowl and sat up straighter to eat. Helmi Gwynlaithe came up and sat herself down beside him, her own bowl of soup in hand. When the Marshal of the Order had informed them that an oracle would be accompanying their detachment north, Rhys had been skeptical, as such a thing was a rare occurrence — perhaps unprecedented. The girl had proven tougher than she looked, however, and maintained a good sense of humor throughout the journey.

"Show me where we're going again?" she requested, pulling her dark hair over one shoulder. Once away from the citadel, she had made a habit of wearing it loose.

Rhys pointed north to the nearby mountain peak, just visible through the warm haze of the fire. "The pass we're aiming for is just west of the Ymr, there."

"No, I meant on your map."

Rhys sighed and dug into the pouch at his belt that held the square of vellum. Unfolding it in his lap, he found the mountain range and marked it for her with his finger. "We started here," he pointed with his other hand at a small emblem of the Eldric

Citadel, home of the Knights Seraphin, and traced his finger along their path through their homeland of Carthannas and up into the far north of Fjalvard to the little village of Kaninholm, only a short distance from where they were camped, "now we're just outside this village here. And we're headed…" he followed the painted valley at the foot of the Ymr north and west, stopping at a line drawn across a section of the mountain range, "there. Hrokar's Pass."

"Let me see it." She snatched it from him, a gleeful twinkle in her eye. Helmi was obsessed with all things written; part of her duties at the Eldric Citadel was the research and cataloguing of documents collected by the Knights. She was so preoccupied with books and scrolls, in fact, that she had insisted on bringing a whole chest full of them along with her; they had been forced to requisition an extra mule in addition to the two they had already been given for the journey just to lug the heavy chest along.

Helmi pored over the map, studying the details with her nose nearly pressed against it. "Are you sure you drew this yourself?"

"Quite," he replied, and took another sip from his bowl. "Why?"

"She doesn't think you've got the skill for that, Sergeant!" one of the twins hooted. Felix and Fergus Comstock were the other conscripted fighters in the detachment, men who were decent in a fight and took orders well enough, but did not have either the necessary potential or the desire to be initiated into the Knights Seraphin.

"I've enough," Rhys replied casually, "though just barely."

"Whatever you do" — it was Fergus speaking, Rhys knew, due to a scar over the right brow that his twin lacked — "don't let the captain get his hands on it. He'll have us over the edge of a cliff or down to some monster's lair in half a dozen steps, no matter the direction." He and his brother both snickered.

"You should listen to him, Sergeant." With impeccable timing, Captain Thorne swept out of the tent and sauntered up to take his bowl from Grim. "I want no part in trying to figure out where I am or where I'm headed — I'm just here to shout orders and generally be commanding." He ran a hand through his blond mane and flashed a winning smile.

Arran Thorne had only recently taken command of the detachment, and though he was very young, Rhys judged him to be of a competent sort. Certainly the Marshal of the Order believed he was a supremely promising officer — the mission into the Ymr was known to be of great importance, and such a command would not be given lightly to so new a captain. Rhys had also heard of some of Thorne's previous exploits, and if the stories were true, he had more than earned his right to lead the vital expedition.

Felix snapped his fingers. "See, that's what the king's army's missing — officers who know what they're good at and what they're not."

"Too right, Comstock." Thorne called both of the scrawny men by their surname, never concerned with telling the two apart. "Besides, if I were to try and riddle out where we were headed, we'd have no use for our poor old scout." He lifted his bowl in a toast to Brother Holywell, the oldest, tallest, and greyest member of the party. The mute returned his toast with a good-natured grin.

"Blackhart!" Rhys called. "Supper's cooling, write later."

"I don't care if it's cold," came the answering shout. "I'm busy."

"Well, I know the lady would enjoy your magnanimous company, so put down your quill and come join us."

Helmi put a hand to her mouth to hide a smile as the huge hospitaler ducked out of the tent and glared from under his perpetually furrowed brows at Rhys. He took the bowl from Grim's outstretched hand and sat on a rock beside the fire, grumbling under his breath.

"Whose work did you copy?" Helmi asked Rhys, her supper forgotten on the ground beside her as she traced the lines on the map with slender fingers. "The illustrations look a little like Harding's."

"I copied no one. Those are all places I've been. I simply scribbled everything I saw on the vellum." She looked at him incredulously, and Rhys could not help but grin. "I don't know whose work it was, Milady. I just found a recent enough map and replicated it as best I could. The notes are mine, though."

"I told you, dispense with 'milady'." She squinted to read the tiny marks. "Ogres in Blackpine Wood, specters in Overdell, Djinn in the Caliphates.... Have you actually seen all of these?"

"Seen, fought, and killed. Lost a number of good men in the struggle, too, gods rest them."

"Gods rest them," Thorne and Grim repeated and raised their bowls.

She shook her head. "I can't even imagine. I've read about all of these creatures, of course, but to see them in person, to face them, fight them.... You all truly are a brave sort, aren't you?"

"Are you missing the citadel already, then?" Fergus teased.

"Hardly. Whatever horrors we are on our way to find, they can't be worse than spending a lifetime locked away in that place."

Grim stepped outside the little ring they made around the fire and brought a bowl to the ninth member of their company. Aedric, the man from Ilba, sat apart from the rest, away from the fire, and gazed up at the stars starting to poke through the pale sunset sky. He quietly accepted Grim's offering, and the young soldier came back to his pot.

Rhys leaned closer to Helmi. "Will you please tell me why we've brought that man along with us?"

"I've already explained," she answered coolly, "I cannot tell you or any else what I may or may not know about him."

"You're quite infuriating for such a generally agreeable young woman."

She smirked. "Why, I'm flattered, Garret."

He grunted and stared at the Ilban, wondering for the hundredth time since they had departed what it was about the stranger that had made the marshal insist he travel with the detachment.

"I will tell you this, though," Helmi said, quietly, so the others would not hear her. "I think we ought not to trust him until we know him better."

"I rarely trust easily." He gave her a skeptical look. "Why do you say that, though?"

"I told you — I can tell you no more. I've taken an oath of silence on the matter." She persisted in that silence, though Rhys tried his best to goad more from her, and returned to the diagram in her lap.

"So, anyone interested in another story?" Grim asked, finally filling his own bowl. "I've remembered a new one what my father's brother used to tell."

"No!" the twins groaned simultaneously, and Fergus added, "For gods' sakes, Grim, no more stories."

"Tough biscuits, boys," he waved aside their objection, "I'm telling one anyway. Let's see, how'd it start…? Oh yes, there was a man once who was quite rich, and he was on the hunt for a grand treasure. No wait, that's not right — he wasn't rich until *after* he found the treasure. Oh, but you're not supposed to know that yet…. Damn, maybe I don't remember it so well, after all. Wait here, I'll go practice and come back."

"Actually, Grim," the captain stopped him with an upraised hand, "I think perhaps it's best to forego any tales tonight. We'll likely start the climb up the slope before tomorrow evening; in the morning, we'll head over to the village and stable the horses. It'll be on foot from there on out, so I would suggest we all try to go to sleep early to prepare."

"Oh." Grim's shoulders slumped. "Yes, Captain."

"Holywell has first watch, then Felix, myself, Grim, and the sergeant. That should see us until dawn." The mute nodded and handed his bowl back to Grim.

Rhys hoisted himself up and offered his hand to Helmi. She stood gracefully without his help. "May I keep this for the night?" she asked, holding up his map.

"As you wish, Milady. But do get some sleep tonight — as the captain said, we've a long day ahead of us tomorrow."

"Helmi," she corrected him. "I will — fret not. Goodnight, Garret."

"Goodnight, Helmi."

She wished the others pleasant dreams and went into the tent, which the captain and Blackhart vacated at night for her use. Rhys started to lay out his own bedroll as the captain came to set up near him.

"You gave the girl your map?" he asked, incredulous. Thorne had been less than enthused about bringing Helmi with them; he saw her as little more than a burden and a liability, and had not shied from letting Rhys know it.

"Just for the evening," he replied, not wanting to engage the captain's misgivings.

"I wish you wouldn't encourage her like that."

Rhys shrugged. "She's an oracle, and likely better-read than you or I."

"She may be an agent of the Order, but she's no Knight," he grumbled. "I don't have a choice about her being here, but I don't like the way she insinuates herself into our business."

Rhys said nothing, hoping Thorne would let the matter drop. After another mumbled complaint that Rhys did not pay particular attention to, he did, and Rhys finished establishing his little sleeping area.

As he stood, he looked over at the Ilban again; the man consistently separated himself from the detachment. Being that he was an intolerably sullen sort, Rhys was partly glad of this, but with Helmi's advice not to trust him, he had decided to be less dismissive of Aedric from then on.

While Grim and the twins went over to the nearby stream to wash the cookware, Rhys sidled over to Holywell. "Keep an eye on that one," he said, indicating the Ilban with a slight inclination of his head. "Tonight and every night until we're rid of him." The mute nodded solemnly.

Once everything was put away and the men were all laid out and drifting off, Rhys finally pulled off his boots and laid himself down under his heavy wool blanket. He tossed fitfully for a while, the fire in his achy joints subsiding slowly. Holywell came over to drop a few more branches on the fire and stoke the embers; as it flared, Rhys saw the Ilban, still sitting alone in the dark outside their camp, staring up at the stars, clutching at something he wore around his neck that Rhys had not noticed before.

When he finally fell asleep, it happened suddenly, without him remembering even closing his eyes.

Something ripped Joren from his dreams. It was still dark and without the fire, the cold had seeped into the hall. He reached up and pulled his fleece tighter about him, still groggy. Instead of falling back to sleep, though, the surreal haze slowly lifted until he was fully awake. It was only then that he became aware of what had woken him.

All over his body, the little hairs were standing on end: from his neck down to his legs. He rubbed his arms to try to banish the goosebumps, but they persisted, their sickening tension flowing into his mind. He thought maybe the cold was causing them, so he groped in the dark to find another fleece to pull over himself.

Finding nothing within reach, he rolled over to his other side, facing Pedr and Vandra. He flailed his hand around on the loft, searching, desperate to be rid of the angst that had inexplicably taken hold of him. His eyes gradually adjusted to the dark even as nausea swept over him and he sat up to look instead of feel. He rubbed his eyes and waited for the bit of moonlight that came in through the smoke holes in the roof to help him see.

The darkness faded slowly until he was able to see his brother and sister, still sound asleep. Beside him, Pedr lay on his back, fleece kicked off in his dreams, snoring softly. The blackness above him lingered longer than the rest.

Then it shifted.

Joren stiffened, and the familiar fear from earlier that evening lanced down his spine again. His breath came hard and fast as panic seized him, though he was stuck in place with terror. The shadow twisted, slowly turning toward him.

Long midnight hair fell away to reveal the blanched face, mouth agape, eyes glassy pools of shadow. Wrath was still written in her features as she turned to regard Joren, a mere arm's length away. The stark whiteness continued down a slender neck to her bosom where her emaciated skin turned black and sooty. As she held his gaze with unblinking eyes, one charred, bony arm unfolded from her side and rose to cover her mouth with a skeletal hand.

After a moment, she turned slowly away from him, fixing her attention on Pedr. Joren watched as the black hands reached out and slid delicately underneath his little brother's head and knees. As she lifted him up, Joren tried to call out and warn his father and mother. All he could manage was a tiny squeak. At the little sound, though, the burnt lady's face appeared suddenly just in front of his, screaming at him in cold, bitter silence.

Joren leapt as he seemed to wake again. His breath came in heaving gasps and he sat up and looked desperately for Pedr. His brother was still there, and the burnt lady, nowhere in sight. Joren's breathing slowed, and he realized he was sitting in a puddle of urine.

Vandra stirred and cast a fleece off her, propped herself up, and looked over at Joren. "Are you alright?" she asked, pulling the hair out of her eyes. "What's happening?"

"Nothing," he answered as smoothly as he could manage. "Nothing, I think…. I think I just had a nightmare."

She wrinkled her nose. "Did Pedr pee himself?"

"Go back to sleep, Van." Joren rolled over onto his knees, cast aside the soiled fleece, and grabbed a new one. Once he had arranged himself, he was terrified to close his eyes. It was a long time before he fell asleep again.

2

LAST DAY OF PEACE

W hen dawn's light finally pierced through the smoke holes in the roof, Joren woke fitfully, his body aching from the stress of his nightmares. He did not want to get up, but neither did he want to remain in bed where thoughts of the burnt lady seemed impossible to escape. The latter urge finally won over and he kicked the fleece off of himself. His linen bottoms were soiled as well so he shucked them and put on just his woolens instead. Then he roused Pedr for their morning trip to the latrine.

The early-summer morning was chilly on the Ymr; Pedr danced around as they walked to keep himself warm. On their way back to the hall, they each picked up a few small logs from the stack next to the shelter.

Inside, their father had brought the embers back to life and added the new wood to the fire. Breakfast was oatmeal and cheese, though Joren found himself without much of an appetite.

"What's wrong with you?" his mother asked unceremoniously, placing a hand on his forehead. "You look like you haven't slept a bit."

Joren cast a sidelong glance at his father, then shrugged. "Nothing, Mama, I'm fine."

"Well, eat up — I don't want you tired *and* hungry."

Joren did as she said and finished his meal, even though he still felt nauseous. Then he remembered his soiled fleece and linens, and the feeling worsened. While his father was still eating, he made his way casually up the ladder, bundled the bottoms up in the sheepskin, and climbed back down.

His mother's eyebrows rose as she saw him. "Joren, what are you up to?"

He froze, trying to think of a likely excuse. Instead, Vandra answered. "I told him and Pedr that we all need to wash our fleeces today. It's starting to get smelly up there." Joren looked at her, still flustered, but she betrayed nothing.

"Oh," their mother shrugged. "Well go on and get it done quickly."

"You boys hurry with that," their father echoed after downing the last of his oatmeal. "We're headed farther out today, east and up the slope, so we need all the time we can get."

Pedr sighed loudly, apparently believing Vandra's lie. They hauled their fleeces down from the loft and went with Joren out into the chilly air.

"Why did you tell Mama that?" Joren asked his sister once Pedr had moved a ways off in front of them. He kept a wary eye on the distant tree line as they walked to the length of stream closest to the hall.

"Because the look on your face told me *you* were the one who peed himself last night," she whispered back. Joren's cheeks flushed. "You haven't done that in years. It must have been a terrible nightmare."

"It was. I just didn't want Papa to find out."

"He wouldn't have cared, Joren," she chided.

"Like he didn't care about Old Havar's grandson?"

Vandra's eyebrows sunk low and she turned and punched him in the arm. "I was trying to make you feel better, you nit!" Her pace quickened.

"Ow!" Joren rubbed his arm and lengthened his stride to match hers. "I'm sorry, Van, I shouldn't have said that." She continued to stomp down the hill, ignoring him. "I'm out of sorts, I'm sorry, please don't be mad at me."

"What are you two fighting about already?" Pedr hollered

over his shoulder as he reached the stream and plunged his fleece into it.

Joren ignored him and grabbed his sister by the arm to stop her. "Van, please!" She whirled to face him, but the angry lines of her face relaxed when she saw the tears welling in his eyes. He reached up and wiped at them preemptively. "I didn't mean anything by it, honest. I'm just… tired."

Vandra stared at him for a moment and then huffed. "It's alright, Joren." She continued down to the water, motioning him to follow. Stopping a few yards upstream from Pedr, she knelt on the bank and started washing. "Why don't you tell me about your dream," she said as he joined her. "It will make you feel better."

"Well," he started, lowering his bundle into the rushing water, "last night, Hala and I had to go fetch a lamb who had wandered away from the flock." He pointed toward the forest. "The sun had already gone down and it was really dark in the trees, and I thought I saw something: a… a face. A terrible face."

"So you dreamt about a face?"

Joren shook his head. "I dreamt about the lady who *had* the face. She was all burned and dead-looking. She was…" he leaned closer and lowered his voice so that it would not carry over the babbling stream to their little brother, "she was hunched over Pedr. She looked at me and then started lifting him up in her arms to take him away." Joren's heart beat wildly in his chest at the vivid memory. "I tried to scream, but I couldn't, only a little squeak came out. Then she turned around and screamed at me… and I woke up."

Vandra's eyes widened as he spoke. "Nydheim's gates, Joren. How did you come up with something like that?"

"I don't know," he wrung out his fleece, squeezing against the pain of the bitter cold water. He could feel her eyes on him as he rolled the fleece back up, and before he was able to think better of it, he asked, "You don't think it was real, do you?"

"No, of course not!" she exclaimed. "Don't be ridiculous. Why would a burnt up old lady try to steal Pedr?"

"She wasn't old, just really skinny, like she was starved."

She waved the comment aside. "Besides, you said she

screamed at you, I would have heard that, the whole family would have."

"She screamed in silence," he corrected her.

"What? What does that even mean?"

"I don't know, but that's what she did!"

"Joren." Vandra placed her hands on her hips, a habit not unlike her mother's, but far more annoying. "Come now, does that not sound like a horrible nightmare? Dreams are filled with impossible things like 'screaming silently'."

"It didn't *feel* like a dream," Joren muttered.

"Well it was, because it must have been." She sighed and reached out to take one of his hands. "Joren, truly, you don't need to worry. Look at Pedr." She gestured to where their brother was slapping the stream with a stick. "He's perfectly fine! Well, as fine as usual."

He nodded, still sullen, unable to shake the fear and agitation. Vandra returned to washing her fleece and Joren dipped his linens into the frigid water.

"Thank you for lying about the fleeces," he said after a while. "And for talking with me. About the nightmare, I mean."

"You're quite welcome," she replied in her most sisterly manner.

"Were you really crying over Old Havar's grandson?" Vandra's smile melted instantly and Joren hurried to explain. "No, I'm not teasing, Van, I promise! I'm asking honestly. You helped me, I just want to help you."

His sister narrowed her eyes, gauging his sincerity. "No," she replied forcefully after a moment. "If you must know, I actually found him to be quite annoying."

"So did I!" Joren smirked. "He was always whining about the cold!"

Against her will, it seemed, Vandra grinned too. "He kept trying to lift heavy things when I was around."

They shared a laugh and Joren asked, "So what were you upset about, then?"

She sobered, but her iciness was gone. "I'm... I don't want to leave yet."

"Leave? What do you mean?"

"What Papa was talking about last night. He'll start looking for a husband for me soon."

"He was only joking, Van — you're not old enough yet."

"Mama married Papa when she was sixteen, Joren. I'm fourteen already."

He felt a pang in his belly as he realized she was right. He had never thought about it before, but she was getting older and would be leaving them soon. He tried to think of something happy to say, to cheer both of them up. "I'm sure he'll find you a good one, a handsome one."

Vandra rolled her eyes. "Oh, thank you, Joren." She gathered up her fleece and stood abruptly. "I'm sure being away from my family with a strange, *handsome* man will make everything much easier!"

"Well," Joren asked, confused, "wouldn't it?"

Fuming, she turned and stalked back up the little hill.

Pedr trotted up beside his big brother, wearing the damp fleece over his head. "What's she upset about?"

"Boys!" their father's voice boomed down the hill and he appeared at the top, waving to them. "Hurry, we have to set out!"

"C'mon." Joren gave Pedr a little push and they started back.

When they arrived back at the hall, both their parents stood outside the door, waiting for them.

"Joren," their mother said as she gathered their damp fleeces from them, a little light in her eyes. "Your father has something for you."

Their father cleared his throat. "This is a little something you've been waiting for awhile, I think, and that your mother and I have been very eager to give you." Joren had no idea what it could be, but Pedr immediately started dancing beside him in excitement. "It's not quite done yet — I thought maybe we could finish it together."

From behind his back, he pulled out a long wooden stick, stripped of bark and crudely-carved with a large hook on one end.

"Your very own crook!" his mother exclaimed, beaming.

Joren's father held it out to him, and he took it, feeling the rough grain on his palms. "I cut the branch from the same tree I made mine from, and your grandfather's." He smiled hopefully. "What do you think, Joren?"

Joren turned it over in his hands. It was thinner and shorter than his father's — perfect for Joren's hands and height. "I love it," he answered truthfully. His father was right — Joren *had* been waiting for this. He held it before him like his father did when they thought there might be wolves about. It felt natural, and a warm glow spread through his chest.

"I even put an iron cap on it," his father pointed toward the foot of the crook. With that, Joren truly could stand against the wolves with his father, side by side. "Now you just have to work on your shepherd's stance."

Joren grinned and planted the staff in front of him, resting his weight on it as he had seen his father do countless times.

His parents erupted in laughter. "The boy's a natural!" his father cried, cheeks rosy, a grin splitting the black beard that so often hid his expressions.

"When will I get one, Papa?" Pedr asked, looking in awe at the little crook.

"Soon enough, Pedr, when you're Joren's age." His wife shot him a skeptical look. "That is," their father quickly amended, "if your mother and I think you're ready by then."

"Can I have a sword instead?"

"Absolutely not!" their mother cried.

"Or a dragon!" Pedr threw his arms in the air at the idea and whooped.

Their father grinned and prodded them both along toward the back of the hall to fetch the flock.

"Have a good day, my loves!" she called after them. "And be careful with that thing, Joren!"

They were nearing the little farming village of Kaninholm, and Rhys's tailbone ached as the horse beneath him shifted back and forth. Each year that passed seemed to bring new pain to his limbs, to the point that he often wondered how long he would be able to continue his service to the Order. Trying to distract himself, he made his mind wander to other things, anything, but the only place they found was the nightmares of the previous evening.

Bad dreams were nothing new to him, and it had been a recurring one, anyhow. He watched various friends and fellow Knights die again, but in a horrific sequence, one after the other, even though in reality they ranged over the course of his lifetime.

Some times were worse than others, and he would wake in a cold sweat; last night had not been so bad, thankfully, but the memory of it lingered a bit more insistently than usual. Rhys told himself it was simply the foreign environment and shrugged it off as best he could.

They wandered through the gaps between fields of vegetables and grains, on the lookout for locals who could be of use in stabling their veritable herd of horses. Captain Thorne's ability to speak the native Fjalr language was dismal at best, so he relegated the duties of communication to Rhys, who had a practiced tongue from years of service in Fjalvard.

The group finally came upon a handful of men tending the fields, and Rhys inquired who might be able to help them, and they all gave him the name Helsik Odursen, pointing him further west.

Continuing on as instructed, they eventually arrived at the largest hall in the village. They dismounted before approaching, and the relief in Rhys's rear end was almost painful as he slid down from his saddle and followed Thorne up to the hall door. The captain gave it three sound knocks before stepping back and waiting for it to open.

When it finally did, an ancient woman, hunched and shriveled, peered up at them with rheumy eyes. She said nothing, but looked from one to the other expectantly.

Finally, Rhys cleared his throat and said a little loudly, "Good morning, Mother. We seek Helsik Odursen. Is this his hall?"

She stared at him another moment before slowly turning

around in place and shuffling off. Rhys glanced at Thorne as the door slowly started to close on its hinges. The captain reached to stop it, but it swung open before he could touch it and there appeared an old man, though not so old as the woman.

"I am Helsik," he said in a raspy voice. "Oh, Knights from Carthannas! Well isn't this something?"

"You know who we are, Master Odursen?" Rhys asked, a little surprised at the immediacy of the old man's recognition.

"I do!" the man answered, stepping outside and allowing the door to close behind him. "Men of your order come through this valley from time to time, though it's been some while since the last. Your emblems are quite distinctive — not easy to forget." The old man peered at the white patch on Rhys's shoulder as though to make sure it was genuine. Then he went over to a bench nearby and sat down heavily, his long grey beard sweeping the dirt at his feet.

"I suppose they are," Rhys agreed as they followed after him.

Helsik's bushy brows lifted when he saw the rest of the detachment idling. "Oh, my. How many of you are there, exactly?"

"We are nine altogether, master."

"Hmmm," he screwed up his face and reached to pick at something in his ear. "Don't know exactly where we'll fit you all, but we'll manage it. A fine honor, to house brave men such as yourselves. Oh, I never did get your name, Sir Knight."

"I'm Rhys, just a sergeant," he fumbled with the words. "But we're not here for shelter, master. Well, not for us."

"Oh?" he retrieved whatever it was in his ear, inspected it, and flicked it away. "For who, then?"

"We're making for Hrokar's Pass, to attempt the mountains, and we were hoping to stable our horses here until our return."

The old man's eyes widened. "Hrokar's Pass? Slain bless me! Why would you do such a thing? It's naught but monsters in the Deep Ymr, anymore. Years since the mountain folk abandoned it." He cocked his brow. "Is that why you're here — monsters coming down from the Ymr? Should I be worried by your presence, Sergeant?"

Rhys grimaced. "Most people usually are. But you have

nothing to fear, master — our destination is further into the mountains, not here, nor does it have anything to do with your little village. A stable for our horses is all we seek in Kaninholm, with fair compensation, of course."

"We can certainly take care of your animals, Sergeant." Helsik gestured at the fields all around. "My sons and grandsons are out now, tending the crops. We have oxen and a few mules here, and I think between all of us we can find a shelter for them, yes. But how long will you be away?"

Rhys looked to Thorne; the young man did not appear to have understood the question, so Rhys answered as best he could. "That, I cannot say, Master Odursen. I think we have only a few more days' travel until we reach the pass, but what we'll find within — and how long we'll be — who can say? However long we're gone, though, we have enough coin to make it worth your while. And of course, if we don't return, you will be free to do with the horses as you like."

"Well, if what I remember about the Knights Seraphin from my youth is anything to go by, Sergeant, we won't have to worry about that."

Rhys gave a little shrug. "Let us hope you're right. Now, master — where would you like us to leave the horses?"

"Well," he intoned, scratching at his chin, "my sons won't be in from their work in the fields until later, so I suppose it's best to leave them here. Those old posts, there," he pointed to the remains of a worn fence that poked up out of the ground, beyond which a field of barley rippled in the breeze. "You can tie them up there, and my sons will take care of them at day's end. I have a couple old pails, too, that you can fill with water to leave for them. They're in that shed." He pointed again.

Rhys explained all they had said to Thorne, who turned and started giving orders to the men. As they hurried to move all of their important gear over to the mules, Rhys retrieved a coin purse from his bag and brought it over to the old man.

"Thank you for your hospitality, master," he held out the offering.

Helsik glanced down at the little leather pouch and shook his head. "We've no need for coin here, Sir Knight." He waved his hand dismissively. "Some traders who come from other parts of Fjalvard have tried to give us coin, but here in the valley, we hold to the old ways — we trade goods here, not bits of metal."

Rhys kept his hand outstretched. "I'm afraid we have nothing else to offer, master. What provisions we've brought we'll need for our attempt on the Deep Ymr."

"Oh, it matters not. As I said, we have the space for your animals and grass aplenty. What you and your fellow Knights do, Sergeant, for Fjalvard and for all the world, is not lost on even us simple folk. I'll not accept any sort of payment whatever for this little bit of help my sons and I can offer." He gave a broad smile, pleased with his righteous stubbornness.

"But surely we can't expect you to take on a burden of nine horses without any recompense," Rhys pushed. "Or at least some show of gratitude."

Helsik's eyes narrowed and he pondered a moment. "I suppose there is something you could do for me, if you insist."

"We do," Rhys answered firmly.

"My daughter married a shepherd, and they live up on the mountain slope, more or less the way you're traveling. We don't see them often, as we can't abandon our crops, nor they their flock. If you're willing, I would send some things to them with you. On foot, as you are, you could be there by sundown, and Olen and my Runa would be so happy for guests. They would surely shelter you for the night — one last comfort before you head for the pass."

"Can you point out the direction of this sheepfold?" Rhys asked.

The old man raised his arm almost due north. "There, up the slope. Younger eyes might even be able to see his hall from here." Rhys could not.

He was hesitant to go much out of the way on an errand, even to repay the man's kindness — that was why they had brought coin. The idea of leaving such a kind deed unrewarded, however, was even more distasteful, and so he told Helsik he needed to discuss the matter with his captain.

"How far out of the way is it?" Thorne asked, once Rhys had explained.

"It will cost us a day at most."

"Then it's out of the question."

Rhys shifted uncomfortably. "I understand we don't want the delay, Captain, but —"

"It has nothing to do with what I want, Sergeant," the younger man replied sternly. "We have our orders from Blessed Seraphe herself; the writ is signed by the marshal. We are to make all haste into the Ymr."

"Of course, but at the same time, we cannot forsake our duties to the people — this man and his sons are kind enough to look after our horses, but he won't take any coin for the trouble. He's asked a small favor instead, it would not be right or in keeping with the purpose of the Order to refuse him, certainly not for one mere day of travel."

"I fully comprehend the need to maintain the Order's reputation, Sergeant," Thorne rested a hand on his hip. "But our mission takes precedence when we do not know the cost of losing that 'one mere day'."

"Look at it this way, Cap," Felix offered as he passed, a saddle bag perched on his shoulder. "It would be nice to have one more night indoors, if we could. Getting colder every step we take northward."

Thorne frowned and signaled for Rhys to follow him away from the others. He sighed and ran a hand through his hair before speaking. "I'm trying to be reasonable, Sergeant — we've spoken about this."

In the first days of their journey north, Thorne had taken him aside, much like he just had, and made a long confession. The young man knew he had a particular intensity, the kind that impressed superiors and wrought dread in the hearts of subordinates. Though he knew its value, he had said, he wanted to temper it, to walk the fine line between absolute authority and a more relaxed command. He was finding it difficult, as Rhys — and every other member of the detachment — knew full well.

"I would like to think I've made great strides with the men since I took charge," he continued.

Rhys nodded. "You certainly have." He meant it.

"But on the matter of the timely completion of a mission, I don't know that I can relax my standards."

"I would be a failure of a sergeant if it was my recommendation to slack in our duties, Captain. Instead, what I ask is that you consider the importance of taking care of the common folk, who — as now — so often support us in our mission to protect all our lands."

The captain chewed his lip for a moment in contemplation. "Damned primitives," he finally cursed under his breath. "Of course he couldn't simply take the coin. This must be the last hole on earth that doesn't use some form of fungible currency." He sighed. "But yes, I suppose you're right, Sergeant. We wouldn't want to sully our reputation in the great city of Kaninholm, now would we?"

"I will support whatever decision you make, Captain," Rhys said, disliking the man's tone.

"Fret not, Sergeant," he grumbled. "Comstock — whichever one it was — will get his night under a roof. Tell the old farmer we'll run his errand."

Rhys gave an impassive nod and went to share the good news with Helsik.

"Wonderful!" the old man cried, and wrung Rhys's hand with both of his. "You do me a very gracious favor, Sergeant."

"It is a kindness repaid, master," Rhys assured him.

His attention was drawn back to the others as Thorne raised his voice in Carthan. "Leave the lady's saddle, Grim."

The sandy-haired youth paused by Helmi's black gelding, a strap held tight in his hand, ready to be loosened. "We're taking this one, Captain?" he asked.

"Yes," Thorne confirmed, "the lady will ride on while the rest of us walk."

"Oh, that's not necessary, Captain," Helmi objected politely, "I'm happy to walk with the detachment."

He shook his head. "You'll ride. Your feet are unaccustomed

to the road — they'll be bleeding before an hour's passed, and we cannot afford to waste any more time." His eyes found Rhys.

"I assure you, I'm well capable of walking beside you all," she tried again, more insistent, but Thorne was unmoved.

"There is no discussion to be had, Milady," his use of the title carried a hint of irritation. "You'll ride and we'll abandon the horse once it can no longer make the climb."

Helmi recoiled. "You'd leave him to die? That's barbaric! Just leave him here with his companions, for mercy's sake!"

Thorne's jaw clenched and he took half a step forward. "Do you really presume to issue *me* an order?" he asked in a low voice.

Rhys, wary of the quick escalation, stepped in and pulled Helmi away. "I'm sure she meant nothing of the sort, Captain," he said deferentially, hoping to defuse the tension. "I will speak with her."

"Do. On this, Sergeant, I will not yield." He gave Rhys a meaningful look. "See that she learns where her place is among us."

Rhys nodded and took Helmi's arm, leading her down a corridor between two fields of grain.

"What on earth has gotten into him?" she demanded, seething.

He did not answer at once, but waited until they were out of earshot to stop and face her. "Helmi," he began, trying as he spoke to maintain some semblance of neutrality. "I know this situation is very new to you, so please heed me in this: it's not wise to disagree with the captain of a detachment. At all, really, but certainly not so brazenly."

"I would not have had to disagree if he had not seemingly lost his mind!" She balled her fists at her sides. "I'm not a fool — I know he doesn't want me here. He has kept his manners very cold toward me this whole time, but now he is openly hostile. Why, Garret?"

"There isn't an easy answer to that question, Helmi. He's very young, you'll have noticed, younger even than you. Typically, a man his age would not be a captain, let alone be given command of such an important and enigmatic task as this. But he is not a typical Knight."

He turned and started to walk slowly down the row as he told her the captain's story. "What I tell you about him, you must not repeat, do you understand? Take an oath of silence on this, as you seem so fond of doing." She rolled her eyes, but nodded. "The marshal made a particular effort to speak with me before we left. He told me about Thorne, where he was coming from and why. The captain's previous assignment was one of his first, as a lieutenant with a larger company. Their mission was to find and eliminate an illicit society of warlocks thought to be hiding in the tropics of Oaxatl.

"It's always a hard slog through those jungles," he mused. "The sweat runs in rivers, swords rust and fuse in their sheaths, and chainmail corrodes before your eyes until it falls off in swaths. Often, men are lost to the giant cats or river monsters that lurk seemingly around every bend."

His mind wandered for a moment through distant memories of his own until she gently cleared her throat. "Thorne and his company went into the jungles in search of the rogue society, and after many weeks, finally found it. But the warlocks were more numerous than they had been told, and in possession of more fell magics. They fought mightily, until the society had been razed, and only Thorne was left of his company of thirty men. He collected proof of the deed and made back to the Eldric Citadel to tell the marshal of their success.

"The marshal tells me he was a broken man at first, and they required him to spend time to heal his mind after the wounds of losing all his brothers to the society. He assures me that Thorne has recovered and is fit to lead, and I'm sure he's right. But a devastating loss like that leaves its mark on a man, sometimes in strange ways."

"That's a horrible thing for anyone to go through," she said, folding her arms and biting her lip. "But are you saying I must endure this maltreatment?"

"We all must endure whatever flaws the man has, so long as he is not needlessly endangering us or the mission. That is the oath we take." He sighed. "He has a particular dislike of you. Why, I can't say, but if you do as he bids, like the rest of us, it will be easier for you. I won't let him get too carried away, but it would help if you don't respond so eagerly to his provocations."

A fire flickered behind her eyes. "I may only be a young oracle, but I'm not afraid of Thorne, nor am I afraid for him to know it."

Rhys held up his hands. "I doubt there's a man among us who would disbelieve you. Still, it would be best for you to follow our example and let the captain be the captain. He'll tire of prodding you as soon as you stop reacting."

Helmi pursed her lips and narrowed her eyes. "Fine, Garret — I will do as you say, because I trust you and like you. For now."

"That's as good a reason as any, I suppose." He inclined his head. "Thank you, Helmi. This mission is beyond all of us and our little squabbles."

"Yes, yes," she waved her hand but failed to hide a little smile. "You've made your point. Let's get back so I can pretend to be cowed by the Mighty Youth."

Rhys laughed aloud at that, something he rarely did in these, his later days. He took her arm again, and the two of them went to rejoin the detachment.

As they returned, Helmi went to stand by her gelding and Rhys nodded at Thorne, who took the gesture as a sign of his victory on the matter.

Once the rest of the horses were divested of their riding gear and tied up to posts, they stored the saddles in the old shed and retrieved the pails to fill for the horses. Then Helsik led a few of the soldiers into his hall to gather things for the shepherd. They came back out with sacks of grain, jars of honey, and canteens and old waterskins filled with mead.

"Thank you again, all of you," the old farmer said, shaking each of their hands in turn. "Give our love to Runa, will you? And the children? They have such good little children. Tell them some good stories of your adventures, will you? They will love that!"

"Of course, master," Grim assured him as his hand was heartily wrung.

"Master Odursen," Rhys said, "thank you again for your kindness. I pray that we may return safely in the following weeks and months and find you've brought in a good harvest."

Helsik's old eyes shone. "I pray the same, good Sergeant."

With Holywell in the lead, the little procession started off again, Grim and the twins each leading a laden mule behind them.

"Oh, remember!" the farmer called after them. "Follow the stream all the way up until you see a trail that wanders away — follow that and it will take you right up to Olen's hall!" Rhys held a hand aloft in thanks as they continued on. "Slain grant you strength, good Knights! And may your own gods see you safely back to our valley!"

3

THE STORY

T he day passed quickly and Joren spent the majority of it walking in circles around the flock, climbing the occasional big rock that jutted from the green grass, and chasing any sheep that wandered too far with his new crook. The temperature had risen steadily until it was comfortably warm with a gentle breeze, and the clouds that slid down off the mountain floated slowly by, granting a little shade here and there.

Any time the forest near their hall was visible from where he was on the slope, he found himself glaring at it. Even with summer's warmth and beauty blooming all around, his nightmare still haunted him. Pedr begged him numerous times to play, but he was in no mood, so eventually his little brother wandered off to torment the sheep.

Joren's mind finally left the bad dreams behind as he gazed out over the landscape before them. Smaller mountains flanked the Ymr to either side, rows of ancient, stoney warriors following their king to battle. The shadows of heavy clouds marched across the slope and down into the valley like conquering armies until they passed over the horizon or melted before the mighty light of the sun.

Joren liked to imagine he was a warrior — sometimes a chieftain's man, but preferably a Knight Seraphin from Carthannas — and would watch himself in his mind's eye, galloping across the hills and fields on a mighty steed, the only soul left after a harrowing battle, riding to the next city in need of his aid. He was the only Knight in the land — the world — who used a crook instead of a sword. Everyone laughed at him... until he slew a dragon with the iron spike on the end.

"Joren, Pedr, come!" Their father's voice cut into his fantasy. He sat on a flat rock upslope, commanding a view of his sons and his flock, down to his hall and the valley beyond. The sun was high in the sky, and the sheep had settled in and were grazing calmly, so while they ate together, he told them a story.

It was one Joren had heard a number of times, but never tired of. As their father recounted the time he and his brother — when they were just about Joren's and Pedr's ages — found a rusted, blunted old sword buried to the hilt in the mountainside, he pointed out where everything had happened. His eyes danced as he remembered finding it; he huffed and puffed as he demonstrated how the two of them had pulled together to try to free the blade from its earthy prison; he laughed until his cheeks were red as he showed them the scar on his hand where the ancient blade had nicked him once it came free.

Joren had always thought that if it were a proper story, the sword would have been magical, or at least his father would have taken it and went off to become a brave warrior and fight mythical creatures. Nothing of the sort happened, though, of course. His father's father had taken the sword away from the two after they were caught with it and given it to a trader for a sack of oats. His father had remained on the mountainside and become a shepherd, too, and never had any adventures in far off lands.

Despite the disappointing end, Joren always enjoyed listening to it. His father found joy in his simple life, loved it, would never choose a different path even if he could. Joren liked their life, too, but he could not help dreaming of so much more.

Finally, as dusk settled over the Ymr, they turned the flock back to shelter them for the night. Traversing the rocky slope was treacherous with the sun below the horizon and Joren had to move slowly so that he did not take a tumble.

Once they arrived, Joren, Pedr, and Hala herded the sheep

back into the pen as their father took the count. The last of them went through the gates and the shepherd frowned.

"We're missing a lamb again," he muttered, looking back the way they had come. A shiver went down Joren's spine, the events of the previous night suddenly horrifically fresh in his mind. His eyes darted immediately toward the forest where he had seen the Burnt Lady. "Do you see her, boys?"

Joren swallowed down his panic and reluctantly turned back toward the slope, standing up on his toes to watch for any movement. "No, Papa."

Their father sighed. "Well, let's get this gate shut and we'll go look for her." Joren found himself repeatedly glancing over his shoulder toward the forest as he helped close the shelter, half-expecting the Burnt Lady to be crawling up behind them in the dim light of evening. Of course, there was nothing, and he scolded himself again for thinking she might be real instead of a nightmare.

They headed back toward the day's pasture, but before they could start the uphill climb, Hala stopped and looked toward the path that ran east along the mountainside and down to the valley. For an instant, Joren was afraid she sensed the Burnt Lady again, but then the halo of faint lantern light grew over the hillocks through which the path wound. The sounds of slow, plodding hoofbeats followed a moment later.

Joren looked up at his father, whose gaze remained fixed on the approaching light. Hala was silent and her tail wagged gently, thumping against Joren's leg.

"Who is it, Papa?" Pedr asked, taking a step closer to his father.

"Chieftain's men, probably," he said, scratching his beard. "Finally doing their job and making their rounds up here."

The light of the lantern finally crested the hill, bobbing as the man who carried it trudged along. More people came into view: men walking and leading three heavy-laden mules. Then another, slender figure sitting tall on a horse. It was arrayed in a dark, hooded riding cloak.

"Hmmm," their father furrowed his brow and screwed up his

face so that his mouth disappeared beneath his heavy mustache. Taking a step forward, past Joren, he eased the heavy shepherd's crook out in front of him and rested his weight on it. Pedr moved behind his legs to watch from safety, and Joren leaned on his crook, too. Together, they stood and waited for the travelers.

When they were closer, Joren's father called out in his warm, powerful voice. "Hallo, strangers!" The man carrying the lantern in front raised his other arm in greeting. "What brings you to our fair mountain?"

Two other men came from further back, one of them motioning for the rest to halt and wait where they were. "Hallo, master shepherd," the older of the two men answered. They were both dressed in leather and chain armor and wore a distinctive white leather patch on their right shoulders: a shield embossed with the image of a robed woman. "My name is Garret Rhys, a sergeant of the Order of the Knights Seraphin. This is Arran Thorne, our captain."

The captain was a much younger man sporting a wispy attempt at a beard. His blond hair was tied back, and his hand rested easily on the pommel of his sword. "Hallo, master," he echoed the sergeant's greeting in a very thick accent. Joren ogled the man's weapon and armor as his stomach did a little dance; it was as though they had just stepped out of one of his father's stories.

"Welcome to the Ymr," their father said, still leaning casually with both hands on his crook. "I am Olen Segurdsen, a humble shepherd. Coming up from Carthannas, are you? What brings you to Fjalvard?"

"You're familiar with our order, then?" the sergeant asked, folding his arms over his chest.

"Of course! I can't imagine the dark corner of the world where your name and deeds are not known."

"Then you'll know our purpose, surely. We go where our goddess commands us and root out whatever evil we can find there."

His father scoffed. "Evil? There's naught but sheep and snow on the Ymr, Sergeant."

"Fear not, master shepherd, we are only crossing through your sheepfold — our destination lies further on. Your wife's father, Helsik, sent us here to you."

"Ah, you've met old Helsik, have you?" Joren's father chuckled. "How is he?"

"He's well, master. He gave us some things to bring to you."

"Well, that's lovely!" he declared with a broad smile, and the last of the tension melted away. "If Helsik has sent you to us — bearing gifts, no less — the least I can do is offer you my hall to spend the night. Consider yourselves welcome guests!" Taking a step forward, he held out his right hand to the sergeant, who took it gladly.

Sergeant Rhys looked at the young captain, then back to Joren's father. "Truth be told, master, we're very grateful. We have a long way to go yet, with no more comfort in sight, so a night under a roof would do us well, I think."

"Of course!" his father spread his arms. "My wife and I love to have guests, especially as they are so rare. Captain, Sergeant, my humble hall is yours for the evening. It will be a tight fit," he admitted, "but we've enough sheepskins to make the floor into as comfortable a bed as you've ever had! Come!"

He turned to Joren and placed a hand on his shoulder. "These are my boys, Joren and Pedr. They'll help you stable your horse and mules. I'll go let my wife know we have more mouths to feed." He leaned closer and whispered in Joren's ear. "If in her wrath she decides to chop me up for supper, make sure your brothers and sisters know how much I love you all." Giving Joren a wink, he straightened and asked the stranger, "How many have you brought us, Sergeant?"

"Nine altogether, master shepherd."

"Nine! Slain take me," he exclaimed. "It might be a little tighter than I promised, then." He turned and made for the hall.

Joren stopped him by tugging at his shirt. "Papa, the lamb."

"Oh, yes." His father considered the matter. "Well, now that I think of it, I'm sure I just miscounted. Don't worry, Joren, just help the good soldiers to the stable and make sure no others escape, yes?" He patted his son on the shoulder.

Joren turned back to the armored soldiers as his father made for the hall, keeping his hand on Hala's flank and trying very hard not to look intimidated, even if he was. "The shelter's this way," he said, indicating with a nod.

"Very good, young master," the sergeant signaled to the other soldiers and the procession started moving again.

Joren watched as the soldier leading the horse — a tall, lean, older man — stopped by the door to the hall and helped the cloaked figure down from the saddle. As it stepped into the lantern light and lowered its hood, he saw it was a lady wearing a dark-blue riding gown. The only women Joren had ever seen besides his mother and sister were his aunts, cousins, and other farmer's wives and daughters down in the valley, and he had never thought much about them. This Carthan lady, though, whoever she was, looked like she had come out of an old, heroic story. Dark hair hung in curls about her lovely face and the warmth of her eyes bespoke tranquility of her soul and —

"Master Joren," the sergeant's calm and forceful voice stirred him and Joren realized he had been gawking. Horrified, he turned away quickly so that his burning cheeks remained hidden as the lady and the captain stepped through the hall door. He stalked quickly on, his heart thumping, and led the soldiers toward the shelter.

Pedr helped him haul open the heavy gate and Hala hurried in to keep the sheep at bay, as she was trained. The group of men led their animals inside and pulled off some of their lumpy saddlebags. It was cramped, just as it would be in the hall, but Joren was sure they would be fine until morning, at least. The sandy-haired man who had led one of the mules came up to Joren and held out his hand, which Joren took as his father had taught him.

"Hallo, Joren," he said in practiced Fjalr, grinning broadly, "I'm Grim. It's nice to see friendly faces so far up the mountain." He knelt down beside him and offered his hand for Hala to sniff. "Who's this, then?"

Joren, still mortified, managed to mutter, "Hala."

"Hala," he repeated, taking the dog's head in his hands and

scratching behind her ears. "That's a good name you've chosen. She reminds me of my da's old dog, gods rest him."

Joren did not know how to respond, so instead of embarrassing himself further, he went to fetch some oats from the shed behind the shelter. Once the animals were all inside and feeding, Grim helped Joren heave the gate closed and fasten it. As they made their way back to the hall, two of the soldiers exchanged in their native language and laughed.

Joren stepped into the warmth from the fire and then hurried out of the way as the soldiers behind him marched through the door.

"Here, master shepherd," Sergeant Rhys said, holding aloft a sack of grain. "The items Helsik sent with us. Where shall we put them?"

"You've seen my father?" Joren's mother asked, surprised.

"We have, mistress. He is well, and he's sent us with grains and oats and mead."

"Mead?" Joren's father cried, his eyes wide. One of the other soldiers offered him a waterskin. He accepted it, uncorked it, and took a deep sniff. "Oh, Mighty Slain be praised! Runa, it's your father's mead!" He turned back to the sergeant. "We haven't had mead since mid-winter," he laughed, "and Helsik uses the finest honey in the world, from bees which must be no less than magical! We'll have some with supper. Ah, what a fine evening this is, eh, my love?"

Joren's mother nodded and addressed Sergeant Rhys again. "Did you see my grandmother, may I ask, master?"

"I believe we may have," he answered hesitantly. "We saw an elder woman who was... very quiet."

"Oh yes," she gave a sigh of relief. "Her speech was taken from her years ago after a bad fever. But she is still alive, I'm so glad to hear it."

"I understand it's difficult for you to go down to the valley and see your family," the sergeant said.

"Yes, we can only make the trip very seldom. Thank you for bearing good news, my lord." She gave him an earnest smile and returned to her cooking.

"Captain," Joren's father said, as his wife added more meat and vegetables to the pot simmering over the fire, "I don't mind if you men bring your weapons inside my hall, but if you would be so kind as to stack them there in the corner so as not to accidentally run my little ones through, I'm sure my wife and I would be very grateful."

The soldiers all looked to Captain Thorne, who in turn looked to his sergeant, who leaned close and whispered a translation. The young captain nodded and removed his sword belt. The soldiers all followed suit and it was then that Joren noticed one of the men did not match the others. Instead of chain armor, he wore only a leather jerkin without the white emblem on his shoulder, and a kind of skirt of various blue hues fell to just above his knees. His eyes were tired and his face hidden behind a heavy beard. The weapon he stacked in the corner was different as well: a bulky, short-hafted hammer whose head was covered in patterns, along with a tall, square shield.

"An Ilban?" Joren's father asked, apparently also first noticing the man. "You didn't mention you'd brought an Ilban with you, Sergeant."

Sergeant Rhys looked to their host and then to the skirt-clad man. In a measured voice, he said, "My apologies, master shepherd. I had forgotten about the recent tensions between your peoples. But I assure you, this man is our companion and means no harm to you."

"Is that true, Ilban? The fighting at the border is bloody, they say. Have you had any part in it?"

"None whatsoever," the man answered in a thick burr. "The clans warring with your people aren't mine."

"And the Fjalr chieftain they're fighting isn't mine." Joren's father folded his arms. "Can I trust that you speak the truth, though?"

He shrugged. "I don't know what I could say to convince you, but for what it's worth, in my youth, a group of us came here to support the Skyhammer in his bid for the throne. Never have I served with a finer man than him, and I would have been happy to lay my life down beside his, had it come to that."

"Asdren Embriksen is a great man, indeed." A light had sparked behind his father's eyes at the mention of Fjalvard's previous Greatthane. Of all the stories with which his father liked to regale his children, none was so often repeated, or told so reverently, as the story of the man who saved Fjalvard with a single blow of his great warhammer. "You claim you served with him? Where?"

"At that final battle outside Rorhavn," the Ilban replied, "and the two that preceded it. I was a new recruit with the Dalbragh at the time and we arrived after receiving a request from the Skyhammer himself for aid."

"So you were there," Joren's father said with a boyish grin, his curiosity cutting through the weight of the moment. "You saw the fateful blow?"

"Aye, we did. It was unlike anything I've ever seen, before or since."

"Then do I have a host of question for you! I'm sorry for my distrust, Ilban, but if you truly fought alongside Embriksen, you're very welcome here." Beaming, he reached out a hand.

"Aedric," the man replied, accepting the gesture.

"Aedric. We'll have to speak more on all this later." He was hardly able to contain his excitement.

Sergeant Rhys, on the other hand, was visibly relaxed by their amity. "Thank you for your graciousness, master shepherd. You have my assurances that we are all here in peace. Now, if you don't mind, I'll introduce the rest of our company to prevent any further surprises."

He clapped a hand on the shoulder of the tall, lanky man who had helped the lady dismount. "This is Brother Leo Holywell. Take no offense at his silence, for he is a mute. And here is Brother Blackhart, our hospitaler and chronicler." The big soldier nodded his bald head, his huge black mustache hiding his lips, making it impossible to decipher his mood. "Grim and the Comstock twins — Felix and Fergus — are conscripted fighters, but they're good lads who have been with us a number of years now." Joren had only just noticed that two of the men were identical.

"And this is Helmi Gwynlaithe," he gestured to the lady in blue, "an oracle of the goddess Othelia."

"Helmi," Joren's father repeated, "that's a Fjalr name."

The lady smiled. "Yes, my mother was from Fjalvard. She married a Carthan farmer." Her accent was softer than the sergeant's.

"Oh, which chiefdom?"

"Sotrgaard."

"Ah, I've never been that far south myself, unfortunately," he lamented. "I would hear more about you, about all of you. You know, it is a tradition here that guests earn roof and meal by sharing worthy stories with their hosts!" His shoulders shook as he chuckled. "But for now, sit, please. We'll have supper ready shortly."

His wife stood up on her toes and hissed something into his ear.

"Ah!" he cried, smacking his forehead. "You have proof now of how seldom we have guests! I have yet to introduce *my* family!" He laughed and gave a playful bow. "I am Olen Segurdsen, master of the hall of my fathers, a humble and simple shepherd." He took his wife's hand. "And this is my wife, the loveliest woman in all Fjalvard: Runa Helsikdottir, my warmth and strength on the mountainside." Joren's mother smiled and blushed, quickly turning back to the fire.

His father then pointed to each of his children in turn. "Our eldest, Vandra; you've already met Joren and Pedr; and of course, the youngest, Agata." He turned to his sons and pointed up to the loft above them. "Now, boys, go on up and fetch all the extra skins we have and spread them over there for our guests." He gestured to the other side of the hall, to the relatively open space between the cook pit and his parents' bed.

Joren gave Pedr a little push toward the ladder and followed him up to the loft. "Did you see the captain's sword?" Pedr asked in an elated whisper as their father started asking questions of the guests below. "It had carvings on the scabbard — a lady I think!"

Joren had indeed seen it, the most beautiful among all the weapons now stacked in the corner of their home. Even the others, though, plain as they might seem in comparison, were marvelous things the likes of which he had never seen but often imagined. "Do you think he's killed people with it?"

"Probably," Joren tossed him an old, soft sheepskin, "but Papa says the Knights usually just kill monsters, not people."

"And the Iliba-man," his little brother worked out the strange word. "I thought he and Papa were going to fight."

"Ilban," he corrected. "I thought so, too." Their father had never told them much of the violence that was happening with Fjalvard's western neighbor, but Joren knew from the news Old Havar brought that things were bad at the border. His father said that was far away, though.

"I wish they had!" Pedr continued, too loud. "Papa would've bashed his head in!" He mimed a punch and fell over, pretending to be dead.

"Quiet, they'll hear you." Joren dragged him back up and together they pushed the pile of fleeces over to the edge of the loft. "Head down and I'll toss them to you."

Pedr gave him a wounded look. "I wanted to toss them."

Joren sighed and gave in, climbing down the ladder instead. The dirt floor of the hall never fully warmed, even with a fire blazing in the pit in the middle of the hall, and he hoped the skins would be enough to keep the soldiers comfortable. He was aware of their guests' eyes on him as Pedr threw him the fleeces, and he suddenly felt very self-conscious. He gritted his teeth and promised himself that if Pedr made a fool of him by throwing too many at a time for him to handle, he would never let him win at swords again. Luckily, he was able to catch them all, and once Pedr descended, they spread the skins around on the floor to make a sprawling, matted bed for the soldiers.

"Come, boys," their father beckoned, "bring some of those fleeces over here so you little ones don't have to sit in the dirt."

The table was occupied on one side by their parents, the captain, and the lady, and on the other side by the sergeant, the Ilban, and the two other Knights. Grim and the twins had spots on the benches near the fire pit, there being no more room at the table. The only time he could remember their hall being so full was years ago when his mother's parents had come up from the valley and brought all their extended family along with them.

While his mother and sister served the stew into wooden bowls, Joren and Pedr laid a few fleeces down between the fire pit and the table, and their father poured the precious mead into cups.

Once everyone had a drink and a steaming bowl in front of them, Joren's father bid them all eat and enjoy. "Now, Captain," he asked around a mouthful of stew, "please, could you tell us more about your order?"

The captain swallowed and furrowed his brow. "The Lady of Light, Seraphe, send us here to... find bad, destroy." He looked up at the ceiling, searching for the words. "We here to protect... you... and all Fjalvard... from... bad."

His father nodded sagely. "I have heard many stories of the Knights Seraphin of Carthannas and shared them with my children, but you are the first we've met. Tell me, what is it that calls you to venture the mighty Ymr?"

"We..." Captain Thorne began, but paused for a long moment before saying sheepishly, "I think Sergeant Rhys do the talk."

Joren's father waved his hand magnanimously. "I understand, my friend! Ask my Runa: when we were young, we traveled east, to be married at the Valdrattr, and there the shamans use a very old and peculiar dialect. Even this I could not master, let alone an entirely different language!" His wife chuckled and patted his arm. "You will learn in time; perhaps even here you will learn something new. But not from that one," he pointed at Pedr, "he has an arsenal of foul jokes, to his mother's great dismay. Though I don't have any idea where he learned them." He cleared his throat pointedly and slipped a wink to his son, who returned a devilish grin.

"The Valdrattr," Sergeant Rhys mused, "that's near Rorhavn, yes? The capital?"

"Yes, not far at all. I think you must know Fjalvard quite well if you have been there?"

"I do," the sergeant replied after draining the last of his stew.

"Mostly with the Order — Holywell was with me there, in fact — but also on my own, when I was a much younger man."

"What did you do then?"

The sergeant gave a demure smile. "I was a trader."

"Noble's son, the sergeant," one of the twins said from the bench. "Made all kinds of gold, then gave it all up to join the Knights."

Joren's father raised his eyebrows. "You gave up a fortune to serve your gods?"

"Well, Felix paints it a little more dramatically than it was, but I did abandon my title and birthright, yes."

"There's not many a man who would do as you, I think, Sergeant."

"Believe me," Rhys said, impassive, "I would not recommend it."

The lady in blue laughed and Joren's father turned to her. "Now, Lady — Gwynlaithe, was it?"

"Helmi, please," she interrupted graciously. "I am not truly a Lady, the good sergeant only uses that title out of kindness." She smiled and Joren's heart skipped a beat.

"Helmi, then. We would know more about you, if you would be so amenable. You must forgive me because I do not know the ways of the southern religions. What did Sergeant Rhys call you?"

"An oracle," she answered, maintaining a very lady-like posture regardless of her claim to the contrary. "I am a vessel of Othelia, the goddess of wisdom. She speaks to me her will and I, in turn, speak it to the Knights Seraphin."

"Ah, so you must be a very important person indeed! 'Lady' is a proper title, then, I think. But the Knights follow Seraphe, do they not? This much, I know. But you are an oracle of Othelia?" He repeated the foreign names slowly and as best he could.

Sergeant Rhys answered. "The Order is devoted to the Lady of Light, yes, but many of the gods keep oracles within our fortress walls, and we hold communion with all of them."

"I see," Joren's father slurped up the last of his broth. "You'll forgive my curiosity: here in Fjalvard — as I'm sure you know — we honor the Slain, our bravely fallen ancestors, and rely on their spirits for strength and guidance. I find it truly amazing that you speak to gods. Our shamans sometimes perform rituals to allow their spirits to fly to the halls of the dead, to learn ancient knowledge and bear messages back from the Slain in Thulheim. How is it with your gods?"

"Ah," Helmi's eyes were alight with curiosity, "how I wish I could have known my mother better, to know more of her culture! You see, she and my father both perished when I was young, and I was raised by the Sisters of the Order. The few books I have relating to Fjalvard are mostly language texts, which record little of your people or history.

"You have intrigued me, Master Segurdsen, and I hope we can speak more before our departure, but allow me to be a good guest and answer your question. I think my communion with Othelia — or rather, the purpose of it — is not so dissimilar to what Fjalr shamans do. Lady Wisdom speaks to me, as I said; often for the purpose of relaying messages from the gods to the Knights of the Order. But like your shamans, she sometimes teaches me ancient rituals and arcane secrets, those that are important for an Oracle to know, but forbidden from being written down, lest evil hands seize and misuse them."

Sergeant Rhys and Brothers Blackhart and Holywell all shifted uncomfortably as Helmi spoke. At a look from the sergeant, the oracle gave an easy laugh and said, "My companions think I have said too much, and perhaps I have. They will forgive me, of course, remembering that this is my first journey out from the Eldric Citadel and I am simply happy to be in my mother's homeland." As she said it, she met the sergeant's gaze. They tested wills for only a moment before Sergeant Rhys relented and looked back down at his bowl with a sigh.

"Er," Joren's father groped for something to break the silence. "You say this is your first trip out from your citadel. Do oracles not often accompany the Knights on their holy quests?"

"No, they don't," Helmi answered with a lingering hint of amusement. "These are somewhat unusual circumstances that bring us north this summer."

"Ah, I see," his smile wavered. "I hope, given the nature of your work, that we are in no great danger here."

"Not at all, master," Sergeant Rhys hurried to assure him. "As we told Master Odursen, we are on our way to Hrokar's Pass, to venture into the Deep Ymr."

"Indeed?" Their father cocked an eyebrow. "The stories of the Knights' bravery must indeed be true, then, if you would traverse that place so willingly."

The sergeant inclined his head. "I suppose that depends on which stories you've heard."

"Wise words, Sergeant." He failed to suppress a grin. "Perhaps you have stories of your own which would prove me right?"

Sergeant Rhys leaned back on his bench. "Very good, master shepherd," he said casually. "Your wife's father requested we share a story with his grandchildren as well. Of what would you like to hear?"

At the mention of a story from the Knights themselves, Joren felt a surge of excitement. Pedr could hardly contain himself, either; he tossed aside his bowl and sat forward, a broad grin spread across his face.

"Tell us a story of your adventures, good Sergeant," Joren's father replied, also leaning back and putting an arm around his wife, "but of your own choosing. I know how dark your business must be, how it must rend the soul of a man. My uncle was a soldier for a time, too, you see. So tell us something light that brings only good memories for you."

"And please," Joren's mother added, "mind the little ears, won't you? Nothing too frightening?"

Pedr moaned in protest. "Mama!"

"Oh!" Grim exclaimed, and slapped his knees. "I've got the perfect one, Sergeant. My little sister asks to hear it every time I'm back home — must've told it to her a hundred times now."

"Very well." Sergeant Rhys nodded somberly.

Grim grinned and rubbed his hands together as he went over to the space by the door. "I call this one 'The Dove Over the Chetwin'."

Joren caught a quick movement out of the corner of his eye

and glanced over to see Sergeant Rhys sitting forward, looking as though someone had slapped him. He recovered quickly, and if anyone else had noticed, they showed no sign of it. Joren's gaze lingered on the sergeant for a moment longer; the man's face betrayed no emotion, but his eyes remained unfocused as he folded his arms and leaned back against the wall again.

Grim cleared his throat and Joren's attention was drawn back to him as the young man assumed a dramatic tone and began his tale.

"In the far north of Carthannas, where the mountains yield before the sea, there stands an ancient and mighty forest. It is a sinister place, known for its feral and wicked monsters. There, we brave souls charged into the darkness on a mission to thin the teeming horde. We made our way, weaving through the colossal tree trunks, hacking through bough and bush," he swung his arms to demonstrate, "cutting a path into the heart of the forest. The darkness pressed close in on us and there pervaded everywhere a terrifying silence, which threatened to drive us mad!" Pedr wriggled up to Vandra, his eyes locked on Grim, and Joren pulled Hala a little closer to him to cradle her head in his lap.

"As we were nearing the center of the wood," Grim continued, "we prepared to find a nest of monsters at any moment. But we did not. Instead, we had pushed on until we were exhausted, and Captain Fielding — this was before Captain Thorne took command of our detachment, you see — finally ordered the halt. He was a grumpy old dog, Captain Fielding, but a good officer, and he let us rest there awhile. Before we had even caught our breath, however, we finally heard the telltale bellowing of some crazed beast. It came from further on, and the captain immediately ordered us back into action, so we charged again, ready for anything.

"We burst out into a clearing with a wide river running through it — the Chetwin, which flows from the mountains down to the sea. Over the river was a crude bridge, and on the bridge, we saw them: huge, made of earth, and simpleminded." Grim pointed at Pedr. "Quick, young master, what kind of monsters do you think they were?"

"Dragons!" Pedr yelled without hesitation.

Grim winced. "Well, no, not dragons. Think of something a little smaller."

"Werewolves!"

"No, they —"

"Golems! Ogres! Gob—" Vandra clamped a hand over his mouth.

"They were trolls!" Grim exclaimed, holding his arms out above his head to demonstrate their monstrous size. "Huge, gnarled, stony trolls, two of them, both standing on the bridge. They were hollering and booming in their deep, mountainous voices and flailing their arms about in the air. We stopped again to watch, stupefied by their inexplicable, wild behavior. The captain ordered us to sneak closer, so we did, and finally we were able to see the cause of their excitement: a beautiful white dove was fluttering all around them and they were trying to catch it, groaning and hollering in frustration at their failed attempts. We were horrified by this, of course, because the dove is one of the blessed creatures of Seraphe, a symbol of purity, innocence, and peace. So Captain Fielding decided it was fate that had brought us there and our duty to put an end to the trolls' petulant game.

"The captain stalked right up onto the bridge — as brazen a man as you've ever seen — and bellowed in his most commanding voice: 'Stop that at once, you lumbering scalawags!'" Grim shook his fist in the air. "The towering trolls — terribly stupid and slow creatures — lowered their arms and turned ponderously around on the captain, seemingly amazed to find him there behind them.

"At the sight of him, one of them rumbled" — he made his voice deep — "'Man-thingy! What you want? We busy!' 'I can see that!' the captain answered hotly. 'But what do you want with that poor, innocent dove?' The troll harrumphed. 'It pet. We keep for fun. Be gone or you be pet, too.' And they turned back, trying to catch the dove again.

"Well, Captain Fielding was not the kind of man to be told off by trolls, so he hollered at them again. 'That bird is a creature sacred to the gods, you oafs! You would not want to anger them, would you?' The trolls let out a stony, earthy laugh. 'No gods here in forest, man-thingy.' This incensed the captain, as it was a horrific insult to the gods and all of us who were so loyal to them. In a fit of rage, he pulled out his sword and held it high to land a powerful blow on the nearest troll's back." Grim demonstrated. "But before he could, our very own Sergeant Rhys rushed in and stopped him, knowing that a blade will do nothing against a troll. Do any of you young ones know how to kill a troll?"

Joren searched his memory for the old stories his father liked to tell. "Oh!" he said, remembering, "they turn to stone in the sunlight!"

"Clever lad, exactly so! But there was a problem — in this dark forest, the sun never pierced through the dense treetops. So what were we to do?" At a loss, Joren looked over to Pedr and Vandra, but they did not know, either. "It just so happens Sergeant Rhys is clever, too," Grim continued. "And he knew another secret about trolls. Their bodies are huge and stony, and their hides are thick and knobby, but they have one little soft spot, here, on the tops of their heads." He turned around and pointed to it on his own shaggy head. "But how to reach them? Well, that's where *I* come into the story!

"We couldn't let those foolish monsters desecrate a holy dove, so we had to take drastic action. If we assaulted them, our blades would do nothing and they would surely have grabbed us up and cast us off of the bridge into the thundering river below. So we had to be smart, and it just so happened that I had an idea. We went a little away from the bridge so the trolls could not hear us. 'If these hooligans want a pet so badly,' said I, 'why don't we find one even more appealing to their childlike sensibilities than a dove?'" Grim turned his head to look pointedly at the twins seated on the bench by the children.

"And that," Felix said with a sigh, "is where *we* come in." The pair stood and crossed over to stand near Grim as he continued his narration.

"Quick, children, what could be more enticing that a beautiful white dove?"

"Dragons!" Pedr cried.

Grim cupped a hand behind his ear. "Did you say *two* birds?

That's exactly right! But not just any two birds — two great, big, awkward birds who sing and dance at a command!" Stooping, he gathered up two of the larger fleeces laying about on the ground and threw one over each of the twins. "So we went about the forest floor, gathering up all the big, wide leaves that were freshly fallen, and laced them with string all around these two, making each a nice coat of marvelous, green feathers. Then we took lengths of stripped bark and made beaks for them, and now they were truly starting to look like the strangest pair of birds in the world." Felix and Fergus moved their arms up and down so that the fleece looked a little like flapping wings.

"They don't look like birds!" Pedr protested, then yelped as Vandra pinched him.

"Quite right, young master," Grim nodded sagely. "They don't now, and truth be told, neither did they then. Luckily, though, we didn't have to contend with a shrewd young man like yourself — rather, we had only to trick two foolish trolls. So, we had their disguises arrayed well and we led them, as though they were trained, back down to the bridge.

"The trolls were still desperately trying to catch the poor dove, who by now was tiring."

"Why didn't it fly away?" Vandra asked quietly.

Grim paused and looked at her. "Er, fly away? I don't…"

"Because," Fergus explained, "it had made its nest on one of the trusses under the bridge. It was trying valiantly to scare off the trolls from its home."

"Right!" Grim said, a look of relief passing quickly across his face. "Just so. And while the dove was continuing to distract the trolls, we came down to a spot a little ways off from the bridge. Captain Fielding shouted to the monsters, gaining their attention. 'You still here, man-thingy?' one growled back at him. 'I am, and I have found you not one pet bird but two. Come and see!'

"The trolls looked supremely suspicious, but they made their way over nonetheless to see what the captain had found for them. They came up and looked upon the 'birds' in astonishment. 'What these?' they asked, and reached out to poke Felix. The captain arrested them with a warning. 'Careful,' he said, 'these are special birds, trained to obey commands and provide entertainment for their masters. For instance, tell them to dance for you.'

"The trolls looked at each other, then back to the twins and ordered, 'Dance!'" Grim stepped back toward the door with a broad grin. "Well, boys? What did you do?"

Felix and Fergus looked at each other from under their fleeces and then leapt into a raucous dance, squawking and flapping, kicking their legs back to smack their own rear ends. Pedr guffawed until he devolved into racked silence, tears streaming from his eyes, and Joren could hardly breathe he laughed so hard. Their father pounded the table and roared in laughter, and Vandra and their mother were unable to suppress their own amusement. Even Agata squealed happily in her big sister's lap as everyone laughed around her.

Grim pushed in between the twins and settled them down. "Meanwhile," he announced, "as these two fools—"

"*Magnificent* fools, thank you kindly," Felix interjected.

"As you say. As these magnificent fools so expertly distracted the thoroughly stupefied trolls, the rest of our detachment sneaked around behind them. We piled one man on top of the other so that we had two man-towers of three each. I was on top of the one, Brother Holywell on top of the other. We maneuvered masterfully up behind our quarry, swords in hand. Then, with a superlative blow from each of us, the terrible trolls were laid to ruin, and the beautiful white dove flew off to leave the horrid forest for good."

"What about her nest under the bridge?" Joren asked, still trying to catch his breath.

"Oh, yes," Grim hurried to correct himself. "She brought her little dove-lings with her out of the horrid forest and they lived a peaceful life from then on in the beautiful green hills of Carthannas. The end!"

Though mildly confused, Joren clapped and cheered with the rest of his family as Grim and the twins bowed and retook their seats. He looked back at those around the table and saw that Sergeant Rhys still had the strange expression, staring down at the tabletop as though it was miles away.

Joren's father chuckled and dried his eyes. "Ah, Master Grim, you have quite a talent at weaving a tale! Do tell us, how did you acquire such skill?"

"Well," the young soldier said, sheepishly, "I have spent a good amount of time in Fjalvard with the Knights, and on one of our last forays here, we fell in with a traveling skald. In exchange for our protection on the roads, he taught me some of the tools of his own trade. I have much more to learn, though, of course." He blushed.

"Nonsense!" the shepherd cried, resting his large hands on the table and standing from the bench. "It was a fine story — I'll have to remember it for my grandchildren! Oh, er," he leaned in close to his wife and muttered, "is there any supper left, love?"

"Oh, yes," their mother's cheeks were still flushed from laughter, "I believe so."

He turned back to Captain Thorne and his men. "Would you men like some more to eat, then? Milady?" Without waiting for an answer, he grabbed up their dishes and started refilling them with what remained in the big cook pot.

The sergeant finally stirred, and Brothers Holywell and Blackhart shared a look behind his back. Joren was clever enough to know that something had happened, but he could not figure out what it was.

Joren's father called to him and pointed with his chin. "You and Pedr go take Hala out to the shelter for the night and make sure the gate's shut tight."

"Yes, Papa." Joren rose and grabbed Pedr's wrist, dragging him along toward the door as Hala padded after them.

"Then all you pups get up to bed, it's late already."

Still pondering Sergeant Rhys's shift in mood, Joren took up the remaining scraps piled near the door, and they led the sheepdog outside. It had grown just cold enough that he felt the need to lift his shoulders to his ears to try and block the wind. He had to push Pedr along as he kept stopping to imitate the dance the twins had done, giggling like a madman.

The sheep were huddled against the stone walls and the mules and horse stood alongside each other. He and Pedr sat with Hala for a bit, rubbing her belly while she gnawed the scraps, and then rose and shut the gate behind them.

After making use of the latrine once Vandra was done, they went back into the welcome warmth of the hall.

"I would have news of the fair south," their father was saying, as the captain pushed his twice-emptied bowl to the center of the table. "We have not heard ought of Carthannas since Old Havar, a trader, came up two seasons ago."

As Pedr kicked off his leather shoes and scurried up the ladder, Joren knelt, taking his time scraping the dirt off his boots so that he could listen to the conversation.

Sergeant Rhys took a moment to respond, and when he did, he sounded very tired. "I don't think much has changed since then, master shepherd, but I'll tell you what I can." His second helping sat untouched on the table in front of him.

Joren's mother stood from the bench, Agata nodding off in her arms, and bustled up to him. "Go on, Joren, up to bed with you," she whispered as the sergeant spoke too quietly for Joren to hear. Reluctantly, he stood and she gave him a hug and a kiss before prodding him up the ladder.

Pedr already had his eye pressed to a space between the boards to watch and hear what was going on. Joren scrambled over beside him, dragging his fleece over to the spot.

"What are you doing?" Vandra asked quietly. They both glared up at her before returning their eyeballs to the gaps in the floor. Vandra sighed and rolled over, leaving them to their snooping.

Grim had taken over for Sergeant Rhys, who remained inexplicably sullen. He was giving an answer to some question by their father that Joren had not heard. "… and the Order sends detachments of Knights out to nearly every known land, you see — but I suppose you already knew that." He gave a self-conscious laugh.

"Indeed," their father said, turning on his bench to better see the three men by the fire. "All the tales I've ever heard hold that peoples of all nations are glad at your coming."

"Except the ones we're sent to kill, eh?" one of the twins snickered.

Their father downed a gulp of mead. "I thought you were monster-slayers."

The other twin nodded. "That we are."

"But you kill men, too?"

"Well, only when those men are monsters," Grim explained. "I'm sure you know as well as we do, master — there are all kinds of evils in the world. Some are more mundane than others, surely, but nonetheless horrible."

"I suppose I do," their father answered, "though our little valley seems peaceful compared to the places you've been. I guess not every story ends so happily as that of the trolls and the dove, eh?"

Even without being able to see most of what was happening, Joren felt the mood suddenly shift.

"No," Sergeant Rhys answered bitterly. "No, they don't all end so well." Through the crack, Joren watched as the man's knuckles whitened on his interlocked fingers. "In fact, I'm not sure any stories we have end happily."

"Well," his father's tone held the same note of apprehension Joren felt, "that one, at least, seems to —"

"It didn't," the sergeant cut him off. Brother Holywell laid a hand on his shoulder, but Sergeant Rhys ignored it. "Trolls on a bridge," he scoffed, "trying to catch a dove. What utter nonsense...."

Their father gingerly set his mug down on the table. "I don't understand."

"I'm sorry, Sergeant," Grim said quickly, sounding guilty, "I forgot, honest, I didn't mean to —"

"Grim," Sergeant Rhys interrupted him, and Joren watched as the muscles in the man's jaw tensed, "tell him the real story."

Moving his head swiftly over to another crack, he saw the young soldier sigh and rest his elbows on his knees. "The trolls and the dove... it's a story I came up with; told my little sister once when she asked what I do with the Knights. What really happened was, we were on our way to a town called Darrow-by-the-Sea, and we had to go through Mosglau Wood, where the Chetwin flows. Well, we came up close to the bridge, but heard a disturbance before we could cross it — just like in the story. Only it wasn't trolls. It was two boys, about your Vandra's age. They were carrying something wrapped up in a blanket between them, trying to hoist it over the side to the waters below. The captain had a strange feeling, so he ordered us to investigate. We ran up and seized the two of them before they could get away.

"They were massively afraid, those boys, with all of us looming over them, demanding what they were up to. We asked what it was in the blanket and one of them burst into tears. We unrolled it and, well…. It was a girl, beaten, bloody, and dead. When he saw her, Captain Fielding smacked them both about until he got the story out of the one that was weeping.

"They were from a nearby village, so was she, and they had fancied her. Not she, them, however. So they forced themselves on her, even though she wanted none. He swore it was an accident, that they hadn't meant to hurt her, and so on, and they decided to throw her in the river to keep anyone from finding out. Before that night, I didn't know children could do something so wicked." He sighed again. "Anyway, the captain had us string up the lads right then and there, from the same bridge. 'Rapers that age won't magically turn to good men,' he said. We carried the girl back to the village so her ma and da could mourn and bury her, and told folks where we'd hanged the boys.

"Couldn't rightly tell my little sister about that, could I? And the sergeant's right — none of our other stories are fit for little ears, either, really." He glanced at Sergeant Rhys and gave a nervous shrug. "So I make some of them story-like, give them happy endings — like the innocent little dove escaping, like it should have been."

Joren's mouth had gone dry. He looked up at Pedr; drool ran down his little brother's cheek as he lay fast asleep. A knot in his stomach, Joren returned his eye to the space in the boards.

Their father was pallid. "I…" he swallowed hard, "I had no idea."

"You told me to pick a tale of my choosing." Sergeant Rhys glared at him. "'One that brought only good memories'. For men like us, there *are* no good memories. Only painful struggle and bloodshed." He sat forward, leaning over the table, and the Knights on either side of him shifted in response, as though readying to intervene if necessary. "You're a blessed man, living a peaceful life; you have no idea of the things men like us do — are forced to do — or the toll it takes on us. And you have the gall to ask me for good memories?" His hands trembled on the table. "I tell you, I have none."

Captain Thorne cleared his throat and without another word, the sergeant rose and pushed passed the others, through the door, and out into the night air, a chilly gust fanning the flames of the cook pit in his wake.

"You idiot," one of the twins said, slapping Grim on the arm. "What'd you have to tell that story for?"

"I forgot," the young man moaned, his cheeks flushed. "I've told the fairy-tale version to my sister so many times, I forgot not to tell it around him."

"I'm sorry," Joren's father said, at a loss. He looked to the others at the table, desperate to understand what had just happened. "I'm so sorry, I meant no offense by what I said, on my honor!"

Helmi took one of his hands in hers. "Be at peace, Master Segurdsen," she bade him. "You did nothing wrong. The sergeant carries many wounds from a life in a violent service."

"She's right, master," Grim nodded. "It's my fault. You see, there's a bit I left out of that story about the boys on the bridge." He shifted uncomfortably for a moment before continuing. "Not long after that, Captain Fielding killed himself — stepped off a cliff after we reached Darrow-by-the-Sea. That hit Sergeant right hard, harder than the rest of us." Holywell gave a solemn nod. "I didn't remember how bad that story could hurt him. So it's my fault, master shepherd, not yours."

Joren's father shook his head. "Whether I meant to or not, I've offended one of my guests. This does not stand among my people. I must make it right."

"If I know the sergeant," Grim sighed, "there's naught anyone can do to calm him. He's got to do that himself. But please don't hold this against him. Sergeant doesn't mean anything by it, sometimes he just gets lost in the bad things that happen. There really have been good times, honestly — some men just have a harder time seeing them, is all."

Helmi drew the attention of Joren's father again. "Fret not, master, I beg you. You have been a good and honorable host and done nothing wrong. Leave Sergeant Rhys to us. For now, go to your wife, sleep, and in the morning everything will be right."

Reluctantly, he rose and did as she said, managing to bid the soldiers a good night on his way. The captain said something to his men in Carthan and they all stood and started preparing to bed down for the night. Helmi passed gracefully by and out through the door after Sergeant Rhys.

Joren rolled over on his fleece and his eyes drifted to the smoke hole in the ceiling, through which a few stars were visible. Grim's true story had surprised him, and he felt foolish that it had. They were men, soldiers — of course their stories were not cute and funny.

As someone heaped the ashes up and the flames died away, he thought about the poor girl, the boys they had hanged, and Captain Fielding killing himself. It left him with a strange tightness in his chest; perhaps Joren did not want to be a Knight so badly after all.

Rhys took a deep breath, filling his lungs with the chilly mountain air. He never used to get so angry. As the years passed, however, his patience waned, and he was realizing an unpleasant truth about himself: he hated anyone who was happy. Naive shepherds, simple farmers, idiot fisherman — they lived such fragile lives, blissfully ignorant of the the horrors that could rain down on them at any moment. And of course, once the terrors came, all they could do was beg Rhys or other Knights to save them. He clenched and unclenched his fist as he tried to calm himself.

The door of the hall opened, spilling light across the darkened hills, and then closed. Rhys prepared for Thorne to give him the same lecture he had given the captain in Kaninholm, about fostering relations with the common folk, but it was Helmi's voice that broke the silence.

"Are you alright, Garret?"

He cleared his throat before answering. "Fine, Milady."

"I've asked you not to call me that."

"Of course." He sighed. "My apologies, Helmi. I'm… slightly out of sorts, I suppose."

"I should say so." She smiled at him and he relaxed a little. Tilting her head back to gaze at the stars that blanketed the night sky, she said, "The shepherd is quite distressed. He's convinced he insulted you somehow."

"I'm an old soldier with a bad temper — he insults me with his happy existence."

"Garret!" she admonished him gently. "I did not take you for a bitter man."

He grunted even as his frustration began to ebb. "I try not to be, gods help me."

"I'm so sorry to hear about Captain Fielding." She laid a hand on his arm and gave a little squeeze.

"He was a good man." Rhys had never spoken of his death with anyone — not once — since reporting it to the marshal. "I've spent the last few years wondering why he did it. He didn't say anything beforehand. I think…" he folded his arms, and Helmi kept her hand on him, which he found oddly comforting. His temper had cooled and was giving way to melancholy, and something about Helmi seemed to coax the words from him. "I think he was tired. I think seeing that girl and having to hang those boys — even though it was justice — was the last bit he could take. It just became too much for him."

"Oh, Garret," he looked over to find her eyes glistening in the moonlight. "I'm so sorry."

Rhys shrugged and forced a hollow chuckle. "I never talk about such things. Better not to. But they say men soften in their old age; it would seem they're right. I…" he hesitated, wondering why he kept talking. "I often wonder what happens to brave men who kill themselves," he sighed, looking up at the stars. "Men like Marcus Fielding, who were selfless and honorable their whole lives, accomplished everything demanded of them and more, but at the end could not bring themselves to go on, for whatever reason.

"They never sing songs for those men, do they? The ballads and epics are always about fallen warriors who die in battle, never about those who end their own lives. More often than not, they're ignored, or written off as cowards." His fist tightened again. "But that's not right. It's not for a bard or minstrel to presume to know the heart and soul of a warrior. Would the gods damn a man for breaking under a burden he never should have had to carry? Or are their souls brought to Eirna, that they may be honored in the afterlife just the same as any others who die in service of gods or king?"

Helmi laced her other arm under his and hugged it, but gave no answer. In truth, he was thankful; as an oracle, she may very well have had the answers to such questions, but learning the truth was not worth the risk of receiving a bad answer.

"Anyhow," he said, clearing his throat, "I suppose I'll have to make things right with the shepherd."

"In the morning," she said softly, finally releasing his arm. "They've all gone to bed now."

"Very well. I'll be happy to leave in the morning, I think." Rhys was uncomfortable with the silence that followed, so he asked the first thing that came to his mind. "Have you had any word from your goddess?"

Helmi chuckled. "No, Garret. How many times will you ask me that question on this journey?"

"Until the answer is 'yes', I suppose."

"You have a while to wait for that. Othelia told me that she would speak to me again once we'd arrived at our intended destination, and I don't expect there will be anything before that. Besides, you would know it if I had. Communion with the gods is quite taxing; it's not something that can be hidden."

"How do you mean?" Helmi had not spoken to him about this before.

She frowned. "I don't know precisely. The friars who attend us never speak of it, but once Othelia releases me, I see the fear and distress written on the faces of the neophytes; I'm exhausted, and my own legs can hardly hold me for hours afterward."

"I see." Rhys had no idea what happened inside the sanctum, and apparently it was vastly different than anything he might have imagined.

"Have you never seen an oracle commune with the gods before?"

"Of course not. Have you ever seen anyone other than the friars or officers of the Order in the sanctum with you during your communion?" She shook her head, but he already knew the answer. "To bear witness to such a thing is not meant for men like me, but for those pure of spirit."

"You're a holy warrior, though," she offered.

"We are warriors in the service of a holy order," Rhys corrected her. "There is a world of difference there. We're little more than tools in the hands of the gods."

"That's ridiculous," she chided, "I'll not stand here and permit you to speak about my road family like that."

"Your what?"

"My road family — you, the captain, and all the rest. You're brave, peerless warriors who deserve fame and wealth and peace in the afterlife."

Rhys could not help but chuckle. "Where did you come up with a name like that?"

"Well, what else would you call us? We're a little family on the road, and I'm the newest member. Except for Aedric."

They were quiet for a time after that, watching together as the stars spun slowly around the earth. A few of the others came out of the hall one at a time to make their obligatory trip to the latrine, but no one bothered them.

After a while, Helmi leaned closer and asked in a low voice, "Do you want to know a secret?" He cocked his brow at her impish grin. "I lied. I *do* know someone besides the friars who has seen my communion with Lady Wisdom."

"Who?" he asked, skeptical.

She threw a glance over her shoulder, then whispered, "Aedric."

"The Ilban?" Rhys turned to face her, surprised. "The friars allowed him into the sanctum?""

"Yes!" She bit her lip, her eyes dancing in excitement. "Not only did he witness it — Othelia spoke to him herself."

"What?" Rhys's heart leapt in his chest. "Well, what... what did she —" he stopped himself. This was startling and unsettling news to be sure, but he was conflicted about asking after a goddess's business that was not meant for his ears.

"What did she say?" Helmi shook her head. "I do not know. She used me as her conduit, but I could not hear their words."

"I thought she speaks to you, and then you relay her words to others."

"Usually, yes. But sometimes she takes over and I can't hear or see or feel and she speaks directly. Usually to the marshal or matron."

"Do you know why he was there? Did she seek him out?"

Her eyes flashed in the moonlight. "I don't know why he was there, but before his arrival, I did hear the friars whispering about an irate foreigner at the gates of the citadel, demanding an audience with the gods. Then she spoke to me, told me to inform the friars she desired to see him. As soon as he arrived in the sanctum, her spirit overwhelmed me and I heard nothing else. I returned to consciousness and only just saw his back as he left. The friars offered no explanation." She still wore a thrilled little smile.

Her giddiness annoyed him. "You're far too amused by all this." The full implications of what she was saying were beyond his grasp, but he understood their dire importance nonetheless. He had never heard of the gods granting audiences to the uninitiated. His suspicions about the Ilban were confirmed, then: there was much more to the man than it appeared on the surface.

"Not amused," Helmi insisted, "Intrigued! Who is this man, that the goddess should speak to him?"

Rhys wondered the same, but instead of speculating, he asked, "Is this why you told me we shouldn't trust him? But if Othelia wants him here, why wouldn't we?"

She pursed her lips. "The goddess of wisdom is not like Seraphe. Your Lady Light is pure and righteous, while Othelia can be crafty and guileful. One can never assume her motivations or intentions as readily as Seraphe's."

"That strikes me as being... worrisome, to say the least," he mused.

"Your goddess agreed with mine," she shrugged, "otherwise I would be here on my own. Regardless, back to the matter at hand — Aedric seems harmless enough, but there must be a reason Othelia wanted him to come with us."

"He's absolutely not harmless," Rhys disagreed. "Not if he was with the Dalbragh, as he claims."

"You know of them?"

"I've crossed paths with them a time or two over the years. They're an Ilban mercenary band, fighting for whoever has the deepest pockets. Honorless churls, but nonetheless dangerous. And if he speaks to gods... perhaps even more so."

"So what do we do about him? Should we tell the captain?"

He cast a sidelong glance at her. "I thought you swore an oath of silence on the matter."

"I did," she waved a hand, "to myself. In case I wasn't supposed to say anything. But I simply couldn't keep the secret any longer. Besides, now I know you better: you're the noble Sergeant Rhys. Surely no harm can come from telling you."

"Well," he watched his breath frost in the light from the heavens, "I will speak with the captain tomorrow about the Ilban. In the meantime, I do not foresee much sleep for me tonight."

"I suppose we had better get back and try, though," she suggested, hugging herself against the cold.

"You go on ahead. I need another moment to clear my thoughts."

She gave him a reassuring smile and returned to the shepherd's hall.

Rhys frowned as he watched her go. For the past week or so of their journey, his interactions with the girl had been stirring foreign emotions in his mind. At first, he was afraid that the feelings were more than friendly, but it was not that. She was a beautiful young woman, certainly, but he was old and tired, and had no capacity for romance anymore.

Instead, he was struggling with a growing sense of regret. The mere mention of his past life — something he never thought about anymore — during supper had awoken thoughts of what an alternate life might have looked like for him. Seeing the shepherd's happy little family only made the feelings grow.

Rhys imagined what it would be like if he had not joined the Order, but married the girl his father had chosen for him; they could have had a whole slew of children by now. Maybe they would be happy, like the shepherd and his wife. He could almost see himself bouncing a little baby girl on his knee, and he wondered what she would have been like once she grew up. He smiled as he realized he hoped she would be like Helmi.

As soon as the thought entered his mind, though, he banished it. The idea suddenly became too painful for him to go further. All of that was impossible now: he was an old misanthrope who knew nothing anymore but death and heartache. It was far too late for him to try for that kind of happiness, and there was nothing useful in feeling sorry for himself about it.

Rhys sighed and ran a hand through his long, greying hair and stuffed the thoughts back down. He was tired, and increasingly aware of his advancing age. His father had not made it past fifty-three years; Rhys was not far from that mark himself.

He stared up at the stars for a while, appreciating their independence from his own troubles. After a moment, though, all the heavens seemed to fade, flickering briefly. He cursed his old eyes and rubbed the weariness from them. When he looked back, the stars were shining as bright as they ever had. Reluctantly, he surrendered to his exhaustion and made the short walk up the hill to use the latrine.

In the shepherd's hall, the faint glow of the moon through the smoke holes gave him just enough light to step over Felix's form, sprawled out on the fleece-covered floor. He looked down at the spot next to the captain, left for him to use, but did not feel ready for sleep yet, tired though he was. With a sigh, he decided he might as well pull watch. Sitting down on the bench by the table, he scooted back and kicked his feet up, stifling a groan as the gravel in his joints shifted.

As his eyes adjusted to the darkness, he saw two icy flashes on one of the benches along the wall. The Ilban's eyes reflected the moonlight as he looked up at the ceiling, and Rhys thought he saw a tear slide down into his rough beard. The kilted man quickly rolled over, hiding his face and leaving Rhys more bewildered than before.

4

DISAPPEARANCE

Again Joren woke while it was still dark. This time, though, there were no goosebumps. Instead, it was the creaking of the loft boards that stirred him from his sleep. He lifted his head and cast about groggily just in time to see Pedr move past him, climb onto the ladder, and start down.

Assuming he was heading to use the latrine, Joren reluctantly threw his top fleece off and crawled after him. "Wait, Pedr," he mumbled, "I have to go with you, remember?" The rule had always been that no one was to go out at night alone, but Pedr was still young and occasionally forgot. His little brother did not respond, nor did he wait when he got down to the bottom of the ladder.

Joren hurried to catch up with him, but as he reached the ground, Pedr threw open the door and dashed outside, barefoot and wearing only his thin linens. The bleating of the restless sheep could be heard on the other side of the wall, and Sergeant Rhys grumbled and stirred where he sat at the table as Joren quickly slid his boots on and went after Pedr, annoyed that he would not listen.

The sky was clear on the mountainside and the moon was bright as it hung near the Ymr's peak. Pedr was already halfway to the latrine, taking long, jarring steps. "Pedr, wait!" Joren hissed, and followed after him.

Coming up alongside him, he grabbed his little brother by the shoulder to try and slow him, but Pedr shrugged him off. "What's wrong with you, you little gnat?" Joren grabbed him again, more firmly, and Pedr flailed his arm, smacking Joren hard across the face. He stumbled back and fell, tasting blood where his teeth had bitten into his lip. Angry tears made his vision waver but he climbed back to his feet and dashed after Pedr again.

His little brother was walking even faster; not running, but taking long, odd steps, his hands loose at his sides. Joren thought for a moment that he would arrive at the latrine first and shut him out, but he walked right past it, continuing on up the slope of the mountain.

Joren had to sprint to catch up to Pedr and his lungs started to gulp the air greedily as he finally reached him. He tackled his younger brother, dragging him to the ground. They wrestled for a moment before Pedr started moaning and crying. "I have to go to her," he wept. "She needs me, let me go!"

"What are you talking about?" Joren demanded, some of his anger wilting to fear. "Wake up, Pedr!" He held his brother's wrists tight as they struggled.

"She needs me!" he shrieked again. "She needs! She needs me!" His shrill cries tore along the mountainside and he pulled out of Joren's grasp, kicking him off and scrambling to his feet. Joren tried to seize him again, but Pedr leapt away and started running.

Giving chase, Joren pumped his legs hard and fast, knowing his little brother could not outrun him. But he did. Joren could not even get within arms' reach again and after a short time, his lungs were burning and the gap between them widened. He pushed himself as hard as he could, terrified to let Pedr escape, but his legs gave out and he tripped over the stones that littered the mountainside and fell, heaving for breath. His shin smacked against a rock but he tried to ignore the pain.

"Pedr!" he croaked, watching the shape of his little brother as it dwindled up the slope. Joren started to crawl after him, fear thrumming through his mind.

A large hand closed on his arm and he whirled, lashing out in panic. Brother Holywell held Joren still until he realized what was happening and calmed. The mute shrugged with his hands and pointed at him.

"Pedr ran away," Joren replied, understanding the silent question. "There's something wrong with him, he wouldn't stop!" He turned and pointed out the direction.

Brother Holywell nodded and stood, motioning for Joren to remain where he was, and pointed down the hill; lanterns swayed back and forth as the other soldiers made their way up the slope. Then he took off after Pedr.

As the heat from his exertion left him, the cold began to seep through his linens and Joren started shivering violently. It was only a few moments before Sergeant Rhys and the others got to him.

"What's happened?" the sergeant asked without ceremony, keeping one hand on the hilt of the sword at his waist.

Brother Blackhart knelt and threw a fleece over Joren as he repeated what he had told Brother Holywell. The sergeant translated for his captain and there was a brief exchange between them and the big hospitaler in their own language. Brother Blackhart pulled Joren's lip down to inspect the damage and shrugged. Then Sergeant Rhys placed a hand on his shoulder and said, "Don't worry, young master, we're going to go find your brother. Grim will take you back down to your parents."

Joren felt like he should protest, insist on going with them, but he knew they would not allow it; in truth, he was spent, his face and leg hurt, and he felt sick in his stomach. So he simply nodded and Grim picked him up in his arms and carried him carefully down the slope.

His mother and father, also in their linens, met them halfway to the hall. "Oh, Joren!" She cried, her face pallid. "What's happening? We heard your brother screaming—" She searched the darkness behind Grim. "Where is he?"

Grim set Joren down and his mother took him by the arms to inspect him. His father stood with his big crook in one hand and a lantern in the other. When the light illuminated Joren's face, his mother gasped. "What's happened to you? Where's Pedr?" she asked again, panic tightening her voice.

"He ran." In the safety of his mother's presence, the fear overwhelmed him and tears flowed freely down his cheeks. "I thought he was just going to use the latrine, but he kept going and when I tried to stop him he hit me! Then I grabbed him but he got away and started running so fast I couldn't keep up with him." He collapsed into his mother, ashamed of the tears that would not stop. Hala's barking echoed up from down in the shelter, and in that moment, he wanted nothing more than to go to her.

"Master Grim," his father demanded, "what's happened, do you know?"

"I know only what Joren here told us. They fought and your younger one ran off. The captain and the rest of them are off chasing him now."

"We didn't fight!" Joren protested, but his mother held him tight against her bosom.

"Olen," she looked fearfully up at her husband.

He laid a hand on her shoulder. "Don't worry, my love. I'm going after them."

"I don't think there's a need, master," Grim said, turning as the shepherd passed him. "Brother Holywell's chasing after Pedr right now, and that man is the wind. I imagine they'll be coming back down the mountain with him any moment."

"Oh, I don't doubt your man." Joren's father frowned. "Still, I think I'll follow after so I can carry him back down. Runa, you and Joren go back to the hall. I'll bring Pedr back soon, love. Master Grim, will you see them down for me?"

"As you wish, master," Grim nodded, and Joren's father continued on after the others. The young soldier turned back to Joren and his mother. "Come, mistress, let's get you two back to the hall, and to warmth. They'll be just behind us, I have no doubt." He went ahead of them to light their way with his lantern while she kept Joren pulled tightly to her.

Inside the hall, Vandra sat on a bench, bundled in a fleece, with Agata asleep on her shoulder. Helmi sat as regal as ever next to her, and the Ilban, Aedric, was busy feeding kindling into the fire pit. Joren sat on one of the benches at the table and his mother grabbed water and a swatch of clean wool to scrub his battered face and leg. Hala had ceased her commotion and there was no sound from the shelter behind the hall.

"Mama," Vandra asked in a small voice, "what happened? Where are Pedr and Papa?"

"Your brothers had a fight and Pedr ran away," she answered with a sniffle.

Joren pushed her hand away from his face. "We didn't fight!" he insisted again. "Pedr went crazy, he wouldn't listen to me!"

"Hush," she ordered, wiping his split lip firmly with the swatch.

Vandra shifted in her seat and Agata's hand twitched against her chest. "What do you mean, Joren?"

"I tried to stop him, but he wouldn't listen," he felt the tears welling again but blinked them away angrily. "He just kept shouting nonsense."

"What nonsense?" she pressed.

"He said he had to go to 'her', that 'she' needed him." As he said it, a horrific thought entered his mind, and when the blood drained from his sister's face, he knew she understood it, too. Helmi had also straightened and fixed her eyes on him.

"He was having a fit," their mother explained, scrubbing at the large scrape down his shin. "A nightmare."

"No, Mama," Vandra whispered. The Burnt Lady's awful face hung in Joren's mind and his heart started pounding, thumping in his ears. "Tell her, Joren."

"Tell me what?"

Joren swallowed hard, looking away from his mother's gaze. He still felt like a foolish child, believing in his own nightmares, but he had to say something. Vandra's fearful countenance confirmed it.

"The other night," he began shakily, "I thought I saw something in the woods by the stream. Some kind of creature — not like a wolf or fox, something else. A face." He did not know how to explain it and his mother's skeptical frown was not encouraging. He was thankful, at least, that his father was not there to hear his silly fantasies. "Then that night, I woke up and saw a woman, a burnt and withered woman, in the loft with us, crouching over

Pedr. She tried to steal him, but I made a noise and she screamed at me — well, she didn't make any sound, but she tried to scream. Then I woke up again and she was gone."

He noticed as he spoke that the others had all turned their attention toward him, even Aedric. "She tried to steal your brother?" Grim asked, narrowing his eyes. He and Helmi shared a meaningful look.

"I'm sure it was just a nightmare, but —"

"What did she look like, exactly?" the lady in blue interrupted him in a kindly voice.

"Do you think she was real?" Joren asked, afraid to hear her response.

Helmi stood and came over, kneeling beside him. "I don't know, sweetheart. But if you can help me understand what you think you saw, we can find out."

"You can't be serious?" Joren's mother turned to look at the other woman. "He had a nightmare."

"Sometimes," Grim said, "nightmares are more than simple dreams."

"What did she look like?" Helmi asked again.

"Well," Joren looked up at the rafters, trying to ignore the fear the memories brought so he could recall the details, "she was thin and bony — like she was starved. Her eyes were too large for her head and they were all black. She had pale skin, whiter than mine, but only her neck and face. Everything else was black, like she was covered in soot. And she had long, oily, black hair."

Helmi gave him a reassuring smile. "Randolph," she said, looking up at Grim, "will you please help me get into my travel chest?" The young soldier went immediately over to the pile of gear they had stacked in the corner earlier that evening and started rummaging through it.

Helmi took a seat at the table across from Joren and cleared the space before her. Once Grim had moved the other equipment off the trunk, he opened it up and started bringing over stacks of books, setting them down on the table with a thump. Shuffling through the different volumes, Helmi pulled one from the middle of the first stack: a big, aged tome, bound in embossed leather.

"What are those?" Joren asked, leaning over to get a better look.

"These are ancient books of the Order," she answered, already leafing through one. "This one is a bestiary; a collection of many bestiaries, actually. It has been compiled over centuries by the friars and has much information about nearly every creature that walks the earth."

"So you think the Burnt Lady was real?" he asked, afraid of what that meant.

"Perhaps. You have given me much information, Joren, thank you."

"Do you mean…" his mother's voice broke, but she cleared her throat and continued. "Do you mean that Pedr didn't just run away? What happened to him, then?"

"It's alright, mistress," Grim said, taking her hand and guiding her to sit on the bench next to Vandra. "Whatever may have happened, the captain and the rest are after him, and they'll find him — you have my word."

Their mother took Agata from Vandra and propped the toddler on her shoulder, fighting back tears as she struggled to understand what was happening. No one slept the remainder of the night.

～

Rhys plodded his way carefully in pursuit of Holywell, the lanterns they carried throwing their paltry light only a few yards before melting against the darkness. The further up the slope they climbed, the more the grasses gave way to rocks, many seemingly the perfect size for a man to trip over and snap his ankle.

Holywell was moving more quickly than they, though not by much; his silhouette was just distinguishable in the moonlight past the haze of the lanterns, a hundred yards or so away. He alone had seen the boy run off up the slope and presumably was now following his trail, stooping every so often, then continuing on.

"Why are we trudging up this damned mountain in the

middle of the night, exactly?" Fergus grumbled, breathing heavily. "Could someone please remind me?"

"Boys must've fought," his twin answered. "The little one popped him in the mouth but good! Did you see it? Lip split clean open." He laughed.

"Well, how'd he get away from Holywell? How fast is this little bugger?"

"He's tiny, reckon he lost sight of him among the rocks."

"Like as not he's already filling a wolf's belly, and we're chasing a ghost. No point in being out here, you ask me."

"As it happens, no one did ask you, Comstock," Rhys snapped, his own breath coming a little harder than he liked. "Keep your mouth shut until you can say something useful."

"Sergeant!" Thorne called from a few paces ahead of them. Rhys lengthened his stride and caught up with him. "As I'm sure you can imagine, I'm not thrilled to have our men losing sleep, risking their safety on this mountain at night." Deep, rasping breaths punctuated his sentences as they continued the low climb. "I'm willing to do it, however, for our host — following your example." He looked pointedly at his sergeant. "But as unfortunate as it might be, if we aren't able to find him soon, we will be on our way as we already agreed. Nothing has changed."

Rhys nodded; he was quickly learning the extent of Thorne's intensity firsthand. Without answering, he purposefully changed the subject. "There's something I need to talk to you about, Captain. Earlier, Helmi and I spoke privately."

"Yes, I'm aware of that, Sergeant," Thorne answered gruffly. "I wasn't able to follow much of your exchange with the shepherd, but whatever happened, you did not handle yourself very well. The marshal warned me about your temper. I'd hoped it wouldn't be an issue."

Rhys's cheeks flushed. "I make no excuses for my behavior, Captain."

"Good — there aren't any. For gods' sakes, man, you were the one who lectured me in Kaninholm about taking care of the common folk!"

"You're right," Rhys answered through gritted teeth. The man certainly knew how to press an issue. "I apologize for my outburst and won't allow my temper to best me again."

"Likely you won't have the chance — as soon as we find the boy, we'll head back, finish the night, and leave as soon as the sun is up."

"Very good, Captain. Now, as to what I want to discuss — Helmi told me that the Ilban spoke directly to Othelia."

That caught Thorne off guard. He cocked his brow. "What do you mean?"

"She claims that he was allowed access to the oracles' sanctum and that while she was in communion with the goddess, he spoke to her himself."

"That can't be," Thorne shook his head.

"It's what the girl claims." Rhys pulled at his collar, releasing some of the uncomfortable heat that was building from the climb. "What did the marshal tell you about him? Did he offer any explanation as to the man's presence among us?"

"No, nothing. You have already heard every word spoken to me on this matter. But faith and trust are always necessary in our line of work — you know that, Sergeant. If Othelia wants him here, as the marshal says, then I remain unconcerned."

"I trust the marshal, but I most certainly do not trust the Ilban, not an inch. Helmi doesn't, either. Enough that we were sent on an unknown errand, but now we have a stranger with us who speaks to the gods? I don't like this, Captain."

"Really, Sergeant, every mission we undertake has its risks, this is no different."

He heard in the younger man's voice that his patience for the subject was waning. Rhys was discontent to remain silent, though. "I know of your reputation in the Order," he said, choosing his words carefully. "You have seen much in your few years. I heard about the business in Oaxatl — I have seen bad days, as well." Thorne's face fell at the mention, but he said nothing. "I have been forced to bury more men than I can count, men I will forever hold as heroes. The only reason I have not taken my spot amongst them yet is that I have learned to listen to my instincts when they choose to speak. And so I beg you to heed my warning,

Captain: for good or ill, the Ilban is dangerous, and I think we need to keep a much closer watch on him than we have thus far."

"I respect your experience, Sergeant," Thorne answered tersely. "And neither am I quick to trust a stranger. I do trust, however, and will continue to trust, the words and commands of the goddesses and the marshal. They would not have insisted on his presence if he had no part to play. I think you would do well to remember that we are the tools of the gods, and very rarely granted the answers we may seek."

The older man sighed. "All I can ask is that you bear my misgivings in mind, Captain."

Thorne did not favor him with a response and so they spoke no more, continuing on up the hilly slope in strained silence.

After only a short way further, Rhys saw Holywell's shape stop, then turn around and start gesturing to them. As they approached, Captain Thorne took a lantern from one of the twins and held it aloft to see the scout's face. "No sign of him?"

Holywell pantomimed shading his eyes from the sun, then pointed down to the ground where he stood and shook his head.

"You lost sight of him here?" Rhys asked, and the other nodded. The hills rose and fell like waves crashing down the slope of the Ymr, and any of them was tall enough to hide young Pedr from their line of sight. Holywell walked two of his fingers across the palm of his other hand and shook his head. "Can't find his trail by moonlight." Rhys frowned. "It's too damned dark to be tracking. Here," he handed Holywell his lantern.

The mute stooped down low and began searching. The others kept behind him so as not to disturb whatever signs of the boy's passage there might be. The Brothers all had some skill in following a trail, but Holywell was a specially-trained scout and by far the most practiced, so they let him work.

Some time later, however, there was still no sign of Pedr. The wind had risen with nightfall and bent the sparse grasses this way and that, lessening any evidence of the boy's footfall. Holywell finally stood and threw up his arms in frustration.

"Peace, Brother," Captain Thorne said. "Finding the boy like this will be nigh impossible."

"How'd a little boy manage to outpace Holywell?" Fergus wondered aloud, again. The mute swept his arm and let out a sharp whistle. "And how's a child get to be so fast, eh? Going up this rocky mountain? Are we not going to talk about how strange that is?"

"Maybe he's half mountain goat," Felix suggested.

His brother scoffed. "What good would it do him to have the head of a mountain goat, you idiot?"

"Who says which half has to be which?"

"Blackhart," Rhys said, massaging his weary eyes, "smack the two of them for me, please."

The hospitaler raised his meaty hand, and Felix and Fergus both ducked away, throwing up their arms in submission.

"Joren mentioned it, too," Rhys continued, "that his little brother outran him. I thought nothing of it, but... something is not quite right here. I wonder..." he mused, scratching at his beard.

"You think whatever we've been sent to find is here, Sergeant?" Fergus asked. "Not further in the mountains?"

Thorne shook his head. "No, that's not possible. Othelia told us to go to the Deep Ymr, specifically. But it could be that something else took the boy. There's no shortage of wicked creatures who have a hunger for children."

"Then should we consult with Helmi, Captain?" Rhys asked. "Talk to the brother again? If there's something out here, I would prefer to know what it is, if possible. It might also be that there's a better way to find the boy than stumbling about in the dark."

"I agree, Sergeant." Thorne picked up his lantern from where he had placed it on the ground. "Our deadline of dawn still stands, which gives us only a few hours, I reckon. As loth as I am to leave a young boy alone and cold, I cannot allow this endeavor to take precedence over our mission. For now, though, you and Holywell start up a search. I'll leave Blackhart and the twins with you to help, and I'll go speak with our oracle."

"Yes, Captain," Rhys answered. "You should take one of the twins with you, though, to be safe."

"I'm quite alright, thank you, Sergeant," Thorne called over his shoulder as he started back down the mountainside.

"Cocky little shite," Rhys grumbled under his breath. The twins chuckled. "Neither of you heard that."

"Heard what, now, Sergeant?" Felix feigned puzzlement.

"Good man." He turned to Holywell. "Now, which direction was the boy heading, could you tell?" The scout turned and pointed northwest. In the distance, the trees loomed dark where the forest encroached upon the Ymr. "So perhaps he's hiding. If we cannot follow his tracks, we'll at least head there and look for him." They started without delay.

Wind whipped through the hills and rocks around them, and the different pitches sounded almost like a faint song to Rhys's ear as they went along. Overpowering the heat in his chest from the climb, the cold started creeping through his mail and leather, and he found himself wishing he had had the foresight to bring one of the heavy fur coats they had packed for the Ymr.

As they crested the final hill before the edge of the wood, another lantern came into view, carried by a barrel-chested man. Judging by the long staff held in his other hand, Rhys guessed it to be the shepherd.

"What's he doing out here?" Felix wiped his nose across his sleeve.

"If I were a father, I imagine I'd be out here searching, too," Blackhart noted dispassionately.

"Master shepherd!" Rhys hailed him over the wind as he stalked down the hill.

The big Fjalr waved in return. "There you are. No sign of my boy, I take it?" He seemed more or less unworried.

"None yet. Do you have any idea why he ran? Where he might have gone?"

"They're boys, they fight," he shrugged. "Slain only know what about. I know they love playing in the woods; never this far up the slope, though. Pedr's prone to angry fits, but he's never run off before. I'll beat him soundly for this, you mark me." He sighed. "Thank you for lending me your help here, Sergeant." He sounded sincere.

Hoping to leave his earlier embarrassment behind them, Rhys said, "It is the least we can offer for your hospitality, master. We attempted to follow his trail, but he is too small and the slope too dark for us to track. So for now, it was our plan to spread the men out and search for him; hopefully his temper will cool and he'll tire of the cold and seek out our lanterns." There was no point in worrying the man about a possible supernatural cause of his son's disappearance, especially as they had no proof.

"I hope we can find him soon," the shepherd replied. "We have not seen any wolf packs for about a month — they know too well the sharp end of my crook — but I still shudder to think of my boy out here by himself at night." As if to illustrate, a shudder literally ran down the shepherd's spine and his shaggy head shook like a dog's. "For your help, you'll have all the mutton and cheese you desire from my stores for your journey, I swear it."

Rhys nodded his appreciation and split the soldiers into groups: two to each lantern while he shared the shepherd's. "It is my guess that if he doesn't return to your hall on his own, he'll seek the shelter of the woods to ward off the cold. Do you think I have the right of it?"

The shepherd stroked his bushy chin. "There are a number of caves on the slope that might also serve the purpose, but without his brother around to impress, I think he would be too afraid to venture into any of them. Hard to find in the dark, too. I think the forest is our best chance if — like you say — he's not settled and made his way back home yet."

"Right, then let's not waste any more time. Stay within shouting distance of each other, at least until dawn. If we've not found him once the sun's up, we'll meet back here on the east side of the forest, understood?" They all set off in different directions into the wood.

The firs sighed as the wind moved among them, broken only by the rise and fall of the soldiers calling out Pedr's name. The trees were spaced further apart so high up the slope, and moving through them was not terribly difficult. Occasionally, a den or hollow loomed from the undergrowth, and they were careful to check each one they encountered.

After a while of silence interrupted only by calling for his son, the shepherd looked at Rhys over his shoulder as they went. "I, er, want to apologize to you, Sergeant," he said hesitantly, "for whatever stupid things I said over supper. I'm a simple man; all I know is this mountain, and my wife will happily tell you, I often say things without thinking. So please accept my humble apology, as your host, and as a man who greatly appreciates all you Knights do."

"Peace, master shepherd," Rhys entreated him, waving his hand. Heat flushed his neck as the embarrassment of his outburst at supper hit him full. "I'm getting to be an old man, and sometimes my better sense eludes me entirely. My behavior was inexcusable, and it is I who begs forgiveness. You are a masterful host, and I dishonored myself last evening."

The shepherd stopped and turned to face him. "A brave man, and humble besides," he nodded approvingly. "Truly, you honor my hall with your presence, good Sergeant. But let us forget any unpleasantness." He extended his hand purposefully. "When it comes time to part, I would want it to be as friends."

Rhys gripped it and they shook hands again. "I would not have it any other way, Shepherd. Now, let's find your son and hasten back to the warmth of Fjalvard's mightiest hall."

In spite of the dour mood, Olen laughed as he turned back around and they continued the search for Pedr.

Joren's head slipped off the hand supporting it and he jerked back fully awake. Helmi was still leafing through page after page of squiggly lines and symbols. He had never seen a book before, or a scroll, or a map; she had all of these and more, and at first, he had looked on in fascination. There were some pictures in the books, elegantly detailed, depicting beautiful creatures and horrific monsters. She had quickly moved past those pages, however, and after a while his exhaustion had overtaken him and the unintelligible script failed to keep his interest.

The hall door groaned on its hinges as it opened. "Olen?" His mother stood, Agata in her arms, but when Captain Thorne stepped through and shut the door behind him, she frowned. "Have you found him?" she demanded. The captain held his hand up apologetically and said something to Grim in their language.

"He says the others are still up searching, mistress. I'm sure they'll have found him soon," he added with a sympathetic look.

The captain waved Grim over and they both sat at the table with Helmi. Joren moved down the bench to make room, but his mother called out to him. "Let them be, Joren, come here." He reluctantly obeyed, and as he sat down with his mother and sister, she threw a heavy fleece over his shoulders and bundled him in it, even though he did not feel cold.

While the Ilban remained seated on the ground by the fire, resting his heavy arms on his knees, the three southerners engaged in what appeared to be an intense discussion in Carthan. Helmi pointed to various pages of the largest leather-bound tome as she spoke and the other two asked questions. Joren wished he could understand what was happening and he felt his mother stirring restlessly beside him.

Finally, Captain Thorne asked Helmi a question that she did not answer right away. Instead, she looked over to Joren. "Joren," she asked in Fjalr, folding her hands on the table, "will you please come tell us your story again? From the first time you saw the creature."

He rose and walked over, careful not to put too much weight on his hurt leg. Helmi made room for him to sit next to her and his palms inexplicably started sweating. Regardless, he repeated his story, trying hard to recount everything as exactly as possible. As he spoke, Grim translated for the captain, who asked questions at certain points.

"After last night," the young soldier asked on Captain Thorne's behalf, "when she tried to take Pedr, did he have any strange new marks on his body?"

"Marks?"

"Something that looked like a scar or maybe a burn?"

Joren considered. "I don't think so." Crestfallen, he added, "I didn't think to look."

Helmi laid her hand on his. "You had no reason, Joren," she said warmly. "Don't worry about that, we're just trying to gather all the information we can."

Grim relayed his response to the captain and then asked, "Can you describe again the lady you saw that night, in as much detail as you can remember?" Joren did so. "There's nothing else, no designs on her skin, inhuman features, marks or scars?"

"Just her huge eyes and the black soot," he answered with a shrug.

Grim looked to Helmi, but she was bent over another passage in the tome, dragging her finger across the script as she read. After the two men at the table had exchanged a few more words, the young soldier thanked Joren for his help, which he understood to be a dismissal. He returned to the bed by his mother and sisters.

"Joren, why didn't you tell us about what you saw?" she asked.

"I thought it was just a nightmare. I told Van, but I didn't want Papa to know."

She fretted, her eyes red and tired, and pulled him close against her again. "I'm sure it was just a nightmare. And your brother had one, too — that's why he ran off. I had an uncle who would sometimes walk about in his sleep and cause trouble." Joren knew she was speaking to herself more than to him, and he wondered if she found the words any more convincing than he did.

5

THE SEARCH

The hours before sunrise passed slowly without any sign of Pedr. Rhys and Olen had wandered from the eastern end of the forest all the way through to the tree line in the west — a distance Rhys judged to be about half a league — then further up the slope, and back to the east. All night, he had been hopeful to hear the nearby cries of one of the others once they had found Pedr, but was not wholly surprised when no such call came. He could not rid himself of the idea that the boy had not simply run off. The forest was black and ominous in the night and Rhys was glad when moonlight gave way to pale dawn.

Throughout the night, after their brief exchange, the shepherd's good mood had slowly sobered as the hours passed with still no sign of Pedr. When the time came, it took some convincing to get the man to agree to accompany him to the forest's edge to meet with the other soldiers.

They gathered next to a large boulder that rested by the stream and drank their fill. "Master shepherd," Rhys said, wiping the water from his beard, "I'm sure you're not going to like this, but we must return to your hall for now." Olen's brows furrowed and he made to speak, but Rhys cut him off. "The day grows warmer, so Pedr will be in less danger now if he's still out here. I have orders from my captain, so we must return."

"Sergeant, please," the shepherd implored him, "we can't leave my boy out here alone and scared."

"I'm sorry." Rhys did not relish the idea of abandoning the boy to his fate, but he had no choice. Perhaps he could convince Thorne of a reason to stay and help; he doubted it, but he would try nonetheless. "For now, there is nothing we can do. I need to get these men a meal, hopefully a little rest, and if Captain Thorne allows it, we'll continue the search. It's possible your boy has already made his own way back — we won't know until we return, ourselves."

"Return if you must, Sergeant, but I cannot. If I go back now, without Pedr, and he hasn't already turned up, my wife will end me before I set foot through the door." The shepherd's attempt at humor was halfhearted, but he gave a tired smile. "Go on, get your men some rest. If Pedr's down there, tell Joren to come and fetch me, will you?"

"I will. We'll return shortly if the captain allows. Here," Rhys handed him his own waterskin. "Be careful up here."

Olen nodded his thanks and lumbered away from the forest toward the rolling hills and crags.

"Let's start moving," Rhys ordered.

Before they made it far down the mountainside, however, Grim appeared over one of the hillocks, winding his way toward them. An extinguished lantern swung in his left hand. "Been searching for you lads for ages," he said as he neared. "Were you in the woods? No sign of young Pedr, I take it?"

"No, he's right here, mate," Felix said, "right here in me pocket." The long night had taken its toll on everyone's patience. Grim shook his head in exasperation.

"He didn't make his way back to the hall in the night, then," Rhys said heavily.

"No, Sergeant — we would've come to get you if he had." He shielded his eyes from the morning sun. "But that's not why I'm here. The captain wants you back down at the hall."

"That's where we're headed now."

"No, just you, Sergeant. The rest of us are to keep on the search."

Fergus spat. "Bollocks."

Rhys was surprised to hear it, too; Thorne had been quite vehement about continuing their mission regardless of finding Pedr. His fears that something sinister was at play were nearly confirmed.

"So this is it, then?" Felix asked. "This is where we're supposed to be, not deeper in the mountains? I'm glad of that, if I'm being honest. Already too cold for summer."

Rhys took a few steps downhill. "Don't concern yourselves with any of that until the captain tells you to. Blackhart, you're in command — try to find the boy's trail. We'll be back to join you shortly. I'll bring food."

Following the stream down the mountainside proved to be an easier journey than the route they had taken in the night. Outside the hall, the Ilban was making himself useful and splitting wood for the fire. He nodded in silent greeting as Rhys passed, then continued his work. The hairs stood up on the sergeant's neck as he remembered Helmi's claim from the night before.

Inside, the shepherd's wife was at the fire pit preparing a meal. She looked at him hopefully as he entered, and it pained him to have to shake his head. Sullen, she returned to her labors. Joren, Vandra, and the toddler were all bunched up at the end of their parents' bed, leaning against each other and snoring softly. Helmi scratched feverishly with her quill at a piece of vellum and did not stop at his arrival.

As soon as he saw Rhys, Thorne stood from the table and gestured at the door, a dark look clouding his young features. Rhys ducked back outside. Unwilling to have whatever conversation might follow in front of the Ilban, he led the captain around the back of the hall.

Before Thorne could say anything, Rhys gave his report. "We searched the western forest, the whole breadth of it, with no sign of the boy."

"How do you stand that woman?" Thorne asked with a sneer, ignoring him entirely.

Rhys sighed. "How do you mean?"

"She thinks her role as an oracle gives her some kind of

authority, even out here. Honestly, I'm prepared to truss her up and stow her on a mule's back for the rest of the journey."

"What exactly happened down here while we were in the hills?" Rhys asked, folding his arms.

"She has been in those tomes all night, making lists, and will hardly speak to me." He must have seen the confusion on Rhys's face, because he took a breath to compose himself and started again. "When I arrived back at the hall, she and Grim told me about something the shepherd's son said — the older one, I mean — about having nightmares. Grim translated the boy's tale to me, and it sounds as though they were more than just bad dreams; the young one may indeed have been lured from his bed by some kind of unholy creature."

"I see." Rhys was not happy to have his suspicions confirmed; it was bad news for the boy.

"And so the oracle," Thorne continued, "in her infinite wisdom, has decided the boy's nightmare must be some sort of portent, and that this creature is what we've been sent to hunt."

"Here on the slope?" Rhys asked. "Well, that doesn't make any sense — we were told specifically to go to the Deep Ymr."

"Precisely, but the woman is infuriatingly single-minded."

"Did she offer any explanation as to why here?"

Thorne waved his hand. "None. As I said, she's been lost in her books, and I find it nearly impossible to speak with her. That's why I sent Grim after you. For whatever reason, you seem to be able to get along with her, so I'm going to have you speak to her. Took him long enough to find you — now we're behind schedule."

"As I said, we were in the forest," Rhys commented absently, biting his lip in thought. It was an unexpected turn of events, given that the directions from the goddess had them prepare for the violent cold and much more harrowing journey into the Deep Ymr. The possibility of finding their purpose here, on a quiet mountainside overlooking a peaceful valley, disturbed him. "What did the boy see?" he asked after a moment.

Thorne started pacing. "Apparently, he had a number of dreams wherein a ragged, emaciated woman with burns threatened him and tried to steal his brother. And last night, when the boy ran, he was screaming about 'her', saying, 'she needs me'."

"Very interesting…. Does Helmi have any idea what kind of creature that might be?"

"She's putting a list together now, but that doesn't matter," he huffed. "I don't care what it is. Our orders are to make for the Deep Ymr, where Othelia will contact Helmi again with further instructions. This mission is unusual enough to have me on edge as it is, I'm not wasting any more time here than we have already."

Rhys furrowed his brow, confused. "But, Grim told me you wanted the search continued."

"Only until dawn, as we agreed. But he wasn't able to find you, apparently, and now we've lost even more time."

"Captain, if I may," Rhys leaned against the wall in an attempt to appear as non-threatening as possible, "if the oracle believes there is reason to investigate further, don't you think we would be wise to listen to her? It's the reason we brought her with us, after all, isn't it?"

"Actually, Sergeant," Thorne snapped, "it's not. We brought her because we were instructed to do so, and so far, she is proving little more than a distraction."

"I hardly think that's fair. Let us at least hear what she has to say, what her reasoning is, before we dismiss it out of hand."

"Is that what I'm doing?" The captain scoffed. "Very well, Sergeant, let us go and discuss this with her, so that we might not *dismiss her out of hand.*" He turned and marched back around the hall.

Rhys sighed and followed after him.

The children had finally stirred and were getting fully dressed as the soldiers entered and sat down with Helmi, who had laid down her quill and was studying her texts again.

Rhys looked to Thorne to begin, but the young man sat in obstinate silence. It was up to Rhys to ask the questions, then. "Helmi," he said, and she perused a few more lines before looking up at him. "The captain tells me you believe this is where we're meant to be, rather than the Deep Ymr."

Helmi rubbed her eyes. "I believe it's possible, yes."

"Possible," Thorne scoffed.

She fixed him with an impassive gaze. "Yes, Captain, *possible.* Otherwise, it would be quite a coincidence that Master Olen and Mistress Runa's son would go missing the very night we arrive at their hall."

"Do you have any idea how often children go missing out here in the world?" the young captain asked. "No, you wouldn't, because this is the first time you've ever even stepped foot out of the sanctum."

"Captain, please," Rhys entreated him. Helmi's eyes narrowed to slits and focused on Thorne. "Helmi, we're just a little confused — our orders are to go to the Deep Ymr and to await further orders from the goddess. So how can it be that our intended destination is here, so far south?"

"I never said anything about the Deep Ymr," she replied, keeping her eyes on the captain, "and neither did Othelia."

Rhys blinked. "What?"

"The Deep Ymr was your determination," she said, "not mine."

"Othelia didn't say anything about it?"

Helmi shook her head. "Not at all. The message she gave me, and that I relayed to the marshal, was: 'Take a detachment of Knights and travel north to Fjalvard in all haste, to the mountains of the Ymr, and there await my call'."

Rhys looked over at Thorne. "That is not what I was told. Is this what the marshal told you?"

The young man's jaw worked as he returned Helmi's unwavering gaze. "Yes, this is what I was told by the marshal, and he and I decided together that the Deep Ymr was most likely our intended destination."

Upon hearing that, Rhys stood from the table — perhaps a little too abruptly, as he drew the attention of the shepherd's wife and children. "Captain," he said tightly, "may I see you outside again?" Thorne's cheeks flushed as he saw everyone in the hall watching them, but he conceded and stood to follow Rhys out the door.

At the sound of the Ilban's axe falling and splitting another log, Rhys turned to head back to the same spot they had gone to speak before, but Thorne erupted as soon as the door shut behind them.

"Are you out of your mind, Sergeant?" he demanded, squaring himself off, a furious light in his eye. "How dare you embarrass me like that?"

"You embarrass yourself," Rhys growled. "You kept valuable information from me and used my ignorance to help you persuade Helmi that we must make for the Deep Ymr, when apparently that isn't the case at all."

"It is the case! The marshal and I spoke at length about this before we embarked, and we agreed that a mission of such importance, of such urgency, could only lead us to the Deep Ymr, where the Knights have seldom gone before."

"And why exactly was I not informed of this?"

Thorne relaxed his stance a bit. "You were told what you needed to be told in order to execute your duties, Sergeant, as was the rest of the detachment."

"Astonishing." Rhys shook his head in disbelief, all considerations of decorum forgotten. "You understand that we have to stay, now, yes? If it's possible that we're in the right place now, we have no choice but to investigate the matter fully."

Thorne shook his head. "This changes nothing — the marshal and I agreed that the Deep Ymr is almost certainly where we are meant to go, and I still believe that."

"*Almost.*" Rhys emphasized the word. "Whatever you and the marshal decided is all well and good, but now we have a practical reason to believe you both were wrong."

"You would take the opinion of a novice oracle over that of the Marshal of the Order?"

"Given Joren's nightmares and his brother's timely disappearance, yes," Rhys answered easily. "I think Helmi's on to something, and we need to listen to her, at least for now."

The captain opened his mouth to retort but surprised Rhys by shutting it without actually speaking. He regarded the sergeant with hard eyes. "Is this your official advice to me?" he asked sternly, "as the sergeant of the detachment, that we remain here and forsake the Deep Ymr?"

Rhys did not hesitate before answering. "For now, yes. Yes it is, Captain."

Thorne held his gaze for another long moment. "Fine," he seethed. "You'll have your way then. We'll comb this barren mountainside for some petty child-stealer until you are satisfied." He pointed a menacing finger at Rhys. "Know, however, that if things go awry because we tarried here — if we fail in our mission — the marshal will know who's to blame." He whirled around on his heel and stalked off toward the slope.

Rhys gritted his teeth and watched Thorne depart up the slope. It took every ounce of strength he could muster not to scramble to find little stones he could hurl at the man's back as he left. "I suppose I'll carry provisions up for the men by myself, then," he muttered bitterly. Placing his hands on his hips, he turned back toward the hall to find the Ilban standing there, a stack of split wood in his arms.

"Sergeant," he rumbled in his thick accent, "would you mind, eh...?" He nodded at the door.

"My pleasure." Rhys could not keep the bite out of his voice as he shoved back through the door, allowing the Ilban to follow. Helmi tore her eyes from the page in front of her and Rhys saw the same fire there as in the captain's.

"Really, Garret," she hissed as he sat heavily on the bench opposite her, "that man is becoming an utter nuisance."

The Ilban closed the door with his foot and carried in his armful of logs. The shepherd's wife thanked him profusely and hurried over to lift one of the bench seats, revealing a compartment for firewood.

Rhys reached up to massage his temples and answered in a low voice. "I've taken care of him for now. We'll stay here and search for the boy and this creature — if there is one."

"I know you told me not to antagonize him, and I'm trying," she dipped her quill violently into its inkwell, "but I will not allow him to endanger our mission here out of blind arrogance."

"Nor will I," he assured her. "To the matter at hand, though:

the captain gave me Joren's account. I can say rather confidently that it does not sound like anything I've ever encountered — or heard of, for that matter. Are we sure it wasn't just a nightmare?"

"Sure?" Helmi sighed. "No, not sure. But when the captain returned last night, he expressed your concern at little Pedr's ability to evade Leo."

Rhys frowned and drummed his fingers on the table. "That's true. Holywell may be old, but he's quicker than any man I've ever met, and an excellent tracker besides. That he wasn't able to catch the boy or follow his trail certainly does give me pause."

"Assuming, then, that he was lured from his bed, I believe I have a likely candidate, regardless of Joren's outlandish description."

"And what might that be?"

"I think we're dealing with…" she bit her lip and lowered her voice even further, "a witch."

"I see." Rhys glanced surreptitiously at the family, though he was sure none of them spoke a word of Carthan. "My first thought was perhaps a maira, given the boy's dreams."

"Yes, I considered that, as well." She shuffled through a stack of pages before her and pulled one out to consult it. "It's certainly possible, but maira almost always kill their victims in their own beds, rather than luring them away, as poor Pedr seemed to be. Actually, his behavior is what has caused me so much consternation."

"What do you mean?"

"According to Joren's story, he tried to stop Pedr but his little brother became violent with him, and started crying that he 'needed to go to her'. Don't laugh at me, Garret, but that sounds quite like what happens to sailors when they hear the siren's call, does it not?"

Rather than laughing, Rhys considered. "Well, it does sound a bit like that, apart from a few glaring contrarieties."

"Yes, yes," she gave him a look, "we're not at sea and the siren's song isn't audible to just one individual. I'm not saying I believe it's a siren, just that the similarities required me to go deep into the texts to dismiss."

"And what you found led you to believe this is a witch?"

"Yes." She quickly found a different sheet. "There are still a few things I cannot explain, but witches are infamous child-stealers and have an arsenal of spells and such that could be used to compel the wills of others."

He leaned closer over the table to see what she had written down, but found his eyes too tired for the task. "Have you found specific spells?"

"While there is a small compendium of known witchcraft, all of the texts caution that witches regularly create new magical enchantments, unique in nature and function, and that it might not be possible to know the exact details of each."

Rhys sighed. "I've certainly found that to be true, unfortunately."

"That being said," Helmi continued, stifling a yawn, "I believe I've narrowed it down to the type of magic, which may tell us something about the witch herself. I think she used a hex."

"A hex." Rhys mulled the idea over. "Did the boy have a mark on him?"

"None of the family noticed anything, but it is often placed on a part of the body where it will not be seen. It seems to make the most sense given the sequence of events. The first night, Joren sees her in their loft, bent over Pedr. She disappears and he believes it was all a nightmare, but really, she placed the hex on Pedr and used a simple spell or concoction to quickly put Joren back to sleep, and then escaped. The next night, she completes and activates the hex from her lair or hovel or wherever she may be hiding, drawing Pedr from his bed."

"Are there hexes that do that?" Rhys asked. "The ones I've seen usually just kill people."

"There are. One that is similar enough is even listed in the compendium: a hex of retrieval."

"Well," he leaned back and stretched out his arms, "you've certainly made a compelling case."

Helmi gave a wry smile. "I'd like to think so, whatever the captain may say." Then she frowned. "What I haven't been able to explain is her strange appearance."

"Thorne mentioned she looked starved and burned."

"Yes, Joren calls her the 'Burnt Lady'. It was more than that, though. As Joren described her, she was naked, covered in soot and ash, with a pale face and huge, black eyes. And he said she was whispering to him."

"Foul incantations, as you said, to hex Pedr and fool Joren into believing it was a dream."

"Perhaps.... But what about the rest of it? The eyes, the ash and soot?"

"I saw a witch once," Rhys recalled, "who had imbibed a dangerous amount and combination of her own concoctions. She had become an inhuman monstrosity — not quite like you're describing, granted, but I don't think it's outside the realm of possibility."

"I suppose that's possible," she sighed. "Still, I hope you or the captain packed wax earplugs in that trunk of yours. Better if we had a widower, though, I think."

"What?"

"In case I'm wrong and it actually *is* a siren," she explained, managing a smirk.

Rhys rolled his eyes. "I understood that, and the wax, obviously, but what was that about a widower?"

"You don't know about a siren's greatest weakness?" He shook his head. "Ah, something the wise sergeant hasn't heard of." A gleeful light appeared in her eyes in spite of the dark rings beneath them. Rhys glared at her. "It's an old defense against the siren song, used by ancient Knights, according to the text. Sirens, succubi, and any other monsters that prey on men and their lust have no power against a man who's lost his wife. There are accounts of sailing ships keeping at least one widower on board if possible, paying him handsomely, so that when the ship came upon waters known to harbor sirens, they could tie up every other man and let the widower steer the ship through to safety on the wind.

"Of course, as I said, it's all moot these days since someone long ago decided to stick candles in his ears."

"Well," Rhys replied, "thank you for that bit of education. I doubt we'll need either widower or wax, though — you've made a good case for witchcraft."

"I'm glad one of you trusts me at least," she said dryly. "Speaking of supplies, though, you should take some relevant items from your stores up with you onto the slope."

"Right." He glanced uncomfortably over at the large chest of hunting supplies they had set in the corner of the hall. "Our defenses against witches are largely herbal in nature, and I usually rely on Blackhart for that. I never was any good at telling one leaf from another."

"I can look through the chest, if you like," Helmi offered, "to see what I can find. I'm no expert, either, mind you."

"That would be very helpful, actually. While you do that, I need to speak to our hostess about food for the men. I'll join you in a moment."

They both rose and Helmi went over to the spot where their gear was stacked and hoisted open the large trunk.

Rhys stretched again, his joints clicking, and as Helmi started searching through their supplies, he approached the shepherd's wife. She quickly gathered more food than was necessary and bundled it in a large sack for him.

"Please, Sergeant," she said, wrapping bread and cheese in linen cloths, "I didn't want to interrupt you, but I have to ask...." The woman's face showed deep worry lines, and she was close to tears just speaking to him. "Last night, Lady Gwynlaithe asked Joren all about a nightmare he had about some horrible creature. She seemed to think it could be real! That can't possibly be so, can it? I've been going out of my mind all night with worry. Does my husband know this?"

Rhys suppressed a groan: he would have to handle this delicately. "Mistress Runa, I'm so sorry that we have caused you such angst." He inclined his head to add sincerity, and chose his words carefully. "We have spoken more on the matter. Right now, we don't think your son's dream was anything more than that. Helmi has found no evidence that your son's disappearance is related to an actual creature."

It was a lie, boldfaced, and Rhys told it easily; better that the poor woman be at peace — even if it was a false peace — while they sussed out the truth of whatever was happening than to fret and worry herself. "However," he continued, "after some deliberation, our captain and the oracle have agreed that we must help you find Pedr. It would not be right for us to abandon folk in need, especially as you and your husband have been so kind and generous with us."

"Oh, Slain's graces!" Her eyes glistened and she looked up at the ceiling to keep any tears from falling. "So there's nothing to fear then? No monsters?"

"No, mistress, I don't believe so." Rhys made his eyes as kindly and honest as he could.

Doubt flashed across her face again. "But then, why is Lady Gwynlaithe still going through all those books?"

"We think Pedr got lost in the night," he answered quickly, "perhaps in the forest, and simply can't find his way back. Helmi is searching for a better way of finding him." The shepherd's wife exhaled in relief. "She has not had any luck yet, but she will not cease her research until she does. In the meantime, we're combing the mountainside; we'll have him back to you soon, I'm sure of it."

"Oh, thank you, Sergeant." She handed the sack of food over reverently. "Our humble thanks to you and to all your men for helping us. Please," she took his hand, "when you see my husband, tell him to be careful, and to bring Pedr back to us."

Rhys squeezed her hand. "I will, mistress. Thank you for feeding our men." As he turned to join Helmi, he saw the shepherd's son taking up his little crook by the door.

"Joren, what are you doing?" his mother asked sharply.

"I have to let the sheep out, or they'll go mad." As the boy said it, Rhys realized the sound of insistent bleating was coming faintly from beyond the west wall.

"You can't take the flock out by yourself!" she protested. The shrillness of her voice told Rhys just how frayed her nerves really were.

Joren was about to argue when the Ilban spoke up. "I can go out with the lad, mistress."

"Oh no, Master Aedric, I couldn't ask you to do that."

"It's no trouble. And he's right — it's not good for sheep to spend a warm day locked away."

"Well...." She looked in desperation at Rhys, as though she wanted him to provide an excuse for the boy to remain indoors.

"I'll keep him safe," the Ilban assured her.

"Alright," she huffed. "But you stay right next to the hall — they can graze out front for all I care. You don't go far, Joren, do you understand me?"

"Yes, Mama." He hurried out the door, his cheeks red.

Rhys watched as the Ilban collected his hammer from the corner and followed Joren. His mistrust was not alleviated by the man's seemingly kindly offer; there was simply something... off about him.

After the door closed behind them, Rhys set the sack of food down on the little area of tabletop not overrun with books and went to aid Helmi.

"Something tells me the captain would not be pleased at the sight of me going through your supplies like this," she observed as he crouched next to her.

"You're probably not wrong. Have you found anything useful?"

"Well, these were conveniently marked." She held up a bundle with a pinned note that had the words *hex-bane* scrawled across it.

Rhys took it from her and heard the clink of glass phials. "Convenient indeed."

"Sadly, hardly anything else is labeled so clearly; most are not marked at all. I know the names of some of the herbs that can be of use, but not what they look like. I don't think I trust myself to choose anything else for you, Garret. I'm sorry." She frowned but he waved the comment off.

"This is more than enough to start. Most of what we use to protect against spells and incantations and the rest is only marginally effective anyhow. We each wear our blessed sigil, at least — that may prove useful." He stood and offered his hand to help her up. "There's one thing we need even more, though, that I hope you can help us with."

She took his hand and he lifted her to her feet. "What might that be?"

"The Ymr is a huge mountain, and the slopes are covered in caves and forests and dens. It is more ground than we can effectively cover if we want to find the boy anytime soon. Are there any means of tracking this witch that you might know of? Or perhaps there's something in your books?"

"Captain Thorne asked the same last night, but I'm afraid I don't think there is, Garret. If we knew the particular hex that was used, we could perhaps create a charm that would aid in tracking the tainted trail left behind by the victim. I have not found a match in my compendium, however, and without that to start, I'm afraid I can do nothing. Another witch could perhaps be of help in unraveling the spell used here, but unless you have one of those in that trunk...."

"So we'll have to find Pedr on our own." He sighed. "Or otherwise stumble across the witch's lair."

"I'm afraid so." She gave him an apologetic look.

"Well, I told the shepherd's wife that you're still looking for a way to find him, and that the dream was nothing more than that. I don't think we need to add to their panic."

Helmi nodded. "Agreed." She pondered something for a moment, then said, "There is one other important bit of information I have for you, Garret, now that I think about it: if I'm right about this being a hex, it means the witch who wrought it is likely rather ancient, due to the nature of the magic, and so probably very powerful."

Rhys frowned. "You're not making going back out there any easier."

"I'm sure it's nothing you haven't encountered before."

"Perhaps. We're used to assuming the worst, though, in the hopes that we'll be spectacularly disappointed." He walked over to the table and placed the bundled phials inside the food pack. "Well, I'd best get this food to the men. Blackhart's appetite has been known to make him... unpleasant. Wouldn't want him murdering the twins, now, would we?"

She smiled. "No, I suppose we wouldn't. Be careful out there, Garret."

"I will. And you keep an eye on the Ilban. I still don't trust him."

Rhys thanked the shepherd's wife again for the food and left the hall. He exited to a sea of shifting wool as the sheep teemed about, munching on the short grasses in front of the steading. Aedric stood with his arms folded, overlooking them, and Joren sat on the ground and scratched Hala's neck while she chewed a bone.

Rhys adjusted the pack on his shoulder and started weaving through the flock. As he passed, the Ilban looked at him and asked in Carthan, "Did I overhear Helmi say you're hunting a witch?"

Rhys paused and faced the man. "Yes."

Aedric frowned. "That's not good news for the little brother."

"No, it certainly isn't. There's still a chance we might find him, though. I told the shepherd's wife there's nothing to worry about. Please be mindful of that."

The Ilban simply grunted.

Rhys regarded him for a moment, a dozen questions clamoring in his mind. This was perhaps an opportunity to get some information from the man. If he wanted any honest answers, however, he knew he must proceed carefully.

"You and I haven't had much of a chance to speak since we left."

"No," Aedric agreed, indifferent, "we haven't."

"I've been wondering, what exactly brings you on this journey with us?" He tried to keep his tone neutral.

The Ilban looked at him sidelong. "Your captain didn't tell you?"

"All I know is that the marshal gave his blessing for your presence amongst our detachment."

"Hm." He rested his hand on the heavy head of the hammer at his belt but said nothing else.

Rhys's blood warmed. "Well?"

The Ilban narrowed his eyes. "All due respect, Sergeant, but my reasons are my own."

"I'm happy to respect your privacy, but I'm sure you understand how secrecy can make a man nervous."

After pausing for a long moment, the man finally replied, "Aye, I can understand that. Even if I told you, though, you'd not believe a word of it."

"Does it have anything to do with speaking to gods?" Rhys should not have asked it, but the words were out before he could stop them. Aedric's brows gathered darkly. "Helmi told me of your dealings with Othelia, though not what was said."

"I see." The man's jaw worked angrily behind his beard. "I'd not heard the Knights were the sort to indulge in gossip."

"Only when the lives of my men are on the line." Rhys matched his tone.

"Neither you nor your men have anything to fear from me, Sergeant."

"I would like to believe that. But I know nothing about you or your reason for being here. So how can I trust you?"

The Ilban was silent for a while. "Your goddess requested my presence here," he finally grumbled, glaring at Rhys.

"You mean Othelia?"

"Aye. She needs a favor done, and I need something from her. But, as I said, that's my business — I've naught else to say on the matter."

Aedric folded his arms again and looked away, and Rhys knew the conversation was over. He thought back to what Helmi had said the night before, about never being certain of Othelia's motives. The exchange with the Ilban had taught him next to nothing, but it was just enough to leave a rock in the pit of his stomach. Not only did the man talk to gods, but apparently he exchanged favors with them.

For the present, Rhys pushed the thought out of his mind and started the trudge back up the slope to find the rest of the detachment.

$\sim$

Joren sat on the grass, watching the flock and petting Hala, wishing he could understand the Carthan the two men were speaking to each other. As Sergeant Rhys left, Aedric turned his attention on the sheep, but did not look at Joren. The grass around the hall had already recently been grazed down, but there was enough there for them to forage for the day. While the warmth of the summer sun felt good on his back, Pedr's absence still made everything around him seem grey and cold.

After a long while, Aedric walked over and sat down a few paces from him. The man remained silent, keeping his gaze fixed on some distant spot up the mountain. Joren looked that way, too, and wondered where the soldiers were looking for Pedr.

Without meaning to do so, he asked quietly, "Do you think they'll find my brother?"

Aedric did not appear to have heard him at first, but finally he looked at him and said, "I hope so, lad."

"Oh." Joren had hoped for a more reassuring answer; his stomach twisted at the thought of never seeing Pedr again. "I heard Sergeant Rhys say they don't think my nightmare was real."

"Do *you* think it was real?"

Joren pulled Hala a little closer to him, and she reached up and lapped at his chin. "I don't know. It felt real."

"Well, either way, if anyone can find your brother, it's the Knights Seraphin. They're good men all, and good at what they do. If something did take him, they'll find it, too; cut its heart out and send it back to Nydheim."

Joren guessed the promise was meant to console him, but it did not. He just wanted Pedr back, whatever it took. There could be no alternative.

Rather than saying any of that, though, he merely asked, "You believe in Nydheim?" Aedric's mention of the otherworldly realm of monsters had caught him off guard.

The kilted man looked away again. "I believe in that as much as I do in anything else we can't see or travel to. But I respect the religion of Fjalvard very much. You Fjalr have strong ties to your ancestors, and the Ilbanach can appreciate that."

"What *do* you believe?" His father had never told them much about Ilba, and Joren wanted to think about anything but Pedr.

"My people don't concern themselves with gods or the after-life. We follow the old ways, of sea and sky and stone, of hammer and forge. Our dead live on through us. We hold the fallen close, carry the burden of their deaths; we keep that sorrow and rage safely hidden away, to be called upon when we must remember, so they are never forgotten. That is the religion of Ilba."

Joren nodded even though he had only half paid attention to the answer; as soon as he had asked the question, he had thought of a better one. "Do you know what the Knights believe happens to the dead?"

Aedric's eyes narrowed as he answered. "The Carthans believe their gods divide the dead into those who were good in life and those who were evil," he explained. "The gods bring the good to a place called Eirna, similar to your Lodrheim, where there is peace and happiness. The wicked they send to a place called Hel; a necropolis in the very far south of the world. There, the god of death keeps them imprisoned for eternity." Aedric's hand rested on his knee and it curled into a fist as he spoke.

"You don't like the Knights' gods," Joren asked hesitantly, "do you?"

"No, lad, I don't. The Knights Seraphin do good work in the world, and I respect them for it, but I don't know how they worship those capricious bastards." He turned his head and spat.

Joren had no idea what to say to that, so he said nothing at all. Hala's head lay heavy in his lap and he rubbed her crown, bunching the skin over her eyes and then pulling it back; her tail thumped the ground in approval.

"She's a good dog, isn't she?" Aedric asked.

Joren had been busy enjoying the funny faces Hala made as he massaged her head, and had not realized the man was watching them. "She is." The silence after felt awkward, so he asked, "Do you like dogs?"

"I do," Aedric answered, and the shadow of a smile crossed his rugged face. "We had a pup once — my sons grew up beside him. He was a good dog, too."

"You have children?" Joren was surprised; it had never occurred to him that soldiers could have families, but of course, he realized now that was foolish.

The hint of happiness vanished and Aedric's face returned to its stony setting. He looked away again, off toward the Ymr. "Once," he muttered.

Joren did not ask any more questions after that.

On the slope, Rhys found that Thorne had already called all of the men together in one spot to discuss their new orders. The captain was still sullen, and tension hung in the air among the soldiers.

"The sergeant has finally arrived," Thorne announced as Rhys drew near, "and the shepherd is still in the hills for the moment, so let me speak frankly. I'm sure you've all gathered by now that we won't be headed deeper into the mountains. At least not yet. From the details provided by the brother, our oracle is convinced that whatever monstrosity we've been sent to destroy is here, on this mountain side."

"So we're not just chasing a little boy what ran off?" Fergus cocked his brow. "We're chasing a monster after all?"

"She seems very convinced that is the case, yes," Thorne answered darkly. Rhys started handing out the food from his pack.

"Well, what does Helmi think it is?" asked Grim, taking some bread and cheese.

Thorne looked to Rhys with a disapproving expression. "Did the oracle give you her final determination, Sergeant?"

"She did, Captain," Rhys answered evenly. "She believes it's a witch. The brother saw the thing try to kidnap Pedr the night before we arrived," he explained to the others, "but thought it was a dream. She must have wrought her magic on the boy, somehow created an insatiable need within him, granted him an unholy strength and speed, which is why he was able to escape us last night."

"Gods have mercy," Felix lowered his head. "We know what witches who steal children do to them, don't we?"

Rhys sighed. "There is a chance the search is a lost cause, it's true. We don't yet know any particulars, however, and there's an equal chance he's still bewitched or held captive. Either way, if Helmi's right, we have no other course but to keep on the search. Oh, and no one say a word about this to the shepherd or his family. The last thing we need is hysterics."

Thorne cleared his throat and spoke in a measured tone. "I don't fully agree that this witch is what we've been sent all this way for. However, I trust in the gods, and in their speaker. So for now we will proceed as though this is our quest." Rhys was surprised by the lack of venom behind his words. The captain was finally showing his professionalism.

"Holywell," Rhys asked, "have you had any luck finding the boy's trail?"

The mute shook his head sadly.

Rhys frowned. "Helmi could devise no other means of tracking Pedr or the witch, either. That leaves us with only one course."

Felix groaned. "Searching the whole mountain?"

"Searching the whole damned mountain," the sergeant confirmed.

"And what do we do," Grim asked, "if we stumble upon the witch?"

"Clutch the blessed sigil at your neck and stick her with the proper end of your sword," Rhys answered. "Failing that, I believe we have something here that may be of use. Brother Blackhart." He handed the bundle of phials over to the hospitaler.

Blackhart carefully unwrapped them and drew one out to inspect it. "Hex-bane." He nodded. "What else did you bring?"

"That's all Helmi or I could identify."

"Hel's gates," the big man cursed, "I have an arsenal of witch-hunting supplies in that trunk, and this is all you bring me?"

Rhys glared at him. "For gods' sakes, man — there's an entire apothecary's worth of herbs and medicines in that trunk! We're lucky Helmi was able to find even the hex-bane. Anyway, she believes it was a hex, specifically, that was used on Pedr the night before we arrived, so it's a good bet hexes are our greatest danger."

"Better than nothing, I suppose," Blackhart grumbled. "Here," he started handing them out. "Drink up."

Rhys held up the little glass container filled with the pulpy liquid and grimaced. He hated the stuff.

"Been a while since we hunted a witch," Felix said, tapping the phial with a finger. "What's in this, again?"

"Never mind what's in it," Blackhart growled. "Just drink it back and hexes should be less effective on you until about dawn, probably."

"Probably?" Grim hesitated with the phial at his lips.

"Nothing like exacting standards, eh, Grim?" Fergus laughed and downed his dose.

Rhys followed suit and had an involuntary shiver run up his back as the foul draught slid down his throat. They handed the phials back to Blackhart, who wrapped them gently up again and tied them tight.

The captain sat down on a nearby rock. "Alright, we've already been up half the night and we've a long day ahead of us, so for now, take a bit of time to rest, eat, and prepare yourselves. There's a lot of ground to cover, and from the looks of it, all manner of places a witch could make a home." He scowled. "We'll have to search as many as possible."

Rhys followed his example and lowered himself down on a patch of grass and broke off a piece of bread, happy to get the taste of hex-bane out of his mouth. The day was warming already, with clear skies to the south and only light clouds floating down from beyond the mountain.

"Oi, old man," Felix called, watching Holywell push the food between his teeth with his finger so he could chew. "How'd you lose your tongue anyway?"

"You idiot, you expect him to be able to tell a story like that with his hands?" Grim scoffed.

Holywell shook his head and snapped his fingers to get their attention. When they looked at him, he pointed over to Rhys.

"You want me to tell it?" the sergeant asked. "Are you sure?" Holywell waved his hand and nodded. "How is it you've not heard this tale already?"

"No idea," Fergus shrugged. "It's the most interesting thing about him, that's certain."

"Well, it's been years since I heard the story myself, but I'll see if I can remember it."

Rhys had asked the same question himself of Holywell years before, and the mute had written down a fairly thorough account on parchment when they were in between missions for the Order.

"If you don't know, Holywell's a refugee from the Greater Antiphoenes. Rescued from a slave ship when he was just a boy. The story goes, the slaver that stole him had done the same to a number of children and had them all in cages. The slaver went to grab one of the children out for a whipping, but young Leo got in his way. Fought him off to protect the other child."

Fergus nodded sagely. "So the slaver cut his tongue out to make him an example."

"He held him down had his dog rip the tongue from Leo's mouth," Rhys replied, "to teach him the cost of being a bad slave."

The twins gawked at Holywell, finally silenced, but the old scout kept happily chewing as Rhys was speaking.

"Gods' mercy," Grim murmured. "Right sorry about that, Brother."

Holywell shrugged and waved his hand, as though saying it was in the past.

"How'd he end up getting free from the slaver?"

"The Knights Seraphin rescued him, of course." The mute grinned broadly. "The Sisters took him in just like they did you two," Rhys said to the twins.

"Well, why's he get to be a Knight and we're just swords-for-hire?" Felix demanded.

"Because you can't stop whoring, drinking, or cursing," Black-hart rumbled.

"The sergeant curses!"

"He's the sergeant — he's earned that right."

"Bah!" Fergus spat. "Grim, how's your little sister doing?"

"You two just can't eat in silence, can you?" Grim stretched his legs out in front of him and answered anyway. "She's well enough, I suppose. The gout's still with her every day — apothecary's tonics don't seem to be helping anymore. But she's happy enough. Thank you for finally asking weeks into our journey, by the way."

Fergus shrugged. "Better late than never, eh? I'd like to see her again, though — been about a year since the Order brought us near Creighton Downs, hasn't it?"

"About that, I think," Grim nodded.

"How old does that make her now?"

"Three and ten. Might only have a few years left, gods bless her. She liked you two — always made her laugh."

"A right gem, your little sister," Felix said reverently. "I hope the gods are kind to her."

They finished the rest of their meal in silence. When the captain finally rose and straightened his sword belt, Rhys stood as well.

"Now that it's daylight," he said, addressing the soldiers, "and — as the captain said — there's much ground to cover, we'll be splitting up, each man for himself. If you find anything, start hollering until the rest come running. Gods be with you, gentlemen — keep whatever wits you might have about you."

"I want everyone back here by sunset," Thorne barked as they all started out in different directions.

After Rhys had lost sight of all the others, a quiet whistle met his ears above the breeze. He looked about and saw Holywell a few hillocks further up, gesturing at him. Rhys hiked up toward him, and as he approached, Holywell started making signs with his hands. They had known each other for nearly three decades, and the sergeant considered himself more or less fluent in the man's hand-speech. He was asking what was wrong with Thorne.

Rhys sighed and quickly told him of their conversations. It might not have been protocol to speak behind the captain's back, but Holywell had Rhys's implicit trust. Truth be told, he would not have minded his friend's advice on the matter, either.

"Am I out of line, do you think?" he asked, "siding with the oracle on this?"

Holywell shook his head and started gesturing.

"Yes, he's *very* young.... Right — I'm not trying to be insubordinate, but we'd be fools to ignore an oracle, for gods' sakes."

The mute nodded confidently.

"Thank you, Leo. I don't think this is the last of the captain's temper, and I'm glad to know Helmi and I aren't the only ones who think we're on to something here."

Holywell slapped a hand on Rhys's shoulder.

"Alright, well, let's get on with this, I suppose. I'm going to try to find the shepherd, give him some food. Be careful out here, old friend."

He spent the next few hours combing the hills that climbed over each other up the slope of the mountain, exploring a dozen different shallow caves and outcroppings, calling out Pedr's name, all without any success. When he finally found Olen, the sun had passed its zenith and if it were not for the wind, it would have been hot. The shepherd was relieved to see him.

"Oh, Sergeant Rhys!" he called as he used his crook to navigate the rocky ground. "You're back. Does this mean you've decided to stay?"

Rhys unslung his sack and started pulling out the remaining bread and cheese. "That it does, master. You've had no sign of Pedr, I take it?"

"Still none." Sweat beaded Olen's forehead and his ruddy cheeks puffed out as he lowered himself down on a flat stone.

"From your wife." Rhys handed him the food. The shepherd accepted it gladly. "The captain has decided we will remain until we find your son." He was careful to say nothing of the witch or anything else that would cause alarm.

"But what about your mission?" the other asked, mouth full. "The Deep Ymr?"

"We will continue on soon enough, but first, we cannot abandon our duty here. Also, the Ilban is helping your son with the sheep, letting them graze around your hall."

The shepherd reached out and squeezed Rhys's hand in gratitude. "I would make you all kings for this, if I was ought but a shepherd!"

"I've renounced one birthright already; I'm content not to have to do it again."

"The Slain will welcome you to Thulheim with feast and drink and music nonetheless, good and faithful Sergeant — you and all your men."

Rhys lingered for only a little while before informing the shepherd about meeting at sunset, and then continued on.

After another hour or so in the hills, he ran into Thorne again. They exchanged a few terse words and went separate ways.

A summer shower drizzled down on them during the afternoon. It made the ground shiftier underfoot, impeding his progress, but Rhys enjoyed the cool droplets on his brow and shoulders. By the time the sun had reddened and begun to sink in the west, the rain had subsided and Thorne began calling the soldiers together. Once the last of his men arrived, he bade them all take a knee or sit.

"No one found a damned thing?" he asked in a hoarse voice. Rhys's throat was also raw from calling the boy's name all day.

"I checked three caves myself," Fergus said, "one of 'em went way far back and got too tight to climb through, but even in there, nothing. Walked probably ten leagues up and down, hollering and looking, still not a sign of him."

Holywell stood and pointed up the slope to the distant snow line, far north and above their current position.

Rhys frowned. "You went all the way up there?" Holywell pinched his fingers close together, making an "almost" gesture. "Gods' mercy, man. And even all that way, you found no sign of him?" The mute shook his head grimly.

"It was the same for me, though I didn't range as far as Brother Holywell," Grim said with a sigh. The soldiers' expressions were all glum and exhausted, the only exception being the unflappable Blackhart, whose mustached face remained a dispassionate mask.

"Without a trail," the captain said, "I think we've come to the end of our usefulness here for tonight. We need sleep and a full meal. Any objections to that, Sergeant Rhys?" he asked with a snarl.

Rhys found himself in absolute agreement with the captain for once, but felt guilty at the idea of leaving the boy alone. The needs of the men had to come first, however. "None whatsoever, Captain."

"So we're not staying up here again, Cap?" Felix asked.

"No," Thorne answered firmly. "I won't risk the integrity of our mission by having you stumble around in the dark again. We'll head back to the hall and determine our next course in the morning."

"Shepherd's not going to like that," Blackhart said, gesturing with a nod to Rhys's right. Olen was stalking down the mountain-side toward them.

"Have you found him?" he asked loudly, as red-cheeked as ever.

"Don't give him any details," Thorne whispered harshly at Rhys. The sergeant did not need to be reminded of the importance of hiding all details from the man, but he nodded calmly anyway, hoping his deference would help assuage the captain's misgivings.

"No, we haven't. Have you seen any sign of his passage?"

"None. I'm starting to worry." Olen's fingers fidgeted on his crook. "I don't understand where he could have gone. He must be lost — he wouldn't stay away so long just because he had a spat with his brother."

"We thought of that as well," Rhys said. It rankled him to have to hide the far more likely possibility. "Perhaps in the morning we should move to another area to search."

"In the morning?" Olen looked uncertain. "Are you giving up for the night?"

"We've had our men out all day, master shepherd. The captain wants us back to the hall to get them some rest and food."

"Yes, of course." He turned around and looked up the dark-ling slope. "I suppose I'll come with you to fetch more tallow for my lantern."

"You'll come back out tonight?"

"I don't think I have much of a choice — I can't leave Pedr out here. It's been a full day since he's eaten, who knows if he's even had water...?" He shook his shaggy head.

"I know you won't want to hear this," Rhys said carefully, "but it would be best for you to sleep the night as well, master."

The man looked weary, but also guilty. "How can I leave my son?" he asked.

"You're not leaving him. But you have other children and a wife miserable with worry who would benefit from having you close. Besides," he gestured around at the settling darkness, "we were lucky enough to avoid any injuries last night. Wandering alone in the dark could have dire consequences. If you're hurt, who will provide for your family, tend your flock?"

The shepherd gave him a forlorn look. "What will I tell my Runa?"

"You'll tell her the truth: you're resting up to go back out and search again tomorrow. There are no easy answers to a situation like this one, master."

"I suppose you're right, Sergeant." He looked over his shoulder at the mountain again. "Slain grant you strength, son." Rhys could just hear him murmur over the wind. "I'll be back before first light." After a moment, he faced the soldiers again. "Alright. I'm ready."

Everyone was silent on the way back down; the shepherd's guilt hung oppressively over them, and Rhys's own gnawed at his belly. Breaking through the clouds floating in the west, the sun blazed red just as it touched the horizon and painted the valley in crimson shades. Rainwater still clung to the long grass on the slope and flecked their trouser-bottoms as they strode through it. The scent of summer was strong on the Ymr.

Upon their return without Pedr, the shepherd's wife clung to her husband, fighting back tears. "You can't leave him out there," she begged. "He's all alone."

"I didn't want to come back, Runa," her husband admitted, "but if we don't rest, we're sure to slip and fall out there in the dark. If I die on the slope, what will become of you and the children?" He was near to tears himself and took her hand in both of his. "I'm going back out again in the morning, love, before dawn even breaks, I swear it. I'm not going to leave our boy out there."

His wife nodded and wiped her eyes. "I'm just so scared for him."

"He'll be alright, Mama," Vandra offered. "He and Joren build little huts out of branches in the forest all the time. Isn't that right, Joren?" Rhys noted the heavy circles under the girl's eyes. "Pedr's probably sitting in one right now, eating berries and... pretending he's on some kind of adventure or something." She forced a smile and her mother hugged her close.

Joren did not look convinced, and she pulled him to her as well. "You're right, Olen," she said tearfully, "you need to rest. All of you do. We'll just pray the Slain will protect him another night. I've made supper." Still teary-eyed, she went to her cook pot and started handing out bowls.

Rhys listened to all that was said and felt ill. He dreaded telling the happy family the truth of what was going on. The time for that was not now, though — if they thought anything other than that Pedr was lost, there would be no rest for any of them, and they all needed it.

Tired and sore, the soldiers arrayed themselves wherever there was space to sit and gratefully devoured the meal the shepherd's wife had prepared for them. Rhys, Thorne, Holywell, and Blackhart all sat down to table with Helmi, who had monopolized the space with her books and scrolls.

She finally looked up from her readings. "You haven't found Pedr." Apparently, she had been too engrossed to listen to the conversation. Rhys shook his head. "I've given further thought to what you requested, Garret — another way to track the witch."

Rhys sat up straighter. "Have you discovered something?"

"Yes," she answered hesitantly, "but it is a dire alternative. There is a tale somewhere in this mess," she gestured at the pile of books and scrolls, "that recounts the struggle of a Seraphin detachment against a particularly clever witch who was stealing children from a village in Carthannas at an alarming rate, but whose lair was impossible to find." She paused.

"And?" Rhys prodded.

Helmi shifted uncomfortably, glancing at the miserable family at the other end of the hall, then spoke in a hushed voice. "They lay in wait and observed until another child wandered from his bed, and they followed him to her lair."

Thorne cursed under his breath. "That's hardly a worthy solution."

"I didn't say it was worthy," Helmi retorted, "but it's what I've found. I've gone through every page and scroll I have that relates to witches and their practices, but there is precious little other than what we already know. I have uncovered no other way to find her than this."

"Well, as unfortunate as that is, we appreciate all the work you've done, Helmi," Rhys assured her. "We will just have to keep on the search until we find something."

Thorne looked over at him, incredulous. "Do you have any idea how vast the Ymr is? How long it could be before this witch hungers again, if that proves to be our only recourse for tracking her?" He scoffed. "I went along with you before, but this is ludicrous. Seraphe could not have meant for us to end our journey here; she doesn't send her Knights out on scavenging hunts."

"What are you saying, Captain?" Rhys asked, afraid he already knew the answer.

"I'm saying that my instinct is still telling me we've made a mistake by not heading for the Deep Ymr. How can you disagree with me, Sergeant? Holywell, Blackhart," he turned to the others, "what say you? Is this folly or not?"

Holywell shifted uneasily, and Blackhart merely shrugged.

"Captain," Rhys said, his patience waning, "with all due respect, as inconvenient and baffling as this mission has become, I still trust the oracle's judgment. We're here and there's a monster — that doesn't seem like a coincidence. Let's just kill the damned thing and be done with it."

"And how are we to do that, Sergeant?" Thorne demanded. "Wait on our arses for a month until the witch is hungry again?"

"Are you proposing we abandon our duty here?" Rhys's temper flared. "You don't like the conditions and so you think you have a choice in it? Damned young fool — why they ever give you little whelps command is far beyond me."

Thorne leapt to his feet, furious. "Keep talking like that, Sergeant, and I'll strip you of your rank myself!"

Holywell slammed a gloved hand down on the table, startling Helmi. He turned his head and Rhys followed his gaze to find the entire household watching them. The mute rose and made for the door without waiting for permission, and the others at the table all followed.

Thorne stormed out in front and went a good distance from the hall, then stopped and whirled around to face them.

"How dare you speak to me like that!" he cried, pointing angrily at Rhys. "I'm your captain — you owe me deference. You as well," he looked at Helmi. "Neither of you is the captain of this detachment. You will start following my orders without argument or I will exercise the fullest extent of my authority, is that clear?" His youthful lips trembled at the declaration.

Even Rhys was unsure exactly what Thorne meant, but he understood it was a threat.

Before Rhys could respond, Helmi fired back at him, "You're acting like a child, Captain." Thorne gasped at her insolence, but she continued. "You demand obeisance yet show none, yourself. I am the chosen and appointed Oracle of Othelia, and all I'm trying to do is ensure we accomplish our mission. Why must you disparage me at every turn?"

"Because oracle or no, you're a foolish girl playing at adventure," he snapped. "You have no idea of bloodshed and sacrifice, of the deep consequences of every decision a captain makes! Of the lives they could cost. And yet you would choose our course, without any experience, any guide but your ancient, crumbling books."

His words made Helmi pause, but only for a moment. Speaking carefully, she replied, "I don't pretend to possess your level of experience, Captain, or to possess any experience at all, in truth. But I know my business as well as you know yours, and I have a part to play, otherwise Othelia would not have sent me with you."

Helmi's clemency had no effect on him. "Why the Lady of Light allowed your goddess any say in this mission at all is beyond me. We've never needed an oracle with us before, and we would certainly be better off without you now."

"Othelia is the only reason we're here at all, Captain," she fumed. "Your goddess of light doesn't have the foresight her sister does."

Thorne was livid, the veins in his neck standing out. "Blasphemy! Are you all mad?" he looked wildly around at Rhys, Holywell, and Blackhart. "You would follow her commands before mine?"

"She's not issuing commands, Captain," Rhys pleaded with him. "She's only trying to do her duty and help us complete the mission."

"Enough!" The young officer shook with rage. "Enough of this. Your insubordination has gone too far. I will not allow another word spoken against me. We are leaving this cursed sheepfold and making for Hrokar's Pass."

"You're a fool if you make us leave," Helmi said coolly.

Even as Thorne took a threatening step toward her, Rhys moved between them.

"One more word, Lady Gwynlaithe," the captain seethed. "So help me, I will not allow Othelia's whore to wrest my command from —"

Thorne was cut short as Blackhart's massive hand smacked across his face. The blow landed with such force that the captain stumbled and lost his footing. The hospitaler made no other move, standing as calmly as though nothing had happened.

As Thorne lay on the ground, struggling to regain his senses, Rhys ran a hand through his hair in exasperation. "Alright," he said, "all of you back to the hall. Leave me with the captain."

Helmi wore a shocked expression and did not resist as Holywell respectfully took her arm and led her away, Blackhart lumbering behind.

Rhys went and stood over Thorne, who remained prostrate, holding his head, but did not try to help him up. "Are you alright, Captain?"

"He... he assaulted me." He still had not fully recovered from the power behind Blackhart's hand. "I'll have him flogged for that!"

"Damn," Rhys muttered, taking a deep breath of mountain air, letting it cool his temper. "I was hoping maybe that blow had dislodged the nonsense from between your ears." He slowly lowered himself onto a nearby rock and rested his elbows on his knees. "Since it hasn't, I suggest you listen to me, Thorne, and listen well." He had tried to reason with the man, given him every chance to act like a proper officer, but to no avail. Now he was forced to take a harder tack, loth though he was to do it.

"Helmi's right," he began, "you're acting like a spoiled child. It's pathetic and beneath a man of your status. I have much compassion for the losses you've suffered, and I understand your concerns about your ability to command, but they don't give you the right to act like this. We've all suffered in the service of Lady Seraphe. We've all bled and buried our brothers. And we all must maintain our martial bearing through it all. Are you following so far?"

A little groan escaped from the captain as he was finally able to roll over and sit up.

"Good. Never have I met a good officer who demanded the deference of others. Typically, men in your position *command* respect by their very conduct, but you are quite young, and it's reasonable that you haven't learned that yet.

"So let me tell you this: the men in this detachment would have done anything for Captain Fielding. We would have followed him through the gates of Hel and stormed the necropolis with no hope of return. He could have led us into the desert without any water, ordered us to swim with him across the oceans. That kind of loyalty certainly wasn't earned by stomping the ground and demanding it."

Thorne turned his head and spat blood. After wiping his mouth on the back of his hand, he met Rhys's gaze, but his pride seemed to whither and he quickly looked back down at the ground.

To Rhys, Thorne had never looked so young as he did then,

bloodied, teary-eyed, head hung in defeat. In spite of his anger, a part of Rhys wept for this boy, who had suffered much already, and was trying to be a leader the only way he knew.

The sergeant sighed. "I've met many young officers in my time, Captain. I see in you true potential that few others possess. The men actually do quite like you. You weren't the first captain to take over after Fielding — there were two others between the two of you. Neither lasted for very long. When you're not being a terror to poor Helmi, we enjoy having you in the detachment. You're a good fit."

Thorne made no attempt to answer, and Rhys decided he had given enough unsolicited advice for one evening. "I'm your sergeant," he said, standing and straightening his leather jerkin. "In the end, I will do as you command, Captain, even if I disagree with you. I do hope you'll consider Helmi's recommendation, though — that young woman is quite brilliant and deserves our respect." He started back down to the hall.

"Sergeant," Thorne called, and Rhys stopped. "I hear you." The captain looked up again finally, and his eyes were red and wet. "I hear you, and I know you're right." He gritted his teeth to stop the tears that threatened to fall. "I just... I don't want to make a mistake like my captain did — I don't want to lose anyone else."

Rhys took a step back toward him.

"Gods help me," he continued, "I don't want to go against you and the oracle at every turn, but I don't know what else to do. What if this witch isn't what we were sent for? What if we lose men in this fight and can't complete our mission because of it?"

Rhys weighed his response before giving it. "Command is not an easy thing. I don't envy your rank — it's why I've insisted on remaining a sergeant all these years. No one can make your decisions for you, and none of us want to, but you have the entire detachment at your disposal, all with their own experience and expertise, ready to help. A bit of trust and humility goes a long way in a situation like that, I think."

"I'm terrified of making a mistake and I'm tired of it." Thorne sniffed. "I know you're right, but what can I do now? It's too late — how can I possibly go back and face the detachment after this?"

The sergeant gave a rough laugh in spite of himself. "Do you think you're the first officer ever to be slapped by a soldier?" Thorne had no answer to that. "Your pride is wounded far more than your reputation among the men, Captain, I promise you that. Come." Rhys held out his hand. Reluctantly, the captain took it and Rhys pulled him to his feet. "Do you want my advice?"

The young man answered without hesitation. "Yes."

"Wash your face, go back to the hall, and eat and go to sleep. Pretend as though nothing has happened. Grim and the twins won't have any idea about all this. In fact, they'll probably think you're reprimanding me for insubordination. And Holywell and Blackhart would tear the patches off their shoulders before slandering their captain's reputation. Whatever you do, don't say a word to Blackhart tonight; it's a sergeant's duty to discipline the soldiers, so you leave that to me. When you have a chance, though, take Helmi aside privately and apologize to her. You owe her that."

Thorne nodded and drew a deep breath.

"I would urge you again to follow her advice, at least until we have a better idea what we're dealing with. Nothing has changed, Captain. Except, perhaps now you have a better understanding of how to proceed, yes?" He nodded again and Rhys handed over his waterskin. "Wash up. It's not so bad, actually, only cut on the inside, it looks like."

The captain splashed water over his face and scrubbed the blood away. "Was it really just a slap?"

Rhys chuckled. "You wouldn't want to see what Blackhart can do when he's truly angry, believe me."

Thorne used his sleeve to dry off and they started back. A few paces from the door, he stopped and turned to Rhys. "Thank you, Sergeant." He said it with sincerity.

"You're a good man, Captain. Learn from this and you'll be a step closer to the kind of officer men will follow anywhere. Like Fielding. Now go and get some sleep while I talk to Blackhart."

Thorne opened the door and went through. Rhys stepped

halfway inside the hall and relished the warmth that washed over him from the fire. Holywell, Blackhart, and Helmi had resumed their seats at the table, and Grim, the twins, and the two older children were sitting together on the floor.

Rhys called quietly to Blackhart, who rose without hesitation, and then gestured to Grim as well. The hospitaler ducked past him out the door but Rhys stopped Grim before he came out. "I want you to offer my and the captain's apologies to the shepherd and his wife for the disturbance earlier, please, Grim."

"Yes, Sergeant. Er, are you alright?"

"Fine," Rhys answered a little abruptly. "Why?"

"Well, Brother Blackhart's the hospitaler," he explained sheepishly. "You're not hurt or anything, are you, Sergeant?"

"I'm old, Grim," Rhys growled, "I'm always going to Blackhart for something or other."

"Right, of course. Sorry, Sergeant."

"Just pass my message to the shepherd." His tone was a little harsher than he meant it to be, but he hoped that would only help to take the focus away from Thorne.

Grim apologized again and went back inside. Shutting the door behind him, Rhys turned and led Blackhart far enough away that they would not be heard. A snappy wind was up, so they did not have far to go.

He stopped and faced the big man. Blackhart's face betrayed no more emotion than usual and Rhys thought carefully about what to say to him. He held the hospitaler's gaze for a long moment before finally saying, "The Ymr is certainly beautiful in summer, isn't it?"

Blackhart regarded him gravely. "I've always found mountain air to be good for the lungs."

"I have a blister on my foot that's been quite troublesome the last few days, do you have any of that ointment left?"

The hospitaler rubbed his beard. "Yes, and I should be able to find it quite quickly, assuming you and the oracle haven't made a complete mess of my trunk."

"I swear I had almost nothing to do with that."

"Hmmm…." Blackhart glared at him distrustfully. "I probably shouldn't have hit the captain."

Rhys nodded. "Probably not. You saved the rest of us the trouble, though. And it seemed to be just the thing he needed."

"Lady Gwynlaithe is a nice girl. Couldn't let him get away with calling her what he did."

"I understand, Brother." He let a little more time pass, watching the last of the pink settle down beyond the horizon. "Well, try to look glum when you go back in, eh?"

"Don't I always?"

"And I was serious about needing that ointment."

They plodded back to the hall together.

6

MASSACRE

A little after the captain and the sergeant had shouted at each other and taken their group outside, Grim approached Joren and Vandra and invited them to play a game he had brought with him on their journey. Neither of them felt much like playing anything, but their mother insisted they do, to try and distract themselves from everything else going on. So they all sat down on the floor together.

As Grim hurriedly finished off his supper and went over to the pile of gear to fetch the game, Helmi and Brothers Blackhart and Holywell came back inside. Joren wondered idly where Sergeant Rhys and Captain Thorne were, but after rummaging around for a while, Grim finally returned with a rolled up length of leather and a pouch with drawstrings, and the thought disappeared.

Grim unraveled the leather and laid it out on the ground, revealing patterns dyed on its smooth side, then dumped the contents of the pouch next to it. A dozen or so little wooden discs and a pair of dice landed on the fleece. Joren knew about dice; his father would play Old Havar sometimes when he came to trade. Everything else was foreign to him, though.

The young man looked at him and Vandra, and in a dramatic voice, asked, "Have either of you ever heard of —"

He stopped and looked over his shoulder as the door swung open again, and the captain stepped through and went to retrieve the supper he had left unfinished. He did not look as angry as he had before, but an uncomfortable tension nevertheless settled over the hall again. Sergeant Rhys remained in the doorway and called Brother Blackhart and Grim to him. Joren kept his head down, inspecting the leather game board so he would not have to look at anyone in case there was more shouting.

There was not, though, and once the sergeant had closed the door again, Grim crossed over to Joren's parents.

"Er, master shepherd," he said in a low voice, "Sergeant wanted me to tell you he's sorry for the disruption earlier."

Joren's father blinked. "Oh, there's no trouble, Master Grim. I trust everything is alright? You haven't changed your minds about staying, have you?" Their mother sat with her husband and clutched at him a little tighter.

"Oh no, nothing like that," Grim assured them. "It was just a... personal matter, I think; certainly nothing for you to worry about."

The sandy-haired man resumed his seat on the floor and rubbed his hands together, his eternally good humor oddly comforting. "Alright, now where was I? Ah, yes. Have you two ever heard of... the Game of Twenty Squares?" Joren and Vandra both shook their heads. "It's an ancient game, played for hundreds and hundreds of years, especially popular in the Caliphates, far south of here. I bought this off a merchant we met in Ainsley, near the border, right where the sand dunes meet the green. You remember that, boys?"

Felix and Fergus sat nearby, slurping down seconds. "Oh, we remember, Grim," Joren believed it was Fergus speaking, "we remember taking about a month's wages off you in the first few games." They both cackled.

"Yes, yes," Grim blushed and cleared his throat. "Never mind them. We're not playing for coin now, obviously. It's a beauty, though, isn't it?"

It was indeed quite beautiful, Joren thought. The leather was warm and ruddy and the twenty squares were stained a rich, dark brown. There were three rows of squares by four, and the middle row extended out to twelve. Every fourth square featured a complex device of various patterns.

"Each of those ornaments represents one of the elements: air, water, earth, fire, and wood." He pointed each one out. "Anyhow, here's how you play — two players each get four pieces, and the goal is to get all your pieces around and to the end before your opponent does. You roll one die before each move to see how many spaces you can go with your piece. Then you move that many spaces, and it ends up being like a race. I'll explain the finer details as we play." He took up four of the little round pieces and held them in his open palm. "Who wants to go first?"

Joren looked at Vandra and she nudged his arm, so he reached up and took the pieces from Grim.

"Excellent, Master Joren," Grim declared, "let's test our skill, each against the other's, shall we? Now, take one of these dice, too, you'll just need the one. Go ahead and roll it, and that's how many spaces you move."

As they played, Joren became subtly aware that he had stopped thinking about Pedr. He could feel the angst lurking in the back of his mind, waiting for the fun to end so it could take over again. It faded into the background as the game went on, though, thanks to Grim and the twins, who were nothing short of a walking comedy.

When Grim's pieces started pulling ahead of Joren's, Felix and Fergus tried to mouth silent advice to them behind his back, and when the man found out, he trapped one of their heads beneath his arm and pretended to pop it off. Then, once Joren and Grim's game had finished, Vandra had a turn against Fergus, who took an early lead. On the secretive advice of Felix, she stole the man's die and inspected it, only to discover that it was loaded, set to roll a six every time. She tried to look appalled, but giggled as the other two men dragged Fergus away and Felix took his place. They made an affair of carefully inspecting both dice after that.

Agata even toddled over after a while and started jabbering and clapping alongside both players whenever someone's piece made it to the end. Her hearty giggle made Joren happy.

He was so distracted by the game that he hardly noticed when the sergeant and Brother Blackhart returned from outside. Sergeant Rhys came over and watched for a while, standing over them with his arms folded. Agata stumbled and fell, landing on his boot, so the sergeant stooped to help her stand back up and she grabbed his beard. His hard eyes wrinkled as he laughed and gently extricated her little fist. Joren seized his baby sister and kept her imprisoned on his lap for the remainder of the game.

Brother Blackhart came over and handed the sergeant a little jar, and then Sergeant Rhys spoke in Carthan to Grim and the twins and went over to the table to sit with Helmi.

"Our Da says we can't play anymore," Felix grinned. "Wants us to get a good night's sleep so we can go back out, first thing."

Grim started gathering up the game pieces. "We'll have to play again, maybe tomorrow night, eh?"

"I hope Pedr comes home tomorrow," Joren said, and immediately regretted it. Grim's face fell and the twins would not look at him or Vandra.

Grim tried to sound casual, but failed. "I'm sure we'll find him soon, young master."

"Vandra, Joren," their mother called to them, "bring your sister and come here."

Joren hoisted Agata up on his hip and carried her over to their parents' bed. Their father sat on the edge, resting his elbows on his knees, and their mother was curled up next to him with a fleece over her. She was always cold. As she took Agata from Joren, their father said, "It's time for bed, you two."

"Yes, Papa," Vandra answered.

Their mother planted a kiss on each of their foreheads. "Don't worry about your brother," she said, even though her eyes were wet again. "Go offer your prayers to the ancestors and the Slain, ask them for strength and bravery for Pedr."

Joren was not able to say anything.

"We will, Mama." Vandra took Joren's wrist and led him over to the loft ladder. Joren's mind was numb. As soon as the game had ended, the oppressive bitterness of their situation had returned to loom over him. He felt his little brother's absence as though his arm was missing.

Joren allowed Vandra to lead him up, and she even threw a fleece over him once he laid down. Then she pulled her own bed closer to him.

As they lay there, Joren found himself unable to sleep in spite of his exhaustion. "Do you think they'll find Pedr?" he asked his sister. She didn't respond, so he rolled over to look at her and found she was already fast asleep; everyone was so exhausted. He sighed and turned back over.

Beneath him, Joren could see the soldiers getting ready for bed, too. The sergeant and Brothers Blackhart and Holywell stayed up for a while, taking old bits of cloth, coating them with tallow, and wrapping them around gnarly branches from the firewood bin. They were making torches, he realized, in case they needed to go outside at night.

He looked away to watch the smoke from the fire dance and twirl up, out of the hole in the roof, trying to let his imagination wander, to become a roaming warrior in his mind and ride around Fjalvard saving people in need, but it did not work. Finally, his exhaustion won out and his eyes fluttered shut. Just before he fell asleep, the image of the Burnt Lady flashed through his mind, and he was afraid.

When Joren woke, he was very confused. There were a lot of noises all at once, and in his grogginess, he could not tell what was happening. Shaking his head to clear the sleepiness, he looked down through the slats and saw that the fire still blazed; no one had put it out for the night. The soldiers were starting to wake, talking to each other in Carthan, and Joren watched his father roll out of bed and grab his fleece coat.

Besides the clamor of everyone in the hall, there was another noise. It took him a moment to recognize it was the bleating of the sheep, their irritated cries carrying through the wall.

"I'm sorry, Sergeant," Joren's father said, rubbing the sleep from his eyes, "I'll go take care of them — you men go back to bed." Joren had no idea how much time had passed, but almost everyone looked as though they had woken from a deep sleep. The only exception was Aedric, who sat by the fire as though he had been tending it all night.

"What's that sound?" Fergus asked loudly, sitting up from his bedroll. No one bothered to answer him.

Joren's father went over to the door and retrieved his crook.

"Hold a moment, master shepherd," Sergeant Rhys said, standing from his spot on the ground. "Wait a moment before going out." He turned to Helmi, who still lay on one of the benches, propped up on her hand.

The sergeant said something to her in Carthan and she responded. They had a brief exchange and Captain Thorne joined in as well. Helmi sat up straighter and Joren wished he knew what they were saying. He was almost fully awake, and so was Vandra; she lay beside him, her eye pressed likewise to the space between boards.

"Is something the matter, Sergeant?" their father asked.

Sergeant Rhys did not answer him right away, but exchanged a bit more with Helmi in their native tongue. "Nothing's the matter, I'm sure," he said, finally, "but I think we'll handle your sheep tonight."

"Does anyone else hear that sound?" Fergus asked, rubbing his ears. Felix nudged him into silence.

"Nonsense!" Their father waved his hand. "The sheep sometimes get restless in the summer when it is too warm for them in the shelter. I'll just go and prop the gate open for a bit until they calm."

His hand went for the door, but the sergeant stopped him. "Wait, master, please," he said commandingly. He looked at Helmi again and the oracle nodded. "In case of danger, I must insist a few of us go with you — or better, in your stead."

"Danger?" Joren's father gave him a strange look. "What danger?" Sergeant Rhys seemed at a loss for words. "What's going on, Sergeant? I thought you said we had nothing to worry about here on the slope."

"Master shepherd, please. I can't explain, I just need you to trust me. Felix, Fergus, come with me." Felix clambered to his feet, but his brother remained on the ground, still pulling at his ears. The bleating of the sheep was growing louder; louder than Joren had ever heard from inside their hall.

"I certainly do trust you, Sergeant," Joren's father replied, but his tone had hardened. He stepped in front of the door, barring the soldiers' passage. "Please, though, explain what you mean. Do we have anything to fear or not?"

"I'm only trying to take precautions, master," Sergeant Rhys replied tightly. "Fergus, get up."

"Precautions for what, Sergeant?"

"What is that bloody sound?" Fergus demanded.

"It's the sheep, you idiot." Felix gave him a light kick in the hip to rouse him. "Get up already."

"Not the sheep, the song!" Fergus shrieked, digging violently in his right ear. Everyone in the hall turned to look at him. Blood ran down his hand from his ear and dripped onto the matted fleece beneath him.

"What did he say?" Sergeant Rhys asked, taking a step toward the man on the floor. He did not wait for an answer. "Fergus, what are you talking about?"

"The song! The song! Can't you hear it?" Fergus insisted, trembling. "Can't you hear her song?"

"*Her* song?"

The bleating from the sheep suddenly turned into wretched, harrowing screams.

"Grab him!" Sergeant Rhys bellowed over the cacophony, just as Fergus leapt to his feet. He was instantly tackled by his fellow soldiers, and they pinned him down on one of the benches opposite the door. Joren clamped his hands down on his ears to block out the grisly sounds, and in the corner, his mother scooted further back in her bed, trying to quiet Agata as the toddler began to cry.

"What in Nydheim is going on?" Joren's father demanded, but everyone else was focused on Fergus. "Joren," his father called up to him. "Come help me quiet the sheep!"

Terrified, Joren scrambled down the ladder and threw his boots on. Vandra was just behind him and dashed over to where their mother sat with Agata. After thrusting Joren's little crook into his hands, his father grabbed one of the torches the soldiers had prepared and held it into the fire. It burst into flames and he headed out the door.

"I'll come with you," said the Ilban, grabbing his hammer from the corner. Clutching his crook in front of him with both hands, Joren hurried after them out into the dark.

Even louder outside, the screams of the sheep were joined by intermittent wet, thudding sounds, and the tiny cries of the lambs were just audible over their shrieking mothers and fathers. The three came around the corner and Joren's father hurriedly slammed back the lock bar on the gate and drew it open.

A sickly odor poured out over them as the light from the torch spilled into the shelter and screams pierced the night. Joren felt his knees go out under him at the sight within, and his father cursed loudly.

The sheep were killing their lambs. They rose up and slammed their hooves down on their young, shrieking and bucking, tongues lolling out of their gaping mouths. Tiny bodies littered the floor, streams of blood and streaks of pulpy tissue running among them.

The horse and mules were rearing and snorting and screaming, kicking each other and trampling on lambs and sheep alike. Behind the slaughter, two sheep slammed their heads into the shelter's stone wall. One fell and lay twitching on the ground while the other rebounded, walked backwards, and charged again, this time impacting with a sickening smack.

Hala was curled up on the ground, crying in pain, blood leaking from under her tail. She nipped at the air all around her wildly. Joren took an instinctive step toward her, but his father's big hand grasped his shoulder and held him back. The horse jumped away from one of the mules and landed on Hala's flank. She yelped and another hoof came down on her head, silencing her. Joren cried out and struggled against the hand restraining him.

"Joren," his father pushed him back toward the hall, not taking his eyes from the carnage, "stay back. Go get help!" He and Aedric both took cautious steps into the shelter, and his father almost lost his footing as he slipped on the gore that covered the ground. "Go for help!" he bellowed again, and Joren turned and ran, warm tears streaking cool across his face in the summer evening.

~

Rhys, the captain, and Blackhart remained stooped over Fergus, holding him down as he writhed and groaned. "What's happening to him?" Thorne demanded, dodging one of Fergus's flailing arms, grabbing ahold of it, and forcing it back down. All his trepidation from earlier in the evening was gone; he had an air of command again.

"I think this is what happened to the brother," Rhys grunted, shifting more of his weight onto Fergus. The louder the man moaned, the stronger he seemed to become. Rhys looked around and found Helmi standing in the corner wide-eyed. He called to her and she hurried over. "Is this what happened to Pedr?" he asked. "He said he heard a song. Can a hex do that?"

"I..." she looked uncertain. "Possibly. Technically, a hex could do all kinds of things, as I said before. If it *is* a hex, Fergus would have had to come into contact with her at some point."

Rhys shook his head. "He would have told us."

"He might not even have been aware of it," she insisted. "She could have incapacitated him first, as she did to Joren. Check for a mark."

Struggling to keep his hold on the man's wrist, Rhys tugged his sleeves and pulled up his shirt, looking for any sign of a hex. He found none. "I don't think it's a hex, Helmi. Think quickly, there must be something else." She nodded and went over to her books, still laid open on the table.

"I thought this was a child-stealer!" Felix said angrily. "Why's it going after Fergus instead of one of the little ones?"

Rhys had no answer to that, so he ignored the question and instead looked over his shoulder at the hospitaler. "Blackhart, can you do anything for him?"

"Short of cracking him in the head?"

"Preferably."

"I can try a phlegmatic. It's not meant for this kind of hysteria, but it might calm him down a bit. Do you have him?" Once Rhys and Thorne had a better grip on Fergus's writhing limbs, Blackhart let go and lumbered over to the chest. He kicked the lid open and dug around inside briefly before returning, a small phial in hand.

"She needs me!" Fergus wailed desperately.

Rhys heard the door behind them slam open and looked over his shoulder. The shepherd's son stood there, sobbing. "Help." He could barely manage the word.

Thorne apparently understood him. "Grim, Holywell, Felix — go with him."

"I'm not leaving my brother," Felix protested as the others grabbed a lantern and a torch and made for the door.

"I gave you an order—"

"I need to go to her!" Fergus screamed, kicking his legs.

The shepherd's wife handed her toddler over to Vandra, pushed both of them to the very corner of the bed, and threw a fleece over top of them. "Stay there with her," she commanded, "and don't move until one of us tells you." Then she came over by the fire, lit another torch, and followed Grim and Holywell outside.

"Ready, Sergeant," Blackhart announced, pulling the stopper from the phial. "Open his mouth." Rhys placed his hand over Fergus's face and squeezed his cheeks hard as the man was still crying out, forcing his mouth to stay open.

The hospitaler brought the phial to Fergus's lips. As he tilted it, Fergus recoiled, coughed, and lunged forward, sinking his teeth into Blackhart's fingers and shattering the glass tube. Bellowing, the hospitaler tried to jerk his hand away but could not get loose. He smashed his other fist into Fergus's hawkish nose and sent a spray of blood across Rhys's face.

Felix leapt on Blackhart, pulling him away from his brother while Fergus continued to scream. His nose was a wreck and shards of the broken phial remained in his mouth.

"You're supposed to help him, not hurt him!" Felix shouted.

"Little bugger nearly took my fingers off," Blackhart growled, shoving him away.

"We need something to hold him," Rhys said, struggling to keep Fergus down. "If not a draught then rope!" As Felix started rummaging around the hall, Rhys looked up at Helmi, who was reading furiously down an old scroll. "What have you found?"

"A spell, possibly," she answered without looking. "Does he have any missing hair, teeth, or nails?"

Rhys looked over Fergus again quickly as he continued to writhe. "No more than usual, I think. I can't tell."

"It could be a malediction," she said uncertainly, "a powerful one."

"Blackhart," Rhys called. "Malediction, what do we have for it?"

"Any normal dagger will do the job," he answered, applying a balm to his wounded fingers. "You and I both know there's no medicine for a malediction."

Rhys knew, but had hoped for a different answer anyway.

"We won't be doing that, obviously," Felix said, coming up to the captain. "Rope." He held aloft a bundle that looked unused.

"Tie him quickly," Thorne ordered, straining to hold Fergus. "He's getting stronger by the moment, it seems."

Over the man's constant moaning and occasional wailing, Rhys could hear an eerie, shrieking chorus coming from the other side of the west wall, where the animals were sheltered.

Joren watched, terrified and powerless, as Brother Holywell and Grim helped his father and Aedric in the shelter. More sheep had charged and dashed their heads against the stones and now lay dead, urine and excrement mingling with the pools of blood on the ground.

The mules, too, were dead. One had tumbled violently while trying to attack a sheep and broken its neck. Another had killed itself against the stone wall, like the other animals. Aedric had been forced to smash in the head of the third with his hammer when it came after him; two mighty blows and the mule lay still.

The horse was still alive, shrieking and batting the air with its hooves. Brother Holywell rushed in to take its reins and calm it, but it jerked savagely away and turned to kick him. The spry older man leapt out of the way and circled around to try again.

Joren's mother came around the corner and froze as she saw the slaughter. The horse evaded Holywell again, turned, and charged for the open air. Joren's mother grabbed him by his shirt and yanked him out of the rabid animal's path, and they landed in a heap.

Holywell and Grim dashed after the horse while Joren's father and Aedric each wrestled a sheep down to the ground. The few that were left continued to charge the stones, cracking their skulls and falling onto the growing pile of corpses.

A panicked whinny drew Joren's attention away from the shelter to the open field behind them. The horse was bucking in place, throwing and twisting its body in unnatural motions. Holywell approached it again, but this time he had his sword drawn. Grim circled around and positioned himself on the other side. Nostrils flared and eyes rolled back, the beast swung its head, trying to bite them. Holywell slid out of the way and as it exposed its neck to him, he landed a swift chop with his long blade. The gelding shrieked again and the blood that sprayed and poured from its wound painted the ground black in the moonlight. Twice more it bucked wildly before sinking to its knees and falling over.

The only sheep that remained were the ones wrangled by the two men on the ground; all the rest had killed each other or themselves. Holywell walked swiftly back and into the shelter. Drawing a dagger from his hip, he bent down next to Aedric and pierced the screaming sheep's throat. A dark spurt followed as he withdrew his blade and then went over to where Joren's father wrestled the lone surviving animal. He knelt and stabbed that one, too.

"What have you done?" his father cried when the blood welled and flowed down his arms from the sheep's neck. He stood, shook some of the gore from his hands, and looked around him.

"They're all gone," he said, ashen. "Every last one of them, gone. We could've saved at least those!"

Holywell shook his head emphatically and crossed his arms in front of his chest. "He's saying they were cursed," Grim explained. "It would not have been wise to eat them, or to use them at all."

Joren disentangled himself from his mother and dashed into the shelter, where Hala lay a little apart from the rest of the death. He placed a hand on her flank, waiting desperately for a breath, even a twitch. There was nothing. The blood around her had started to congeal already, and the warmth under her coat was fading.

"Slain's mighty halls." Joren's father stared at his blood-soaked hands. "What happened?"

Before anyone could answer, however, wild howling erupted from the hall. His father and the other men all dashed out of the shelter, but Joren did not move, his mind too numb to do anything but sit there next to Hala. In the light of the torch his mother still carried, the red all over was slowly turning brown. She came over to him and hugged him close, pulling him away from the scene despite his efforts to remain.

As he was dragged away, Joren blinked through warm tears and watched Hala's face fade into the darkness.

"I can't hold him any longer!" Thorne shouted, looking desperately to Felix. He was wrapping the rope as quickly as he could around his brother's legs, but his efforts were impeded by Fergus's kicking and flailing. The man's wails were bestial, rending Rhys's thought, louder than he had ever heard a person scream.

"Ahhhh! I need her, need to go to her! She needs me to go! She needs me! She needs!"

The sergeant tightened his grip around the man's wrist, but it was no use; Fergus finally pulled away and threw him off. Rhys stumbled back, nearly crashing into Helmi before righting himself.

Shaking off the captain as well, Fergus kicked wildly, catching his brother in the jaw and knocking him to the floor.

The rope around his feet came loose and he scrambled up and bolted away. Felix grabbed at his ankle but to no effect. Pausing just long enough to open the door, Fergus charged through at the same moment the shepherd appeared, bowling him over. There was an audible snap as the big man fell and he howled in pain while Fergus took off into the night.

Rhys leapt through the door after him to see Holywell and Grim there, covered in gore. The captain was just behind him and as he came outside, he pointed at Fergus. "Holywell, get after him! We'll be just behind you." Without a moment's hesitation, Holywell obeyed, coursing up the mountain after the madman, his lantern in hand.

Rhys made to follow, but Thorne stopped him. "Wait, Sergeant — we need supplies, quickly." Felix flew past them as they headed inside, but neither attempted to stop him; they knew he would go after his brother regardless of what they said, and there was no time to argue.

While Grim and the Ilban attended to the shepherd — it looked to Rhys as though he had snapped his ankle — Thorne barked at the hospitaler for help going through the chest. Blackhart went over, and together they started quickly pulling out items and handing them to Rhys to stuff into a pack.

As they worked, Rhys looked over at Helmi, who was still turning pages over desperately. "What kind of black magic is this, Helmi?" he asked. "We need to know what we're dealing with."

"It's too similar to what happened to Pedr," the oracle answered, her voice wavering. "It has to be a hex."

"I didn't find any mark on him."

"It must have been some place inconspicuous, just like with Pedr," she said. "When you were up in the hills, was he ever on his own?"

"Well, yes, we all went our own ways to find the boy."

"Then she could have incapacitated him with a spell, placed the hex on the sole of his foot for all we know, and he would have been none the wiser."

"Gods-damned witches," Rhys growled, carefully placing the last item from the trunk into the captain's pack.

Grim and the Ilban came sideways through the door, the shepherd suspended between them.

"What on earth happened out there?" Rhys asked, appalled at the amount of blood on their clothes and hands.

"The witch put a curse or something on the sheep," Grim explained. "They went mad, killed each other, and themselves; the mules were rabid, too, and the horse. Tried to kill us."

"How did you stop them?"

"Had to kill them instead."

"All of them?" Thorne asked sharply.

"All of them, Captain."

"Gods' mercy," Rhys looked at Helmi. "How could she have managed that?"

The oracle blinked and stared, tapping her finger rapidly on the table. "I... don't know. Curses are powerful, but require much preparation and much knowledge. This must be a very powerful witch. Or else..." she swallowed hard. "Or else the work of a coven."

Thorne sighed. "From one witch to gods know how many."

"That's not the answer I was hoping for," Rhys frowned and adjusted the items in the sack and cinched it tight.

"What's going on here, Sergeant?" Olen demanded, his face ashen beneath the blood spatter, hopping on his good foot as the men helped him over to a bench. "You lied to us — something is out there, killed my entire flock!" He slammed his fist down on the table. "And Pedr? Is this why we can't find him? Did something take him?"

"Joren's nightmare," Runa said, shaking in anger. "You told me it was just a dream, nothing to fear!"

"Yes," Rhys answered, pitiless. "I lied to you — not out of cruelty, but compassion. But there is no more pretending now. Your son was taken by a witch, and apparently she is not done with us yet." The shepherd's wife let out a sob. "If you want my advice, flee this mountain. We're going after our man, and if we find your son, we'll return him as well."

"Damn you!" Olen bellowed. "We trusted you!"

"Trust us still," Rhys said, handing the pack to Thorne, "or don't. Either way, we're leaving and you would be wise to try and save the rest of your family."

The shepherd wanted to say something else, but Rhys ignored him and turned away. "Are we ready, Captain?"

"Almost," he pointed at Rhys and Blackhart. "We're doffing our armor. We won't need it against witches and we'll be quicker without it."

Rhys did as he was commanded without hesitation, removing first his jerkin and then pulling the chain shirt off and over his head.

"What about me, Captain?" Grim asked, wiping bloodied hands on his trousers.

"You're staying here with the Ilban." Thorne's tone brooked no argument. "Guard the oracle and try to keep the shepherd and his family out of trouble, too."

The young soldier said nothing, sinking glumly down onto the bench next to Olen.

"If the witch's lair is high up," the captain continued, "we might have a need for those coats." Before he finished the thought, Rhys went and started going through their equipment.

"Blackhart, how is your hand?"

"Fine, Captain," the hospitaler rumbled. He had applied some balm to his torn fingers and wrapped them in linen bandages.

"Gather up some food, then — enough for six of us for at least a day."

Rhys found the heavy fur jackets, pulled three of them out, and handed them out to the others. Once everything was prepared, they stepped outside into the night's chill.

Helmi appeared at the door behind them. "Captain," she said, respectful but firm in her tone, "all the signs are now showing that — at best — we're dealing with a truly powerful and insidious creature. Whatever your opinion of me or Othelia, please use caution and... be safe."

The captain turned to her and his expression softened. "Lady Gwynlaithe, I owe you an apology," he said earnestly, "and this might be my last chance to give it. My treatment of you was unwarranted. Please forgive me."

Helmi blinked nervously, unsure how to answer. "There is nothing to forgive, Captain," she managed. "Just please — be careful."

"We will, Milady." He turned and took off at a jog up the mountainside, Blackhart beside him, following the path Fergus had taken.

"You be careful, too," Rhys told her as he slipped on the fur jacket. She did not say anything but held out her hand; he took it briefly in his and gave a gentle squeeze, then headed off after the others.

7

PURSUIT

R hys knew from the start that they had no chance at catching up with Holywell. The man was at least a decade his senior, but lithe and energetic as any youth, and had spent many years as a scout, ranging ahead of his detachment in all kinds of terrain. The ground was still wet beneath their feet, and Rhys could see in the halo of light from the captain's lantern occasional footsteps where there was a bare patch of earth. Three different tracks lay over top one another where first Fergus had gone, and then Holywell and Felix had followed.

Their pace lagged as the slope steepened, and before long, Rhys's chest was heaving as he worked his tired legs ever further. Ahead of them, a tiny light appeared and vanished randomly, like a ship traveling the waves at sea, as Holywell carried his lantern up and down the hills. Every now and again, he could see Felix's silhouette in the scout's lantern light, and he was glad that at least they were together.

After only a little while, Rhys began to slow against his will, his lungs burning in the chilly air. Blackhart was also struggling, and Thorne reluctantly shortened his stride to match theirs.

"How are we going to catch that old bastard?" Rhys asked between breaths, flapping the front of his fur jacket to help disperse the uncomfortable heat their exertion had created.

"I don't think we'll have to," the captain answered, noticeably less winded. "As long as he and Felix can track Fergus, and we can keep Holywell in sight, we'll manage to find the lot of them."

"I pray you're right about that."

They continued on in silence for a long while. Rhys watched the waning moon arc across the sky, sliding behind errant clouds and back out again to loose her silvery light over the Ymr. Holywell's lantern disappeared for long periods occasionally and he worried that they had lost him. He always managed to come back into view, however — over a ridge or from around a bend — and so they continued the struggle up the mountainside.

After many hours without stop, Rhys's knees ached and his back was sore. The captain's lantern had finally gone out and they relied on moonlight to guide the way. Blackhart slowed considerably after that and they were forced to stop and take a number of rests, for which Rhys was secretly thankful.

Their initial passion and fervor to recover Fergus had necessarily been tempered by the sheer distance they were required to cover: Rhys guessed they had come half a league at least already and had no idea how much farther was left. The Ymr still towered impossibly high above them to the north, and the witch's lair could be on the very peak, for all they knew.

The eastern horizon was just turning to a slightly lighter shade of blue when Rhys noticed the ground crunching underfoot. He looked up and saw they were not far from the snow line. As they came about a hundred yards or so from where white began to blanket the rocky mountainside, a sharp whistle cut through the air and echoed down toward the valley. There were Holywell and Felix, outlined against the snow a little ways above them, waving their arms.

By the time they reached the two, Rhys was thoroughly exhausted. Blackhart was in even worse shape and trailed behind.

"How far ahead is he?" Thorne asked without ceremony.

Felix answered impatiently. "A good way. We lost sight of him hours ago, but were able to follow his tracks." He gestured to the unmistakable trail of prints that Fergus had carved along the damp mountainside and now traced through the crusty snow. "We can catch him, though, maybe, before he gets… wherever it is he's going." He made to start off again.

"Wait a moment, Comstock," Thorne halted him. "Let Black-hart catch us up, and we'll rest for a moment."

"I'll just go on without you."

"You won't," was Thorne's firm rebuke. "You won't catch him. Even if you do, you saw how strong he was — he'd snap you in two."

Felix paid him no mind and started stalking off through the snow.

"Just a moment's rest, that's all we ask," Rhys called after him. "Let us catch our breath, drink some water, and we'll continue on beside you, I swear it. I don't intend to lose your brother today, but I'll be damned if we lose the both of you."

Felix hesitated and turned back toward the others, fixing Rhys with a dangerous gaze. "Fine. Have it your way, then. A moment's rest. But if we get to him and he's two moments dead, I'll send you all to meet him."

Rhys's jaw tightened, but he let the comment pass. Squatting down, he drank deep from what remained in his water skin, then packed snow into the empty vessel. Blackhart finally made it to them and sat his rear right down in the snow. Rhys reached into the bag the hospitaler wore on his back and pulled out hunks of bread and cheese and jerky. He passed them around and they quickly devoured half of what they had brought.

Thorne had the others drop their heavy chain shirts as well; they could recover them on the return journey. The cold started to sink in past the heat of exertion and Rhys finally fastened the ties on the front of his fur jacket.

After what seemed like only a few moments, Felix cleared his throat noisily and the party started up the mountain once again.

～

As soon as the captain, sergeant, and hospitaler left, Joren's parents assaulted Grim and Helmi with questions. They demanded to know more about what was happening, what it meant for Pedr and the rest of the family.

Helmi calmly explained that there were no definitive answers — all they seemed to know was that Pedr had been lured away by a witch and that apparently, the same had happened to Fergus. Beyond that, Helmi insisted she could tell them nothing. They asked her why the sergeant had lied to them, but Helmi would not answer, and Grim said only that they had not wanted to worry the family unnecessarily.

Joren understood what it all meant: the Burnt Lady was real, and Pedr would probably not be coming home.

After two nights of near sleeplessness, Joren was exhausted and beginning to wonder whether he would ever sleep again. The sight of Hala's lifeless, battered corpse haunted him every time he closed his eyes and fears about his brother's fate twisted his stomach into knots.

His parents continued to badger the others for answers for some time. His father even tried to go back out to follow after the soldiers, but on his damaged leg, he could hardly make it to the door; he had turned his ankle badly when Fergus knocked him over, so Joren's mother put him on their bed and attended to the swollen, purple mass.

The three children had again spent the remainder of the night at the end of their parents' bed, clinging to each other under bundled fleeces. Neither he nor Vandra spoke, but Joren was grateful to have his big sister near. Helmi delved back into her books, occasionally consulting with Grim in their language, and Aedric sat quietly, tending the fire, his face the same stern mask it always was.

Joren, his father, Aedric, and Grim were all still covered in the animals' blood, unwilling to risk a trip in the dark to wash. His mother had taken a damp cloth to their faces, but their clothes remained stiff and crusted.

After a while, as the sky lightened and turned pink through the smoke hole, Grim stood and walked over to Joren's father.

"Master shepherd," he said gently, rousing him, "Lady Helmi thinks it best that we dispose of all the animals outside, seeing as it's not good to keep cursed things about. And the sooner we do it, the better off we'll be." With weary countenance, Joren's father nodded and tried to rise. His wife held him back forcefully. "The Ilban and I will take care of it, master," Grim said kindly, "I just wanted your leave to begin."

"You have it," his father grumbled. "I know better than to argue with you, even if it means our entire livelihood will have been destroyed in a single night." His meaty knuckles went white as he balled his fists, and his wife put a hand to his cheek.

"Papa, what will we do with Hala?" Joren asked, unable to bring his voice much higher than a whisper.

His father's glazed eyes held his for a long moment, and his face softened. "She was a good dog, wasn't she, Joren?" The question came gently, as a consolation. Joren nodded, afraid his voice would break if he tried to answer. "We'll build her a pyre of her own, separate from the others. Can you do that for us, Master Grim? Once you've done with the flock and all the rest? That way, we can send her off as a true Fjalr."

He took his wife's hand from his cheek and took it in his. "Do you two remember when we sent your grandfather on to Lodrheim?" Joren and Vandra both nodded. "If shepherds go there, surely must their faithful companions, also. So that's where we'll send Hala, and it will be a better place for her presence."

Grim bowed his head slightly and made for the door, motioning to Aedric. Joren leapt off the bed to follow, earning a sharp rebuke from his mother. "Joren! What do you think you're doing?"

"I have to take care of Hala." His voice was raw from all the shouting and crying the previous night.

"I don't want you anywhere near those cursed beasts!"

"She was my dog," Joren said, "I have to see to her."

"He's right, Runa," his father said quietly. Her head whipped around and she stared at him, wide-eyed. "Let him go. Master Grim will look after him, won't you?"

"Yes, of course."

"They're warriors," she insisted, "they're trained for this sort of thing. They don't need a boy's help. Are you so eager to lose another child?"

His father's face fell and he let go of his wife's hand.

"Go with them, Joren," he growled. "Do as they say. Go on."

Joren nodded, grabbed his little crook from the corner, and followed the men outside.

The morning sun was just cresting the horizon and it warmed his cheeks. Thin, lofty clouds hung high above, painted purple, pink, and yellow as sunlight dashed against their dipping bellies. The world was silent all around them but for a whisper of wind; not even the chorus of birdsong broke it. Joren's step faltered as Hala's absence echoed around him again.

They made their way warily to the back of the hall, where the dark blood had fully browned and hardened from the night before. Finally, a sound other than the wind filled the air, and it was perhaps worse than the silence: a swarm of flies nested on the corpses, pulsing and buzzing maddeningly in erratic flight. The stench of decay had overpowered that of death, and it billowed from the open shelter in wafts batted around by the breeze.

Joren's eyes immediately found Hala, but he hesitated, disgusted by the sight of her and ashamed of his disgust. Aedric rested a hand on his shoulder, and with the other, lifted his linen shirt up over his nose to filter the bad air. Joren imitated him.

"We'll have to burn the lot of them," Grim said. "It's a damned waste, but it must be done." Aedric nodded. He first made for Hala, and Joren hurried after him.

"Joren, stay out of here." The kilted man motioned him back with his free hand.

"I want to help with her!" Joren went right up to the lifeless form, forcing himself to be unafraid of whatever curse might linger, and waved his arm in the air to clear the flies. Hala's tongue still lolled out but was now dry and cracked. Her body was stiff as, together, he and Aedric peeled her away from the thick, clotted blood that covered the ground. She seemed lighter than she had in life as they carried her out into the sun.

They laid her down in soft grasses and when Joren pulled his hands from under her, they were slick with a sticky, clear fluid.

He regarded her silently as the men went back into the shelter and began unceremoniously tossing the sheep and mangled pieces of what was left of the lambs outside. She did not look peaceful, exactly, but she was where she belonged at least: under a warm summer sun, the breeze coursing through the grasses around her.

Joren felt the pain and the anguish slipping away from him a little. For some reason, his tears would not come again, even though he wanted to weep over her as any good boy should do for his dog. He tried to cry, watched her death over again in his mind, forced himself to imagine what life would be like from now on without her, but nothing came. Then he thought about Pedr, imagined a witch cooking him in a pot and eating him while he screamed for help, and still his eyes remained dry. Finally, he balled his fists and stood, his jaw clenched tight.

Aedric and Grim were busy heaving the carcasses out into the open. Joren stalked over to the growing pile and took one on top by its rigid legs, dragging it down and over to an open spot where the pyre could be built. He continued the grim work, his anger growing with every corpse he moved, their idiotic faces frozen in death, gaping with graying eyes at the world they had left.

He moved back and forth from the pile until he was exhausted, but he refused to stop even then. Finally, as he took hold of another one and yanked as hard as he could, he tripped and the dead sheep came down on top of him. He scrambled out from under it, rose to his feet, and began kicking and stomping on the corpse. He brought his foot down on its swollen belly, on its face, on its legs. He miss-stepped again and fell to his knees, so he beat it with his fists.

"Joren!" Grim's voice barely cut through the red haze in his mind, but he could not seem to stop himself. He rained blow after blow down on it, putting all his strength and soul into the assault. Grim's hands grabbed him roughly by the shoulders and pulled him off the body. "Joren, what are you doing?"

"It's my fault!" Joren cried, "I couldn't stop Pedr from running away and now he's dead!" He did not mean to say the words, did not even know they were waiting to be said. But as soon as they came out, he wept freely, his chest racked by violent sobs, and collapsed against Grim.

"Don't say such things," the soldier's voice wavered as he patted Joren's back. "Holywell's got Fergus's tracks now — there'll be no stopping him from finding him and your brother, both. They'll kill that witch and have them back before tomorrow's dawn, I'm sure of it.

"Listen," he said, and held Joren away from him so that he could look into his eyes. "Whatever happens, it wasn't your fault Pedr ran. We couldn't stop him, either." Joren was still unable to speak, his head pounding from the grief that suddenly overwhelmed him. "You mustn't blame yourself, young master." The painful sobbing finally subsided and Joren started to catch his breath. Grim's kind voice made his words believable, and he desperately wanted to trust the man's hopefulness.

"Grim," Aedric rumbled from beside them. "I'll sit with the lad for a while till he calms." He took Joren's hand and helped him to his feet. "Go on and we'll be along shortly."

Grim was apprehensive. "Alright, I suppose."

Aedric said something quietly in Carthan that seemed to convince the young soldier, who nodded and gave Joren one more heartening smile before leaving them and returning to the shelter.

The Ilban led him over to a patch of clean, green grass and the two sat down on it as they had the day before. Wiping his eyes and drippy nose with his sleeve, Joren asked, "What did you say to him?"

"That you and I got along well yesterday and that this work is too much for a young lad." He surveyed the peaceful morning around them as he spoke, his pale brow furrowed against the sunlight. "You gave that corpse a sound beating."

Joren glanced down at the ground, embarrassed. "I don't know why I did that."

"Don't you?" He looked up and saw the man's cold, blue eyes scrutinizing him. "You told Grim, just now: you feel guilty that you couldn't save your brother, and you think he's dead. You've also just lost your loyal sheepdog, and now you feel like you're all alone."

Tears built up behind Joren's eyes again and he clenched his fists.

The Ilban sighed and his stern expression softened. "Grim's right, lad; nothing that's happened is your fault. But that doesn't make any of it easier to deal with, does it?" He reached down the collar of his shirt and pulled something from around his neck and over his head. "Let me tell you a little more about my people. Do you remember what I said yesterday, that we believe in honoring the dead and always keeping them close?"

He opened his fist to reveal the pendant of a necklace. "This is part of that. It's called a Braegheath, the broken sword, and worn by all the Dalbragh. It represents all our brothers-in-arms who died a violent death, before their time. We carry these with us always, to remember them."

He handed the trinket to Joren. It was a simple design: the hilt of a sword with half the blade broken off, crafted from silver and tarnished by years of wear.

"There's another part to remembering, though," Aedric continued, "and it's much harder than simply wearing a symbol around your neck. To my people, remembering is more than veneration — it's a responsibility. We hold each death in our hearts, no matter how much it hurts. We embrace that pain to make sure the fallen are never forgotten, because to be forgotten is far worse than to die. Do you understand why I'm telling you this, lad?"

Joren shook his head, tears threatening to spill at any moment.

"I tell you this because it's alright to feel everything you do. The sorrow, the rage — it's good to feel those when you lose someone. I don't know if your brother will come back, Joren," Aedric held his gaze, "but if he doesn't, you remember this. The anger that comes after loss. You keep that with you forever, lad. You weep, you fight, you beat your fists bloody if you must. You do it all, for one reason, and one reason alone: you owe it to those who didn't make it. To remember them always. And nothing keeps a wound like that fresh the way rage does."

Joren trembled as the Ilban spoke. He supposed he did under-stand what the man was saying, but all he could feel was despair and helplessness. He did not want to remember anyone, he wanted them to be alive and to come home. He wanted to pet Hala, to play with Pedr and let him win at swords. Joren would let him win every game for the rest of their lives if he would just come back home.

Tears started rolling unbidden down his cheeks, but he struggled to stop them. Aedric reached out and closed his hand on Joren's shoulder. "Don't ever forget them, lad," he said quietly, and Joren thought he could see a glistening in the man's own eyes. He remembered what Aedric had said about having children, once.

The Ilban stood abruptly and cleared his throat. "For now, though, there's work to be done. We can't let anything stop us from our duties, not even mourning." He took back the pendant and replaced it around his neck. "Try to find a place to keep all those emotions lad, like the Dalbragh and this pendant. It carries all that for us, so we can put it away and call on it when we need it."

He held a hand out to Joren. "Come, dry your eyes, lad. The Knights may yet find your brother. Don't despair for him just yet." Joren wiped angrily at his eyes again and took the man's hand.

Aedric lifted him up and without another word, he walked away to resume the disposal of the dead sheep.

Joren did not follow immediately. He looked up at the Ymr, where the Knights were off chasing Fergus and looking for Pedr. The ache built up behind his eyes again and he shook his head to drive it off. His eyes watered anyway and he blinked the tears away.

While some of what the Ilban had said was confusing or difficult to care about, his advice about putting his feelings aside was not new to Joren: his father had taught him that years ago. He liked the idea of using an object to help him, though. Joren did not have a necklace or any other trinket, but as a shepherd, there was one thing he would have at his side all his life.

Joren walked quickly over to where he had left his crook, grabbed it up, and went around the back of the hall, purposefully not making eye contact with either Aedric or Grim. As he found a bit of privacy, Joren sat down on the damp grass and held his crook in his lap. He closed his eyes and let all the pain and fear well up inside him again without trying to fight it. Then he imagined it going through his hands and into his crook.

After a few moments, the difficult emotions began to ebb, and he was able to take a deep, shuddering breath, clenching his shepherd's staff tight, and a bit of calm returned. Hoping the Ilban's method would really work, Joren got up and headed back to the pile of corpses.

They spent a good while dragging out the bodies. The mules took both of the men's great strength and Joren's little efforts alongside them to haul out into the field. The warring emotions inside him stayed dulled, but whether muted by the hard work or thanks to Aedric's advice, he could not say.

After a time, he grew tired, and instead of thinking about all the bad things, he thought about Hala in Lodrheim. He thought that maybe one of the ancient Slain heroes would see what a good dog she was and take her to Thulheim, where mighty Fjalr warriors feasted. Maybe they would teach her to fight alongside them in their battles in Nydheim, and she would help keep the monsters from clawing their way back into the world of the living. The thought comforted him.

Once they had moved all the bodies, they busied themselves with gathering wood and stacking it into a large pile. Grim fetched a torch from the cook pit inside and held it within the heart of the pyre until the tinder and kindling had lit and spread the flames to the larger sticks and logs. After a little while, it blazed hot and they started throwing on the corpses.

Joren was disturbed that the thing primarily occupying his mind was hunger. Cursed though they might have been, the sheep all roasted the same as a normal, healthy one would, and once the smell of burnt wool had given way to cooked meat, he found himself nearly drooling. It was a long while before the final corpse — the horse with its cut neck — went on the pyre. Grim and Aedric had to take turns using his father's axe to chop the animal into pieces small enough they could lift.

Joren remained numb through it all; no more thoughts of

sadness or anger pulsed in his head or gripped his chest. It was all just a task to be completed.

Vandra came out once with waterskins — mead for the men — which were received gratefully. She kept a good distance and only stayed a moment. Just before she hurried back inside, her eyes found Joren's, and he saw great sympathy there.

As the two men tended the pyre, Joren busied himself with making a smaller one for Hala. He gathered up all the little sticks and twigs he could find and topped them with some logs off the wood stack behind the hall. Carefully lifting her rigid body in his arms, he carried the dog over, laid her down on her funeral bed, and ran his hand along her blood-stained head. He took deep breaths and closed his eyes, watching in his mind as Hakon the Furious knelt and petted her just as he was, welcoming her to Thulheim.

He went inside to invite the others to come out and send her on with him. His father tried to rise, but could not put any weight on his ankle, so Grim came and offered to help him, and the two went out together. His mother set aside the wool shirt she had been darning and put Agata on her hip to follow.

"Are you going to come, Van?" Joren asked her. His sister regarded him with a look of apprehension, but she nodded and walked with him out to the pyre. Helmi had paid no notice to the goings on, being still firmly engrossed in her books.

Outside, his family and the two other men all stood around Hala's bier. Aedric lighted another torch in the flames of the big pyre, which still burned, and handed it to Joren with a solemn nod.

Joren's father centered his weight on his good foot and spoke loudly to the heavens. "We mourn the loss of Hala, a loyal, clever, and trustworthy companion. May the fires we put to her cleanse her of the foul curse which robbed her of life, and her spirit find its place in Lodrheim, where all good shepherds and their helpers, too, rest for eternity. May her guardian soul watch over our family even in death as she did in life."

Joren held the torch to the tinder at the bottom of the pyre and the fire slowly ate it all, then began devouring the kindling and the logs. He whispered a final goodbye as the flames licked higher, finally engulfing his Hala. He felt the sadness stirring again, but as soon as he realized it, it seemed to go away, melting back behind the wall that was building in his mind.

As Hala burned, Joren's father patted his shoulder and allowed Grim to help him back into the hall. His mother gave him a kiss, her own cheeks wet, and followed her husband, the toddler on her hip squirming to be let down. After a moment, and without a word, Aedric also turned away, heading down to the stream.

Vandra alone remained next to him and together they watched the flames whip about in the breeze.

"You didn't cry," his sister said, wiping an errant tear of her own.

"I did earlier."

"But not now?"

He shrugged, the Ilban's words running through his head again, and thought about the new power his little crook had. "I'm sure I'll cry for her again later. But now's not the time for it."

"That's very… grown-up of you." She frowned as she looked at him, but said nothing else. She took his hand in hers and squeezed it tight, heedless of the dried gore that coated his fingers.

They remained there for a while until the flames finally started to dwindle. Aedric returned, his hair, beard, and clothes all wet, but cleaner than they had been. He said nothing, walking past them to return to the hall. Vandra gently released Joren's hand. "You should go wash. Then come and get something to eat. I made a fresh loaf of bread."

He nodded and tried to return the smile she gave him, but could not. He suddenly felt very tired. Vandra went back inside and Joren made his way down to the stream. Stripping naked, he soaked all his clothes and scrubbed them against each other to rid them of the filth of the previous night. Then he stepped into the frigid water and washed himself all over, gritting his teeth against the shock of the cold. Once he was done, he hurried back to the hall to warm himself and dry his clothes by the fire.

Inside, Grim was inspecting Joren's father's foot. He attempted to turn it carefully with his hands and the other gasped in pain and pulled his foot back.

Grim sucked his teeth. "I wish Blackhart could've had a look at it before they ran off." He sat back on his haunches and muttered, "Should've left him behind instead of me."

"Is it broken, do you think, Master Grim?" Joren's mother asked as she sat on the bench beside her husband and took his hand.

The soldier sighed and winced when he answered, as if the words hurt to speak. "I'm no hospitaler, mistress, but... it's mightily swollen and at a bit of a wrong angle. I think it might be."

Joren's father grunted. "That settles it, then. Runa, you and the children are going down to your family in the valley. Today."

"What?" She let go of his hand. "What are you talking about? We're not going anywhere until the soldiers bring Pedr back."

"I'll stay here and wait for Pedr," he replied, shifting his leg so that his foot hung just off the ground. "I don't understand what's going on here, but the sergeant was right — I must think to the safety of my family. The flock's gone, Hala's gone, everything. We only have what's in the larder and that won't last long, Runa."

"I'm not leaving Pedr *or* you," she insisted. "Once the soldiers return, we'll go down to the valley together."

Joren's father shook his wooly head. "No. We'll prepare that old handcart, stock it with as much as it can carry, and if the soldiers aren't back by dusk, you'll take it and the children down to your father's hall."

"And who would pull such a heavy load? Joren's not strong enough, nor Vandra, nor I."

"Between Van and Joren, they can handle it. And if it gets to be too much, leave it on the side of the road — what's important is that you get to safety."

"And if all the food brings wolves?" Her voice was shrill. "What then?"

He frowned, considering. "Ilban," he looked over at Aedric, who was hunched by the fire. "Could I trust you to see my family safely down to the valley below us?"

Aedric jerked his head in Helmi's direction. "I can't leave her side, shepherd."

The oracle appeared too lost in her books to pay attention to the conversation, but Grim challenged him. "She's not your charge, Ilban — she's the Order's to worry about."

"I've business with her and her goddess that's not yet concluded. I'll be damned if I let her out of my sight and something happens to her."

"Master Grim, then," Joren's father appealed to the soldier, "please, will you escort my family away from here? The valley is only a day's walk."

Grim shook his head. "I'm afraid I've already been given a charge, master shepherd. And I certainly can't leave her alone with this man."

"Oh, you've a problem with me now, too, do you?" Aedric sneered.

"Sergeant doesn't trust you," Grim's eyes narrowed. "That's good enough reason for me."

Aedric scoffed but before he could reply, Helmi interrupted them. "Enough," she said, finally looking up from her books. "Master Segurdsen, you are right to want to remove your family from the mountainside. Last night, this situation proved to be more than I had anticipated. But none of us can take your family down to the valley — not before we have completed our task. You want us to find Pedr, don't you?" Her voice was harder than usual, and she regarded Joren's parents with a stern countenance.

"Of course we do," his mother answered quickly. "And I'm not leaving until he is returned to us, Olen." She stood and walked away from her husband, who huffed and clenched his jaw.

"At the least, we will prepare the cart," he groused. "Joren, you and Vandra see to it. Make sure it's in good order, you understand?"

Joren nodded. "Yes, Papa."

Together, he and his sister went outside. She brought some fresh bread along for him, but Joren found his appetite was still missing.

8

THE CAVERN

After a few hours of hiking, with frequent breaks, the party finally came to a spot on a ridge that offered a clear view of the Ymr's expansive slope. Ever-deepening snow and a steep grade had made for slow going since dawn. Rhys's legs were burning from the effort so high above the valley, and the thin air had quickly left him exhausted. He could see the others struggling as well, and even Holywell gulped his air down each time they stopped. Though Rhys had finally cinched the thick fur coat, his toes and fingers still ached from the cold; their leather boots and gloves were no match for the bitter mountain.

As they paused there on the ridge line, the mute clambered onto a towering, snowy rock to get a better view. The tracks they had been following showed no signs of stopping or even slowing, as though Fergus had run full tilt all the way. How he had managed it without his lungs exploding must be the result of the witchcraft, Rhys decided.

Holywell whistled and gestured for them to follow, leaping off the rock and continuing alongside Fergus's tracks. "Is he the captain now?" Blackhart grumbled, hauling his massive frame out of the crater he had made in the snow.

"He's the fittest of us," Thorne replied between deep breaths, "I'll give him that much."

As they heaved one foot in front of the other, Rhys followed the trail of footprints with his eyes. He dared not say it aloud, but it seemed as though they ran the lip of the ridge until it curved to the south and finally terminated in a terrifying precipice that over-hung the slope. While he was sure that whatever awaited them would be a horrific challenge, he would be nonetheless relieved for their trek to reach its end. As though an answer to prayer, once they had climbed far enough toward the cliff, the mouth of a cave loomed into view.

"Well, that's got to be it, doesn't it?" Felix asked, panting.

The captain stood up on his toes to see as far as possible. "It looks as though the tracks go up there, yes. So either he went off the cliff or into that cave. Either way, that precipice is the end of our journey, at least for now. Let's take a moment to catch our breath."

Whether from sense or sheer exhaustion, this time Felix did not object. Rhys happily obeyed as well and thrust his hands under his arms to try to get some warmth back in them. As the wind whipped up the top layer of snow, showering them with icy needles at every gust, Thorne stepped back through his own tracks to come up next to him.

"I think Felix and I will go in first while you and the others wait in reserve, in case she gets the better of us or is able to slip past and escape."

Rhys scoffed. "If that happens, pray our gigantic hospitaler can just fall atop her so I can kick her to death — my hands are next to useless in this damned cold."

The captain unslung his pack and started rummaging through it, paying his grumbling no mind. "Blackhart, come help make sure I know what I'm looking at here." Blackhart ignored him, mumbling to himself and fidgeting with his wounded hand. "Blackhart!"

"What?" the man barked, seemingly startled by the captain's voice.

"Come here, make sure I don't grab a phial of hemlock or something."

"I'm not a poisoner, Captain," Blackhart growled, plodding over to him. "I only packed in that bag what we might need for fighting a witch. Let me have it." He snatched the pack from Thorne and quickly started handing out phials. "Here, camellia extract to fortify your minds against maledictions. It only makes you resistant, doesn't cure them, so be sure to hold on to them and down the whole thing before going into the cave. They don't last long, unlike hex-bane. We also have bundles of asafoetida — put them around your necks — and these," he withdrew a few small glass balls filled with a pulpy liquid and stoppered tight. "Very delicate, made to shatter on impact. She won't like the concoction in there, let me tell you."

"What is it?" Felix asked, holding the fluid at arm's length.

"She won't like it at all, gods help her, she won't like it." Blackhart repeated, shaking his head. Felix shrugged and tucked the glass ball into a pouch at his waist.

After they had taken a little while to rest, Thorne cleared his throat. "Felix and I will go into the cavern first and see what we can find. I want you three to remain outside, at the ready. Understood?"

Rhys did not relish the thought of staying out in the bitter cold, but neither did he particularly want to argue his way into charging headfirst into a witch's lair. Thorne turned and took the lead, making straight up the small climb to the precipice and the mouth of the cave.

Over the sound of the wind, Rhys could hear a murmuring, and at first his heart leapt, thinking he was somehow hearing the witch's song that had overpowered Fergus. On looking wildly around, though, he realized it was Blackhart, scrutinizing his wounded fingers again and grumbling.

They came off the ridge onto the flat area that ended in a precipice, and at about ten yards from the gaping blackness of the cave entrance, Thorne halted and pulled out his phial of camellia extract, motioning for Felix to do the same.

"If things go wrong," the young captain said, holding the phial aloft as though making a toast, "it was an honor to have been your captain, however briefly. And..." he hesitated. "I'm sorry for being such an arse."

Felix raised his phial in turn. "We never expected any different, Captain."

Thorne shrugged and brought the concoction to his lips but paused before drinking it down. "Blackhart, gods, you're not actually crying, are you?"

Rhys turned and saw that the hospitaler was indeed weeping, tears streaming down his wind-blasted cheeks and water from his nose freezing on his bushy mustache. "She's not going to like this," he sobbed, wringing his hands, tearing open the wound inflicted by Fergus, so that a fresh stream of blood leaked down his arm and made dark spots on the snow. "She doesn't want you here, doesn't want anything to do with you, why are you here?"

"Gods' mercy!" Felix exclaimed, taking a faltering step backwards. "The witch has got him, too!"

"You've no business here," Blackhart continued, hunched over and weeping like a child. "She's just lonely, leave her alone."

Rhys moved away, placing his hand on the hilt of his sword. "But how?" He wondered aloud, a sense of dread growing in his heart.

"It hardly matters now," the captain said, downing the extract and tossing the phial aside. "If we find the witch and kill her, perhaps it will break the spell." He drew his blade. "Keep him restrained, Sergeant. Felix, with me!"

"Don't hurt her!" Blackhart bellowed, looking up from his hands, eyes red and swollen from his tears. He leapt forward with incredible agility and made for the captain.

Rhys only had time to turn in an attempt to intercept him, but the hospitaler's huge hand, augmented by the strength of the witch's dark magic, flung him aside. He landed in a hulking snowdrift a few yards from the cave's mouth. Felix was cast aside as well and Holywell was halfway to Blackhart, but before the scout could reach him, the big man grabbed ahold of Thorne.

"You don't belong here!" he screamed, shaking the captain violently by his neck. "You can't hurt her, she doesn't deserve it!" Holywell reached them and grabbed Blackhart's fur jacket but was unable to arrest the onslaught. Instead, the hospitaler took frenzied steps, dragging the captain in front of him, still bellowing and throttling the smaller man.

They reached the edge of the precipice and Holywell drew his sword. "She doesn't like to be hurt! You can't hurt her! She doesn't want you here!" The mute raised his weapon high and brought the rounded pommel cracking down hard on the back of Blackhart's head.

The hospitaler, unaffected, lifted the captain wholly off the ground and hurled him over the precipice.

Rhys scrambled forward and reached out a hand, as though he could help from such a distance. Thorne made no sound as he fell; he simply disappeared over the edge. Rhys watched, dazed, as Felix rushed past him and into the cave, shouting his brother's name. Blackhart whirled and lunged after him, but Holywell was quicker and got between them, slashing at the hospitaler with his sword to keep him at bay. He gestured wildly at Rhys, bidding him to follow after Felix and see the job done. The sergeant rose on shaky legs and made his way through the deep snow and into the maw.

He found himself in a tunnel about a man's height and a half and twice his width. It immediately curved toward the right, going deeper into the mountain. The floor was uneven and littered with hazards, and Rhys had to move slowly to keep from turning his ankle. After only twenty or so paces, the wind from outside had faded to a shrill, distant whistling and blackness loomed all around him. He could just hear Felix's harried footsteps receding over the sound of his own breath.

As quietly as he could, he withdrew his blade from its scabbard and held it before him in the dark, feeling his way along carefully with his other hand against the tunnel wall. His tentative footsteps echoed down the twisting throat of the cavern.

Before long, the passage took another sharp turn, and ahead, Rhys could see a faint, odd light flickering. A wave of warm air hit him as he drew closer and realized the passage opened up into a large chamber.

"Fergus!" Felix's desperate cry rang out from within and there was the sound of a scuffle, then a heavy thud. Rhys leapt forward, ignoring the dangerous footing, and charged through into the cavern, sword held before him at the ready.

He took a quick survey of the scene before him. The chamber was large, filled with a strange light that batted at the shadows hugging the walls. The light was pale, sickly, and came from a strip of fire that burned in the center of the cavern; the flames themselves looked almost black, yet somehow gave off the bad light. He saw that the fire was not fed by wood or coal, but came from a long, narrow crevasse in the floor, a jagged scar cut into the stone.

Between him and the flames were the twins. One was stooped over the other, who lay seemingly unconscious on the ground. Before approaching them, he cast about quickly in search of Pedr, but there was no sign of the boy. Looking at the flames terrified Rhys and made him ill, so he swallowed back his fear and focused on the twins.

"Felix," he said, taking a step toward them. "Felix, what —" The figure on top looked over its shoulder at him, and the strange light illuminated the scar on his brow and small shards of glass sticking from his bloodied lips: Fergus. Felix moaned at his brother's feet, and Rhys could just see the wound on his head that had incapacitated him. "Fergus," Rhys asked slowly, "what happened to Felix?"

Dark shadows fell across Fergus's face, but his eyes reflected the ghastly light. "She doesn't want you here," he croaked. "You should not have come." He stooped back down, grabbed Felix by his boots, and started dragging him toward the shadows.

"Fergus," Rhys said again, his voice faltering. "We came to save you. Tell me where she is, Fergus, and we can be done with this."

Fergus did not respond. As he was dragged, Felix moaned again and twitched, starting to come awake.

Rhys followed them, afraid of what might happen if he let them pass into the darkness. "Fergus, stop!" he commanded, coming up and grabbing the man by the arm. Fergus flailed angrily and caught Rhys on the chin, sending him reeling backward, the tang of blood in his mouth. As Fergus turned, Rhys could see a ragged, bloody wound in the man's neck, bleeding freely, as though something had recently taken a bite out of him.

"Fergus?" Felix asked groggily, trying to sit up and probing the raised area on his temple. "Fergus, what are you doing?" His brother yanked his leg violently, dragging him further, and Felix's head rebounded off the ground again with a smack. "Let go of me!" He started kicking his legs wildly.

Rhys recovered and spat the blood from his mouth, then went after Fergus again. This time, he held his sword in front of him.

"Release him, Fergus," he cried, his voice reverberating off the cavern walls.

Ignoring the order, Fergus reached down and smashed his brother's nose with his fist, and Felix went limp. They were almost to the shadows.

Panicked, Rhys made the decision to use his blade. His heart ached at the thought of killing one of his own men, but he steeled himself and raised his sword. The weapon arced through the air, aimed at Fergus's neck, but the man rolled his shoulder as it crashed into him and the sharp edge bit deep into muscle and bone. Fergus reached out and shoved Rhys violently back, and the sergeant landed painfully on his hip.

Grabbing ahold of the sword with his other hand, Fergus wrenched it free. The edge cut into his fingers and blood poured from both his fist and shoulder as he turned to Rhys and bellowed, "She doesn't want you here!" He turned the sword around, taking it by the hilt, and shook it angrily at Rhys. "Just leave!" When Rhys did not move, Fergus slashed at him.

The sergeant climbed to his feet and backed away. Fergus huffed, tears streaming from his eyes, and stalked back to his brother.

Out of the corner of his eye, Rhys caught a tiny flash of light from the shadows beyond the twins. He squinted and could see two eyes reflecting the pale light, staring back at him from the dark. Two huge, black eyes.

Remembering Joren's description of the Burnt Lady, Rhys fumbled with the pouch on his belt that held Blackhart's myste-rious concoction. As Thorne had said, if this was anything like the dark magic they had encountered before, killing the witch should break the hold she had over his men.

He managed to get the glass ball out without fracturing it and drew it back, taking careful aim. As his eyes further adjusted, he could see the faint outline of her body, sitting calmly on the ground. Her eyes seemed to watch him as he prepared to throw, but she did not react; her lips moved rapidly, but no sound came from them.

Rhys hurled the little globe hard, sending it whistling through the air straight for the witch in the shadows. It hit its target square, shattered, and Rhys could just see the pulpy contents splatter over the creature. His heart pounded in his ears as he waited for the reaction. Nothing happened. The witch remained motionless; only her lips moved, continuing to speak their silent spell-craft.

Rhys waited another moment as Fergus continued to weep and mumble, clutching the sword and shaking with emotion. Finally, he was convinced the concoction had had no effect, and panic and terror lanced through his mind.

"Why won't you just leave?" Fergus seethed, stamping the ground. Felix had begun to writhe again on the floor, but the only sound he made was choked sputtering.

Afraid and unsure what to do, Rhys reached for the dagger at his belt, having only one idea left. Before he made his move, Fergus hollered, "She doesn't want you!" again, and raised the sword over his head. Rhys made for them, but Fergus brought it swinging down like a club toward his brother's belly. Felix coiled reflexively and the blade chopped into his knees, rebounding off the bone and spattering them both with blood. Felix shrieked as Fergus readied for a second blow.

Rhys lunged at them, dagger at the ready, but was immediately arrested by huge hands from behind. "You won't hurt her!" Blackhart screamed, squeezing Rhys tight and yanking him off his feet.

Fergus swung again and Felix rolled over to grab his brother's legs, begging for mercy. The sword cut into his side and he screeched in pain. Rhys struggled as hard as he could, but Blackhart's mighty arms crushed the air from his lungs and kept him pinned, helpless, as he was carried away.

Again and again the sword sang through the air, spraying blood and tissue with each arc, hacking Felix apart. Fergus screamed and wept as he murdered his twin brother, and Rhys could do nothing to help either of them.

He heard a scuffle from behind him and suddenly was released. Falling to his knees, he gasped in the hot air and started crawling.

Fergus brought the sword down and it struck the stone, snapping the worn blade in two. Tossing it aside, he grabbed his brother by the hair and dragged him toward the crevasse. Felix did not move or cry out. Rhys got to his feet, still heaving, clutching the dagger tight in his hand. It was too late to save Felix, but he could help Fergus, if he could just get to the witch.

Rhys could still see her sitting serenely in the black, whispering evil incantations, as he lengthened his stride, breaking into a run to reach her. He was about to cross into the shadows as Black-hart's hands grabbed him again. The hospitaler sobbed as he twisted Rhys's dagger-hand behind his back. "She doesn't want you!" He jerked, hard, and Rhys felt the muscles and sinews of his shoulder rend and tear and he cried out in pain.

Blackhart dragged him back, and though he struggled, Rhys could do nothing to free himself. His eyes went back to Fergus, who had dragged his brother's broken form to the flames that belched up from the long crack in the cavern floor. He took Felix by the collar and unceremoniously laid him over the crevasse. The pain must have been enough to wake the poor man from his stupor, as he moved whatever parts of him remained to try to escape the licking flames. Fergus stepped away, shaking his fists and pulling his hair as Felix burned.

Rhys bellowed wordlessly and clawed at Blackhart's hands, but to no avail; he watched his friend die and still could do nothing.

A little tremor shook the cavern and Rhys looked on in terror and bewilderment as something rose up out of the crevasse. A massive arm — burnt and withered, human in form, but impossibly long — stretched up out of the sickly light, grasping frantically at the air. It curled over Felix, closing around him, the spidery fingers wrapping fully around his waist. The monstrous appendage yanked hard, and something like a shriek came from Felix. The gap was too narrow for a man to fit into, but the thing dragging him down was relentless. Felix contorted as it pulled on him again, harder, and the crack of his spine echoed through the cavern. He sputtered in agony, having not the strength to cry out, as he was violently folded in half and dragged down into the fiery abyss.

Rhys was in shock, unable even to struggle as Blackhart pulled him away. He watched numbly as they came up alongside Holywell, who lay prostrate and unconscious on the ground. The hospitaler stooped and grabbed the man's collar in his other hand and proceeded to drag them out through the tunnel, still raving and sobbing about *her*.

Rhys winced as he was pulled across the rough, rocky ground. The sound of the whipping wind rose and the heat gave way to biting cold. Blackhart threw them out into the snow and Rhys did not even have the strength to get to his feet after landing. All he could manage was to look back at their friend, the hospitaler.

"She doesn't want you!" Blackhart bellowed, raking his nails along his bald head in frustration. A large red stain spread from a narrow wound in his chest. "Just stay away! She doesn't want any more soldiers!" Blood seeped from the gash, pulsing angrily as he howled. Taking an imposing step toward them, he cried, "Fodder for the abyss! Is that what you want to be? Just stay away!" With that, he turned and limped back into the cave, another wound gaping on the rear of his leg.

Rhys looked over at Holywell. His eyes remained closed, and his face was battered where Blackhart had beaten him unconscious. Seeing that his chest still rose and fell slowly, Rhys collapsed back down into the snow.

He lay there, the wind buffeting across his face, his injured shoulder on fire, and for a moment, Rhys wanted the cold to take him. It was too much — to struggle to his feet, to wake Holywell and make the descent, only to have to climb back up and try again to kill the... whatever it was. Certainly not a witch; that much they now knew.

Rhys had been skeptical of witchcraft since Fergus had succumbed without any sign of a hex. The way the creature mouthed silently as she sat watching them all had rekindled that doubt, and the lack of a reaction from Blackhart's special brew confirmed it. Spells and other such verbal magic required vocalization, so what had she been saying, silently? And the crevasse, the sickly flames, the monstrous arm... Rhys had no answer for these.

Holywell stirred beside him. He started and pulled his lean face from the snow, climbing quickly to his feet and searching his hip for the sword that had fallen in the cavern. As he recovered his wits, he stooped down and took Rhys's injured arm.

"No!" Rhys gasped as the pain flared anew. "Not that one, it's displaced, I think." His friend quickly took the other arm and hauled Rhys to his feet. Then he turned and made for the cavern again.

"Wait," Rhys grabbed his sleeve to stop him, "we can't."

The mute looked at him, a storm of emotions written in the deep lines of his face.

"We must regroup," Rhys said, adjusting his bad arm. "We need Grim. And the Ilban, gods help us, if we're going to be able to do this at all." The fire behind Holywell's eyes made him feel guilty for wanting to wait, but they truly had no choice; this creature was far beyond what they had anticipated.

Holywell gestured angrily at the cave.

"I have no sword — neither do you — and even if I did, my arm couldn't wield it."

The other waved him off and started forward again.

"I beg you, Brother, please!" Rhys cried. "We've lost half our detachment already. If we've any hope of killing this..." he searched for a word rank and diabolical enough to describe her, but none came to him through the haze of pain, "this thing, it won't be with just the two of us. It's not a witch. I don't know what it is, and we'll need to consult Helmi. Leo," he entreated, struggling to keep his voice from quavering, "did you see what she did to them? We were not prepared for this. She's not a witch. Please."

Holywell's shoulders slumped. He looked at Rhys, pressed a hand to his chest, and gestured to the cave. The meaning was clear enough: "They're our brothers."

The pain in Holywell's face at the prospect of abandoning Blackhart and Fergus echoed Rhys's own, but he knew that charging in thoughtlessly would mean not only death, but the failure of their mission. They were soldiers; it was their job to die, but not recklessly, and not without purpose. "Fergus is mortally wounded already. It looks as though you had to do the same to Blackhart."

A tear gathered at the corner of each of Holywell's eyes and a gust streaked them across his weathered cheeks. He slammed a fist into his open palm.

"He gave you no choice, I know. It was a kindness, and beneath her foul influence, he knows it. Without whatever evil power she's using to keep them alive, though, they are both already dead. I watched Felix die, too. There is nothing we can do for them now." He inched over to the ledge of the precipice, careful not to jostle his mangled shoulder, and glanced over. The drop was maybe eighty yards — farther than any man could survive. He saw shapes at the bottom, but for the glare of the sun off the snow, could not tell if they were rocks or shrubs or a corpse.

"Come," he said, shading his eyes. "We need the others' help. If we start back now, we can perhaps make it before nightfall." He placed his hand on Holywell's shoulder and looked him in the eye. "Then we'll have vengeance for the fallen. I swear it."

After a moment, Holywell nodded grimly. Then he turned and spat at the ground in front of the cave, and the two started a desperate descent back down the Ymr.

9

MURDER

Joren could not remember their father ever having used the old handcart that sat behind the hall. Before moving it, he and Vandra sat down on the back and shared the bread she had brought outside. Joren took a bite at her insistence, even though he still did not feel like eating.

As he brought a piece to his mouth, Vandra sniffed. He looked over and saw her eyes shimmering in the sunlight, her own bread forgotten in her lap.

"Are you alright, Van?" he asked.

Her lower lip quivered as she looked at him. "No. I didn't want to say anything earlier, because of Hala, but... I'm really scared for Pedr. At first, he was just lost, and that was bad enough. But now they're saying a witch took him. The Burnt Lady, Joren. You saw her, she's real." She shivered.

Joren's stomach started twisting again. "I..." he tried to make himself say something encouraging, but he could not. "I'm scared, too."

"Witches cook children and eat them," she said, her breath coming faster. "What if they don't find him in time? What if...." The tears finally broke free and rolled down her cheeks, and she hid her face in her hands.

Joren put his arm around her like their mother would want him to do. His own eyes started to ache, but he swallowed hard to keep the tears back and eyed his crook, which leaned against the cart next to him.

"What will we do," she sobbed behind her hands, "if Pedr doesn't come back?"

Joren thought about what the Ilban had said, about remembering, but it had not helped him earlier, and he knew it would not help his sister now.

"He *will* come back," Joren said instead, trying to make his voice strong. "The Knights will find him and save him."

Vandra took a gasping breath and removed her hands to wipe her cheeks. "I don't want to go to the village," she admitted. "I feel like we're abandoning him if we do."

Joren thought for a moment. "I don't want to go, either. But think about Mama and Aggy. I don't want them to be in danger." He took his arm from around her and grabbed ahold of his crook. "The sergeant said he doesn't think the witch is done with us yet. So I think Papa's right — we should go, just in case, even if we don't want to."

His sister dabbed her eyes with her sleeve and nodded. "I suppose you're right, Joren."

"And you don't have to be afraid of wolves, either — I have this," he hoisted up his crook and tightened his grip on it. "I can keep us safe."

Her eyes red and weary, Vandra gave him a little smile. "You're really growing up quickly, you know that?" She reached out and tousled his hair.

Joren dipped away and hopped off the back of the cart. "C'mon," he said, "let's see if we can get it to move." She sighed and came down to help him.

He inspected it as he had been told, trying to imagine the things his father would check. He counted all the square nails holding it together, making sure none were missing, and looked for any spots that were rotted through. It seemed to be in good condition, but stuck in deep ruts the wheels had made over years of disuse.

Together, he and Vandra were able to rock it back and forth until it came up and out and they could move it. The grass underneath was pale and sickly, and thick mud was stuck to the iron-bound wheels where they had settled. Joren scraped off the wet soil with his fingers, and then they each took hold of one of the handles. After a few yards, the wheels rotated freely and they pulled it around the front of the hall.

As they approached the door, loud voices carried through. Joren and Vandra both paused outside and listened through the wall. Their parents were arguing again — or perhaps still — about going down to Kaninholm.

"We can't risk keeping the children here," their father was saying. "If a witch lured Pedr, she could do the same again to Joren or Vandra." Joren looked at his sister; her face was drawn. "And whatever happened to the twin could happen to the Ilban or Grim or even to me. It's too dangerous, Runa, you can't stay here."

"I told you," she answered hotly, "when the soldiers bring Pedr back, I'm going to be here. I can't leave our son and you should know better than to ask me to!"

"I'm not asking you, Runa." Their father's voice grew heavy. "As your husband, I'm telling you — you and the children can't stay here." She made no reply, so he said, "I'll wait for Pedr. I can't go anywhere anyhow, with my ankle like this. Do you understand me? Runa?"

"I've already given you my answer, Olen. It's the only one I have to give: I'm not going anywhere."

"Damn you, woman," their father growled. "Won't any of you help me to convince her?"

Joren heard someone cough — Grim, probably, he thought. "Your husband is right, Mistress Runa," the young soldier said hesitantly. "We don't really know what we're dealing with, and I think it would certainly be best for you and the little ones to be as far away as possible until we have things sorted out."

"Wait," their father said, "what do you mean you don't know what you're dealing with? You said a witch took Pedr."

"Well, I…" Grim stumbled over his words until Helmi sighed loudly.

"It *is* a witch," she said, "it's just not quite like any witch we've ever seen before."

"Is that why you're still reading all those books?" their mother demanded. "Slain have mercy, do you even know how to get Pedr back?"

"Of course we do, mistress," Grim answered, sounding wounded. "There's none better than the men up there right now to save your little boy, I'll stake my life on that."

"Do you hear this, Runa?" their father cried, ignoring Grim's testimony. "They don't even know what it is they're looking for! Please, you must take the children to safety." Again, their mother made no answer. "Please, my love," her husband entreated her, "come here. Please, I can't get up and come to you on this damned leg." There was a pause before he spoke again and his voice was softer. "I don't want to send you away. But the truth is, I'm terrified, Runa. Pedr's gone, and I hope he'll come back, but even so, we've lost our livelihood. The flock is gone, and without it, we'll have to go down to your father's, anyhow."

"I don't want to leave him, Olen," their mother replied tearfully.

"I know, my love, I know. But I need you to trust me. If you stay and anything were to happen to you…" his voice broke and he paused before continuing. "Please, Runa, please trust me. I'll wait for him. And if they don't come back, or they come back without him, I'll crawl up the mountain myself if I have to, and get Pedr back. I swear it on my ancestors, on my love for my family."

The sounds of quiet weeping came through the wall, along with the intermittent turning of a page in Helmi's books.

Finally, their mother sniffed and said, "I'll tell the children we're leaving."

"Thank you, my love," came the grave reply. "We're not going to abandon him."

Footsteps came toward the door, and Joren and Vandra both scrambled back to the cart.

A moment later, the door to the hall swung open and their mother came out, tears dried on her cheeks. The corners of her mouth tugged down when she saw them waiting. She spread her arms and came to envelop them both, pulling them close and weeping again, silently. She held so tightly onto Joren he thought his head might pop, but he did not struggle against her.

Composing herself with a deep breath, she loosened her hold on her children so they could look up at her. "We have to go," she said, tears still flowing freely from her tired eyes. "We can't stay here, it's too dangerous."

Vandra shot a look at Joren, but neither said anything.

"We have to think about you three right now," she continued. "The soldiers will remain and rescue Pedr. If anyone can save your brother, it's them. And your father will stay as well." She squeezed her children tighter and held them both captive for a long moment, rubbing their backs and planting kisses on their heads. "We have to load as much as we can onto the cart," she said, finally. "Come, you two. While we do, say your prayers to the mighty Slain and all our ancestors to watch over your little brother."

Joren nodded, and as she led them both by the hand back to the hall, he looked over his shoulder, up the rocky slope of the Ymr, and shuddered.

They found the captain's body at the foot of the cliff, broken, bloody, and already half-frozen. His face, at least, was serene, and Rhys was very thankful for that. Whatever difficulties the detachment had had with him, Arran Thorne was too young a man to be lying dead on the side of a mountain, a hundred leagues from his home.

Rhys took Thorne's exotic sword from the spot it had landed in the snow and handed it to Holywell, knowing his damaged arm would be useless with a blade.

Tears flowed silently from Rhys's eyes and froze in his beard as they heaped snow over the captain's body. The man they buried was hardly out of boyhood, with his entire life and great potential ahead of him, all now wasted in a lonely corner of the world. He had survived a slaughter in the jungles, only to become a victim of that cursed mountain and whatever the creature was that haunted it.

Rhys said a prayer over him once he was covered and kept their other brothers in mind as well. He begged Seraphe to see his soul ferried to the green fields of Eirna; he entreated her husband Oronos, the god of justice, for guidance; and he asked strength of Rheacles, the god of war. Of course, none of them answered him; he was a lowly soldier who was not fit to speak with gods. But he trusted that they heard him, regardless. They must.

He and Holywell marked the spot with rocks so that they could return later to bear him down the mountain for a proper burial. The cold would keep his body from decomposing, giving them time to deal with the creature first. Rhys hoped privately that they would be able to do the same for Fergus and Blackhart, and it broke his heart to think that Felix's body was beyond recovery. Whatever that evil crevasse was, it did not look like a place that mortal men could walk.

Once they had finished marking the poor captain's body, they took a moment to catch their breath and prepare for the rest of the trip down the mountain. Rhys's arm had only worsened since the initial injury and he could feel the massive swelling in his shoulder stressing the seams of his shirt. Holywell had torn a length from his own shirt and fashioned a sling for him, which was at least helping to relieve the pain caused by his arm's own weight. Every step he took, though, sent flames through the joint.

After the brief pause to pay their respects, the two remaining Knights resumed their descent. Holywell took lead, as he always did, but kept looking over his shoulder to make sure he moved slowly enough that Rhys could keep up. Even after his own injuries, Holywell was agile and surefooted, easily finding the quickest routes down the slope.

As they went, Rhys's mind stormed in the wake of their losses. It was not the first time he had seen a number of men fall in quick succession, but this time he seemed unable to recover his calm intent. Over and over he watched Fergus butcher his brother alive, heard the boy's screams, the rending of flesh, the snapping of bone and sinew as he was torn down by the monstrous arm.

The captain — Arran — plunged over the precipice in his mind, wordlessly, then Captain Fielding followed him, dashing himself against the rocks at Darrow-by-the-Sea. He saw the deaths of dozens of brothers since the time he was in his twenties and had freshly joined the Knights Seraphin.

Rhys's vision blurred as tears welled but refused to fall. The wind stung his face, his shoulder throbbed, his left knee repeatedly collapsed under him if he stepped too far, and he was tired. So abysmally tired; tired of the Ymr, of the Knights Seraphin, of life. Above all, he was tired of losing people close to him. Could the gods not be merciful and finally let him be the one to give his life? Apparently not. Not yet. And in the meantime, his list of names to mourn continued to grow.

In his youth, Rhys's anger would have driven him onward, the promise of vengeance lighting a dire flame in his heart. Now, though, that flame was all but extinguished. Vengeance he would have, certainly, or finally earn his death in the attempt; but even if he survived, it would only be to see more deaths, lose more brothers. How much could one man endure in his lifetime?

His legs grew heavy, from both exhaustion and despair, until it was difficult to force one past the other. He continued to follow Holywell, though, pushing past the war in his heart, doing his duty in spite of it all. Together, they charged through the wind and deep snow, defying the deadly mountain, knowing they would only have to turn around at the end to come back and try again.

Joren grunted as he flopped the last sack of oats off his shoulder and onto the ancient handcart; it was already loaded with sundry perishable goods, and there were just a few more items to go. His mother had delayed as long as she could, fussing over each item, making sure it was wrapped or bundled twice over. He knew she hoped the soldiers would come back with Pedr before they had to leave. Joren made sure to leave a space in the middle of the cart, stacked high on all sides, where Agata could safely ride without fear of her falling out or anything falling on top of her.

As he started back toward the hall, Aedric stepped out through the door, empty waterskins slung over each arm. He paused when he saw Joren, regarding him gravely for a moment. "Will you help me fill these, Joren?" He asked, his voice light. "I could use an extra pair of hands to carry them all." Joren shrugged and nodded, taking a few of the empty skins the kilted man handed him.

They walked the whole way in silence. The sky was pink as the sun dipped below the horizon and warm colors glinted off the rushing ripples of the creek. Where once Joren's favorite thing to do was watch the sun set, it was fast becoming a time he dreaded; each of the Burnt Lady's attacks had occurred at night thus far and it made him fearful for what lay ahead. He kept looking over his shoulder without meaning to, as though she herself might be sneaking up behind him.

Aedric dipped the neck of one of the vessels into the water. "Are you alright, Joren?" he asked, noticing his new tick.

"She only takes people at night," he answered sheepishly.

The Ilban sighed. "Aye... all the more reason to get you and your family away from here as soon as possible." He lifted the filled waterskin up and screwed in the stopper.

"I don't want to go. Neither does Vandra, or Mama, really, I think."

"You're right." The Ilban nodded solemnly. "None of you want to go, but I agree with your father that it's best you do. At the least, for your baby sister's sake."

"If Agata was old enough to talk, I don't think she would want to leave Pedr either."

Aedric did not respond to that. They worked quietly for another minute before the man spoke again. "You didn't cry when we burned Hala."

Joren thought back to the flaming pyre that had consumed her. "I tried to do what you said — I put all the bad feelings in my crook."

"That's good, lad. Once you get to the village, when you're

safe, make sure to call those feelings back out and cry all the tears you've held back."

Joren dipped another waterskin into the stream. "I don't think I'll need to — I think I've cried enough already."

"You must," Aedric's voice hardened and his brows furrowed deeply. "It's your duty to weep, to mourn. That's part of it. Who else will remember, if not you?"

Joren looked away from the man's angry gaze. "I just meant —"

"I know what you meant, lad. But I want to make this clear. It's not about us, who survive — we mourn the dead for their sake. We owe it to them. Do you understand?" His fist squeezed the empty skin in his hand hard. "Someday it won't just be your dog. You'll lose people you'd thought would always be there, who shouldn't go before you do. You'll carry those losses with you for the rest of your life, and you'll make yourself remember; you'll make yourself mourn. Because it's right."

Joren bristled at the rebuke; he did not like to think about death, especially while they were waiting to see whether or not Pedr would come back with the others. But the Ilban's anger was intimidating, so he said nothing.

The man's mood quickly softened, though. "I'm sorry, lad," he said with a sigh, "I don't mean to be so harsh. It's just… there are things I wish I could have taught my sons, but I never had the chance. And it's better to learn these things while you're young." He frowned and looked back down at the waterskin in his hands.

Joren felt a little pang of sympathy, but was still annoyed. He already had a father; he did not need another one.

He struggled to find a way to respond, but before he could, screams ripped through the quiet evening, startling him. Joren's stomach dropped as he turned and realized they were coming from the hall. Aedric leapt up and dashed off, Joren hurrying behind, his irritation immediately replaced by sheer panic.

The voice screaming was not his mother's or Vandra's, and as the wordless cries changed into calls of Aedric's name, he realized it was Helmi's. Terrified of what that meant for his family, he ran as fast as he could, memories of his pursuit of Pedr flashing through his mind. He felt ill, but pushed himself to keep up with Aedric.

As they came around the side of the hall, Agata's pained cries floated out from nearby as well. Helmi rounded the corner at almost the same time and the Ilban nearly knocked her over but managed to catch her with his hands as they collided. When they parted, Joren saw that she held his baby sister in her arms. Agata was wailing and sobbing, mucus running from her nose.

"Which one was it?" Aedric barked.

"The shepherd," Helmi answered. She was breathless and near tears, clutching Agata to her. "He's made off with Vandra. Grim gave chase."

"Where is his wife?"

Her lip quivering, she glanced back at the hall door, then looked pitifully down at Joren. "Joren, I—" He dashed past her. "Aedric, don't let him!" she cried, and he could hear the Ilban right behind him. The hall door was open and he flew through it before Aedric could stop him.

The fire crackled happily in the center of the room and the aroma of the supper his mother had been preparing before their departure wafted throughout the little space. He looked around and did not see her at first. She was lying on the other side of the fire, hidden from his view by the big iron pot. Aedric's hands fell onto his shoulders but he jerked violently away and circled around to see her fully.

She lay on her back on the dirt floor. One of her arms sat to the elbow in the fire pit, withered and blackened and hissing. Her face was a ruin, beaten bloody and beyond recognition: her nose had been caved into her skull and her eyes mashed into their orbits. Little drops of blood dotted the front of her dress.

Joren's frantic heartbeat slowed as he looked over her. Part of him wanted to scream and leap forward, to drag her arm out of the fire and cradle her shattered head in his lap. The other part of him, though, was silent, numb. He stood there, conflicted and aloof all at once, until Aedric took his shoulder again.

The man cursed under his breath. He did not try to pull Joren away, but stood their with him. Joren's eyes went from her still burning arm back to her face, then back again. Then they lost focus and he thought maybe he was crying. When he reached up to wipe at them, however, they were dry. His mind grew terrifyingly quiet; the confusion and fear melted away in an instant and was replaced with a profound exhaustion.

He shrugged Aedric off again and went to his mother. Sitting down beside her, he reached over and pulled her arm out of the flames. She was not stiff yet, like Hala had been. He laid her burning limb in the dirt so that it could extinguish itself while he moved her other arm up and lay down beside her.

Aedric took a step toward them and reached out again. He hesitated, though, and finally let his hand fall to his side. "I'll be outside, lad," he said gently. "Come be with your sister when you're ready."

The thought of Agata weeping in a stranger's arms sent a pang of guilt through him, but all he could do was scoot closer to his mother and lay his head on her breast. She was still warm, maybe just from the fire, and he was thankful. Closing his eyes, he tried to ignore the scent of burning flesh and focus on the stew and the presence of his mother beside him. He took deep, calming breaths and the sounds around him faded away; for the moment, it was as though everything was alright.

They were nearing the hall as the last bit of pink faded, chasing the sun. Rhys had underestimated the toll his damaged shoulder would take and as a result, his pace had eventually lagged. He had urged and finally ordered Holywell to move ahead of him, but the old scout paid his complaints no heed, instead remaining close by his side.

Rhys's melancholy had slowly faded the further down they had come, gradually being replaced by a feeling of unease. Nightfall seemed to bring evil things on the Ymr, and Rhys was not willing to assume this evening would be any different. The sooner they reached the hall and made sure the family had left for Kaninholm, the better.

Coming to a prominent hill that overlooked the slope below it, Rhys was able to glimpse the hall and the fire flickering through its open door. "Nearly there," he said between breaths, looking over at his companion. "I don't know about you, but once we send the family off — if they've not gone already — I'll need at least a few hours' rest before we make the climb again." Holywell nodded emphatically.

They had not gone another thirty yards down the hill when Rhys caught a darting shadow out of the corner of his eye. Whirling to face it, he saw the shepherd loping away up the slope and dragging something behind him. "Damn it," he grumbled as the large man disappeared, carried off by the inhuman speed and strength the monster's magic granted. "We're too late."

He took Holywell's arm before he could sprint off in pursuit. "Let him go. We have to hurry and reach the others." After seeing the damage Blackhart had been able to do, he feared whatever carnage the equally large shepherd might have left in his wake.

They started back toward the hall but were again arrested, this time by a ragged holler from down the slope. "Sergeant!" Grim called, breathless. "The shepherd! You've got to stop him!"

They hurried to him. "Hold there, Grim," Rhys ordered.

The young soldier was heaving and leaning on his knees even as he took slow, uncertain steps toward them. "You've got… to stop him." A few gasping breaths, then, "He's got Miss Vandra!"

Rhys shared a grave look with Holywell; it was his daughter the man had been dragging behind him. A touch of guilt prodded his conscience as he decided again not to pursue them just yet.

"That's… unfortunate," he said, and he meant it. "But we can't risk going after them right now. We have to get back to the others."

Grim looked up at him, horrified. "We can't just give up on her!"

"We won't. But there is much more at stake right now than any single life. Come, on your feet." He tugged on Grim's jerkin until he was upright and urged him down the slope. "Is everyone else still… themselves?"

"He killed Mistress Runa," Grim said, disgusted by the words.

"Knocked her and her babe to the ground and stomped her mercilessly."

"The child?"

"No, his wife. Helmi took up Agata and kept her away. He kicked her to death and kept screaming at her. I tried to pull him off her, but he threw me aside, had that same damnable strength as Fergus." He looked over his shoulder, realizing there were only two of them returning. "Oh, gods, where are the others?"

Rhys paused, imagining how to soften the blow even as the events at the cave plagued his memory. "They...." He sighed. "We are all that's left."

Grim stared at him, disbelieving. Then he swallowed hard, trying to compose himself before he came apart. "Did they go well?"

"They went bravely." Rhys said it quickly, and he was unsure if it was a lie.

The young soldier cleared his throat and sniffed while pointedly looking away from the others. "And what of little Pedr? Any sign of him?"

"No. No sign that I could see."

"Ah," his voice trembled on the sound and he kept his face turned from them for a long moment as his shoulders shook. Finally, Rhys saw him wipe furiously at his eyes. "Evil mountain we've stumbled upon, eh, Sergeant?" He asked, trying valiantly to keep his voice steady.

Rhys placed his good hand on the young man's shoulder and squeezed. "That it is, Grim. Will you help us take vengeance for our fallen brothers?"

He nodded vehemently. "I'd follow you into the Necropolis if you asked me, Sergeant. The twins would have, too. I know they got on your nerves, mine too, but..." he wrestled the words out, "but they would have gone anywhere with us, done anything. Brave lads they were." He nodded again as his voice failed him.

"I know they were." They walked in silence the rest of the way.

As they drew close to the hall, they found Helmi and the child sitting on an old stump amid the grass and Aedric bent over a pile of kindling, fostering glowing embers within. Helmi leapt up at the sight of them and rushed over to Rhys. "Thank the gods!" she cried, wrapping her free arm around him. He winced as pain shot through his torn shoulder. Her brow wrinkled in concern. "Oh, what's happened to you?"

"It's nothing serious," he said, forcing a brief smile.

"Are you sure? Has Blackhart looked at it?" She looked around for the hospitaler, and when she failed to find him, gasped and put her hand over her mouth. "Oh, no... where is everyone? Please tell me they've just fallen behind." Rhys said nothing, could say nothing. Tears welled in her eyes but she fought them back. "Did you find Pedr?" she asked desperately.

The sergeant shook his head.

"What about Vandra? Her father took her, we have to help her."

"I know," Rhys took her arm and turned her around, back toward the Ilban's fire, "but right now, there's nothing we can do for her. We have to regroup." Reluctantly, she allowed him to guide her back to her stump. "Helmi, it's not a witch."

"What?" she asked sharply. "How do you know?"

Rhys gestured for Holywell to sit and rest. "Nothing we saw in that cavern suggested witchcraft."

"A cavern?" She rocked the toddler gently on her shoulder and sat forward. "Tell me everything, Garret, please."

"I will, but... why are we sitting out here?"

Helmi's voice wavered as she answered. "Olen... killed poor Runa. She's still in there and... and Joren's with her."

"I see. Is that a good idea?"

"The lad's in mourning," the Ilban growled. "He'll come out when he's ready. Are you really going to leave his sister to her fate?"

Rhys's simmering temper broke through. "If you want to give chase up that damned mountain in the dark, without any preparation or planning, you're free to do so. But I warn you, it's not as easy as you might think."

Aedric set his jaw firmly behind his beard but said nothing. He looked over his shoulder at the hall, and then knelt back down by the fire.

Rhys sighed and started to lower himself near Helmi's stump, but stopped when a rickety old cart sitting nearby caught his attention.

"Grim, what's this cart, here?" he asked, walking over to it.

"Oh, er," the young man stirred from his melancholy, "provisions, Sergeant. Perishables, mostly. The shepherd was about to send his family down to the valley before... before it happened."

"They should have left by dawn." Rhys shook his head wearily as he started rifling through the supplies on the cart. "What's done is done, though, and now we must determine what to do next." He pulled out some more cheese and jerky — of which there was plenty — and tossed them to Holywell.

"Please, Garret, what happened in the cavern?" Helmi pressed.

Rhys steeled himself, wary that his emotions might overwhelm him as they had before.

"Holywell was able to track Fergus," he began, still looking through the contents of the cart. The tale was easier to tell without having to face any of the others. "So we followed him up the mountain, past the snow line. The tracks led right up to the mouth of a cave near a sharp precipice. We rested briefly to prepare and that's when Blackhart started acting strangely."

Rhys lifted a heavy sack of barley and shifted it over onto an old crate, but only found more grain beneath it. "He did not react exactly as Fergus had — I thought he was simply bitter about the climb and complaining to himself. But just as we reached the cave, he started weeping, moaning about 'her', that 'she didn't want us there', or some such. The captain started for the entrance and Blackhart flew into a rage, leapt at Thorne, and grabbed him by the neck." He sighed. "Poor boy never had a chance. Blackhart threw him over the precipice and he didn't even cry out as he fell."

Helmi gasped and Grim hung his head.

"Holywell distracted Blackhart as Felix and I went into the cave, hoping that if we could kill the witch — creature, rather —

it would end the spell she had over the others. Felix ran ahead of me, and when I got to the large chamber deeper in, I saw him and Fergus standing in front of a crevasse."

Trying to hide the shudder that ran down his spine at the memory of the place, Rhys pulled a loaf of rye from the stock of provisions. "It was very… unsettling. Flames rose out of it. They weren't proper flames, but dark and somehow wrong. Fergus was still under the influence of the creature, even as it did whatever it does to control Blackhart.

"It looked as though it had bitten him, taken a part of his neck clean off. Fergus attacked his brother and took my sword from me when I tried to stop him. He flew into a rage like Blackhart had and murdered Felix." Grim made an involuntary sound in grief and disgust. "It was then that I saw the creature, hidden in the shadows.

"She sat there, moving her lips rapidly. I thought at first she was speaking spells or curses, but she was utterly silent. I threw Blackhart's concoction at her, but it had no effect. Then I tried to put an end to her with my dagger, but Blackhart seized me from behind and dragged both Holywell and myself out of the cavern. The last thing I saw was Fergus laying his brother across the crevasse.

"Then…" he swallowed hard, "then something else came out from the flames. An arm. A massive, grasping arm reaching up out of the crevasse. I've never seen something so horrifying in all my life. It took Felix and ripped him down into… I don't know what." He looked over at Helmi and finally gave voice to his terrible suspicion. "But it looked like where the damned go. Helmi, it looked like Hel."

"That's not possible," she answered immediately, though her fearful expression belied her conviction.

"The necropolis is…" Grim screwed up his face as he tried to calculate the distance, "hundreds of leagues, at least, from here, Sergeant."

"I'm well aware of that, Grim," Rhys said, "but if ever I've seen a place that could be the realm of the death god, this was it."

"No, Garret," Helmi insisted, "I have seen Hel." They all

turned to look at her in surprise. "Just… visions — glimpses given by the goddess," she explained quickly. "Though a terrible place, it is a prison, cold and lonely, but not a place of torment. It does not look like what you saw. And it is confined to the necropolis in an isolated desert; no doors exist anywhere else."

Rhys had no choice but to take her at her word. "Whatever it was, I've never seen its like before. Nor have I ever been so terrified in all my life." He reluctantly took a bite of the rye loaf. He felt guilty, eating and resting while the shepherd's daughter was likely being taken to her death, but without rest and food, they would not be able to follow after her.

"After the arm came up from below and took Felix," he continued, "Blackhart threw us out into the snow and left us there. I knew that we would have no success without more help, so we came back down."

"You told me they all died!" Grim exclaimed as Rhys finished. "Brother Blackhart is still up there?"

"No." Rhys's answer was stern. "He and Fergus are both fatally wounded, and only the creature's dark magics are keeping them alive for the present. There is no saving, them, Grim, do you understand? They are dead already, and being used for evil purpose. The only help we can give them is to end their enslavement to this monster."

Holywell put his hand on Grim's shoulder to get his attention and nodded his agreement, for which Rhys was grateful. Grim huffed and finally grunted his understanding, but glowered at the sergeant.

"Blackhart's other herbs had no effect?" Helmi asked.

"No, none of them. Not hex-bane, nor camellia extract, nor… whatever it was in those glass containers. Not even our blessed medallions. None of it had any effect on the monster or its magic. And you tell me, what witch casts her spells and maledictions silently." Helmi frowned. "It's not a witch — but I don't have any idea what it *could* be." He took another irritated bite out of the loaf.

"I was wrong," Helmi said, looking into the flames of the

Ilban's fire. "Gods have mercy, how many have I killed because I was wrong?"

"None," Rhys said firmly. "We all believed it was a witch. Even Thorne, and he thought everything here was little more than a distraction. You are not to blame for any of this, Helmi. In fact, your knowledge of those books might be our final hope."

She nodded, her eyes still wide. "I continued studying after you left, but I only read what I could find about witchcraft." She sat quietly for a long moment, her face screwed up in thought. "I don't have any idea what this thing is, either," she said slowly, "but I do have an idea that might help us: an arcane method that may be useful in destroying such a sinister aberration." She paused.

"What is it, Helmi?" Rhys prodded.

"I'm afraid you'll find this distasteful, but given the circumstances, I'm afraid we might not have any choice." She looked over toward the hall. "Poor Runa — what happened is a tragedy. But it also affords us with a unique opportunity."

Clearing her throat, and throwing an apprehensive glance at Rhys, Helmi continued. "As I'm sure you all know, blood is a powerful catalyst for magic. If that blood has special properties — such as that of a virgin or of a murdered person — it can be even more powerful."

Having lost his appetite, Rhys cast aside the rest of his bread and fixed Helmi with a hard gaze. "I hate blood magic."

"I understand, Garret," she said quickly, "but the gods themselves are known to use it, even the Knights have had occasion. And it might be the only chance we have against this monster, considering we don't know what it is."

Rhys had seen blood magic used before, to gruesome and horrific ends, and he wanted no part of it. Helmi had a point, however. They had no positive answer to what the creature was, so….

Suddenly, he remembered something Helmi had said the day before, and his heart skipped a beat as he realized the implications.

"Wait a moment," he murmured, the idea coming together in

his head. "Yesterday, you said the original attack on Pedr made you think of a siren."

"Yes," Helmi responded hesitantly, "but that's ridiculous, and we discussed why."

"It *is* ridiculous," Rhys agreed, "but that doesn't mean you weren't close to something." He stood and started pacing slowly in an arc around the fire. "She's not a siren, that's certain, as we're not at sea and her song is silent, affecting only one man at a time. But what if she's something similar?"

Everyone was silent as Rhys ruminated. "That crevasse in the cavern," he mused, stroking his short beard with his good hand, "we have no idea what it is, or where it leads. So anything could come out of it, not just the menagerie of evil we're familiar with."

"You think that's where she came from?" Helmi asked, horrified.

"It would explain the burns and ashen appearance the boy described. And her emaciated form could perhaps have fit through the crevasse. It's feasible, at least."

Helmi shifted the toddler over to her other shoulder. "I suppose that's possible, but then we have absolutely no base of knowledge to work from."

The sergeant narrowed his eyes. "I don't think that's entirely true, Ilban," he turned to the man crouched by the fire. "I'll ask you again why Othelia sent you with us."

Aedric sighed. "I've told you, she and I have terms, and hers were that I accompany you north on your journey."

"What I mean is," Rhys clarified, "why you? Why would a goddess of the Pantheon agree to any deal with you, specifically? Unless you offer something the rest of us cannot." He glanced at Helmi and then asked what he knew would be a very important question. "Ilban, you wouldn't happen to be a widower, would you?"

Aedric stood slowly and rested his hand on the hammer at his belt. "Aye," he growled. "What of it?"

Rhys ignored him and turned to Helmi. "A widower, just like you said. That's why he's here. That's why your goddess struck a deal with him. She's known all along what we would face up here." Against his will, his temper began to rise, and his good hand curled into a fist. "Why didn't she tell us?"

Helmi must have seen the anger written on his face, and she struggled to give an answer. "I don't know, Garret, I… she made no mention of it, but I can't believe she would let us go through all of this if she had known."

"'Crafty and guileful'," he said, "I believe that is how you described Othelia."

"Yes," she admitted, "but not malevolent! You don't under-stand, Garret — you all seem to think the gods are all-knowing, but they're not. They know far more than we do, obviously, but even for the goddess of wisdom, many things are hidden. She has visions, bits and pieces of knowledge that make only a small part of the whole, and her oracles see even less." She stood from her stump and crossed quickly over to him, taking his hand in hers. "Please believe me, Othelia is not cruel. If she had known — if *I* had known — we would have prevented this."

"We lost good men up there," Rhys said, furious, the pain of losing his brothers hitting him full again.

Tears welled up in Helmi's eyes as she pleaded with him. "I'm so sorry, Garret. I hold myself responsible, I should have thought of this sooner, listened to my instincts. But if you're right about Aedric, we can end this now." She squeezed his hand.

Rhys nodded, his mind a mess of guilt and distrust. Forcing himself to focus, he said, "I trust you, Helmi. I do. But I cannot trust your goddess."

"They're all a bunch of right bastards anyway," the Ilban muttered, turning back to his fire.

Rhys let go of Helmi's hand. "Did you know?" he asked Aedric. "Did you know what you were to the goddess?"

The man gave him an exasperated look. "I don't have any idea what you're on about. I thought Othelia must have wanted a seasoned fighter along, and I spent long years with the Dalbragh."

Rhys scoffed. "Don't flatter yourself. You're here because your wife died and for no other reason."

"Mind what you say about her," the Ilban warned, widening his stance.

Rhys gently pushed Helmi aside and squared himself to Aedric. "You could have saved them all. Now we'll have half the strength we did when we go to face her again!"

"Don't you put their deaths on me!" the Ilban bellowed back, hands in fists at his sides. "I didn't kill your brothers."

"Whether by deceit or ignorance, the blood of heroes stains your hands, you bastard," Rhys spat. He took a step toward him before Holywell slipped between the two and held them apart.

"Please, you two!" Helmi snapped, hugging Agata tightly to her. "Garret, you did not even know about widowers and sirens until yesterday; surely you can forgive this man's ignorance of the same."

Rhys was unmoved and held the Ilban's icy stare unflinchingly.

"Really!" Helmi huffed and smacked Rhys in his injured shoulder. He winced and finally looked away from Aedric. "We have a common enemy," she scolded them. "One that will not allow us the time for bickering."

The pain running through his arm and into his chest helped to clear Rhys's head of the seething rage that had overtaken him. His eyes found the Ilban's again.

"Point me in the direction of your monster, Sergeant," the shorter man rumbled, "and I'll happily bring my hammer down on its head. But I'll not carry the blame for your fallen brothers; I've too many to carry already. You have my sympathies for them, though, and my hope your rotten gods treat them better in death than they did in life." Aedric's eyes remained cold, but his words were genuine.

"You're right," Rhys relented, a touch of embarrassment heating his cheeks. "Their deaths are not yours to bear."

"They lie with the creature," Helmi said firmly.

Rhys nodded and sighed as a fresh wave of guilt and fatigue hit him. "Let's just kill this damned thing and be done with it."

He and Holywell both sat back down, but the Ilban remained standing. Helmi resumed her place on the stump and said, "Presuming you're right about Aedric, he is our best chance at success. I still think we should use the victim's blood that is available to us, however, in case we're wrong about the creature being related to the family of seducers. It will give us a greater chance of success."

Rhys did not have it in him to argue.

"I don't quite know what you're all talking about," Grim said slowly, "widowers and seducers and all, but will any of that really help against a creature that can take our minds?" His face was drawn and pale as he looked between the rest of the group. "One that can cause a whole flock of sheep, and mules and horses besides, to go mad and kill themselves?"

Rhys looked to Helmi, then Holywell, and finally back at Grim. "Grim, I have absolutely no idea," he said heavily. "But we don't have much choice in the matter, do we?" Grim digested the words, shook his head, and looked away.

As Holywell handed Rhys a bit of jerky, Joren appeared in the doorway of the hall wearing a heavy coat and walked purposefully over to join them, his little half-carved crook in one hand, another very tiny fleece jacket in the other.

Laying down his shepherding staff, he started putting Agata's arms through the little sleeves as she sat, sleepy, in Helmi's lap.

"Joren?" Helmi asked carefully. "Are you alright, sweetheart?"

He did not answer her, but continued bundling his little sister.

The Ilban frowned. "What's going on, lad?"

"Are you going to go save Vandra and my father?" the boy asked, turning to Rhys. Dried tears stained his ruddy cheeks.

"We're going to try."

"Then we're coming with you," Joren answered simply, stooping to pick up his crook.

Rhys shook his head. "You absolutely are not. Where we go, it is far too dangerous for children. The climb alone would be too much for you."

Joren looked at him with a blank expression. "Pedr's gone, isn't he?"

The question caught Rhys off guard. "I… I think so. I'm sorry, Joren."

The boy slammed the iron butt of his little crook down into the ground and blinked against the tears that sprung into his eyes. "Then I have to go after Papa and Van!" he cried, trembling.

"They're all we have left. You can't stop me — I'll go with or without you!" The accumulated trauma of the past few days was finally beginning to take its toll on him.

"We're going to take care of your family," Rhys answered, trying to keep his voice gentle out of compassion. "But you need to worry about your little sister."

Joren gritted his teeth as the tears fell and looked desperately over to Aedric. The Ilban regarded him in silence, and something seemed to pass between them.

After a moment, he sighed. "He's coming with us."

Rhys scoffed. "You're mad if you think—"

"He's lost everything," the Ilban spoke over him, "his brother, his mother, his dog. Now the rest of his family's in trouble and he wants to help. He has a duty to help them."

"He's a *child*."

"After this?" Aedric shook his head. "Do you remember, Sergeant? When you first woke to the world, its violence and its cruelty? You can't be a child after something like this. Will you really stop him from trying to save his family?"

"What you're suggesting is asinine," Rhys argued, "likely equal to marching the both of them to their deaths."

Aedric shook his head. "That's his decision to make. It's his family. He has a weapon. No one — not god or mortal being — has the right to stop a man from doing what he must. I know that you of all people, Sergeant, must agree with that."

At a loss, Rhys looked back at Joren. He had calmed and no longer trembled or wept, but met the sergeant's gaze forcefully, clutching his little staff in a white-knuckled grip. The Ilban was mad to suggest taking the children along. At the same time, however.... Rhys did indeed remember when the peaceful curtain he thought was life had been torn away for the first time, revealing the grim reality behind it. Joining the Knights and watching men die had forced him to confront the horrors of the world, and to decide what kind of man he was going to be.

Joren was far younger than Rhys had been, and very freshly wounded. The Ilban was right, though, and now the boy was having to make that decision as well, to choose what kind of man he was going to be: the kind who stayed behind, or the kind who charged forward. Looking at him there, in the firelight, rage in his eyes, Rhys could not help but admire him.

He sighed and climbed back to his feet. "Very well. If you want to come, I won't stop you." Rhys took a step toward the boy and fixed him with hard eyes. "But know this, young Master Olensen: if you choose to be a man here and now, then you shoulder the burden of that choice. We will still try to protect you, but in times like this, there are no guarantees. The things we saw on the Ymr are far beyond even what happened to your mother. Are you prepared to face that? Are you willing to risk your sister's life for this?"

Joren swallowed hard, finally showing a flash of hesitation. Again, he looked at the Ilban, who showed no sign of either encouragement or disapproval. Another moment passed, and Joren met the sergeant's gaze again. "Papa stayed out all night and day looking for Pedr." There was a little tremor in his lip, and his words came fast, passionate. "He would have crawled up the mountain with his broken leg if he had to, to find him. He and Vandra need us. Me and Aggy won't abandon our family. We have to help them no matter what."

"Good man." Rhys nodded and placed a hand on Joren's shoulder. "In that case, eat something. We've a long trek ahead, and you'll need your strength. The rest of us will prepare quickly and then we'll be off."

"Garret, this is madness," Helmi said, looking at him desperately. "We can't risk their lives like this."

"Joren has spoken for himself," Rhys answered calmly, throwing a glance at the Ilban. "Arguing will only cost us time — as you pointed out, I think."

Helmi opened her mouth to respond, but Rhys turned to Holywell and said, "I'm sorry, Brother, but I think we won't have the time for rest after all. Do we have one more climb in us, do you think?"

The mute shrugged, then nodded grimly.

"Let's get on with this, then." Rhys adjusted his injured arm in its sling. "Grim, those heavy coats we brought — get a few for you, Helmi, and the Ilban. Holywell, fill a pack with as much food as it will hold and make sure we have plenty of full waterskins. Ilban," he regarded the man gravely, "ready a few lanterns, at least three, and make sure they've enough tallow to last." He added in Carthan, "Keep the boy out here, away from the hall, do you understand?" Aedric nodded.

At his insistence, Helmi handed the child over to Joren and Rhys took her by the arm to lead her toward the hall. "Come, I'm going to need your help preparing this damned blood magic." He kept his voice low and spoke Carthan to be sure Joren did not understand what was happening.

"I can't believe you're allowing them to come," she complained as they walked.

"We have no choice. If we're all going up the mountain, I can't very well force him to go down to Kaninholm, can I? The boy will try to follow us regardless, and I'd rather have him close at hand."

As loth as Rhys was to admit it, he agreed with the Ilban on at least one thing: no one had the right to prevent another man from trying to protect his family. Joren was young, granted, but not much younger than many squires and pages that served the King's Army. Helmi did not seem to agree and remained discontent with his answer. He refused to speak more on the subject, though: there were more pressing matters at hand.

They followed Grim into the gruesome scene in the hall. The boy had covered his mother's head with a piece of cloth, but the shape beneath it told Rhys the woman's face was a ruin — another horrible sight he could count on to visit him in his nightmares. Helmi took deep breaths and maintained her composure as they crossed to the big chest the Knights had brought.

"How do you propose we use this blood?" Rhys asked as he crouched down.

Helmi helped him haul the lid open. "I think the best way will be to coat a dagger in it."

Rhys started going through the chest with his remaining useful hand. Beneath the veritable forest of herbs were tools more to his liking. "Does the dagger have to be steel?"

"Pure iron or silver would be better, I think," she said.

He pulled a bundle of suede out through the pungent cloud. Unrolling the soft leather, he revealed two silver-coated daggers, their handles beautifully wrought in the likeness of Lady Seraphe. "We're in luck, then." Setting it aside, he dug further into the chest and withdrew a plain steel dagger, which he slid into his belt; his left hand was useless with a sword, but would be able to manage a shorter blade well enough.

Helping him to his feet, Helmi followed Rhys over to the shepherd's wife, and they knelt beside her. An unexpected wave of grief hit him as he stooped over the woman. He had not realized the warmth and vibrance Runa had brought to her husband's hall, and her absence was striking.

Laying the daggers on the floor, he laid a hand on hers and muttered a brief prayer. "May your ancestors welcome you to Lodrheim, Runa Helsikdottir, first among hostesses, proud daughter of Fjalvard, and may the Slain watch over your son and daughters." He added, "Seraphe, grant us the strength to see this thing done, and forgive us for using this foul blood magic."

He took the first dagger in hand. "Where should I...?"

"Heart's blood is known to be the most effective," Helmi said, her face ashen.

Rhys had learned a bit about the body from Blackhart over the years, so he found the poor woman's breastbone and laid the tip of the dagger to the left of it, between the ribs above her breast. Leaning all of his weight on the hilt, he sunk the blade slowly through the muscle. It came out with a gory, viscous patina. Helmi swayed at the sight of it, and he helped her to sit back while he did the same with the second dagger. Once he was done, he laid the weapons out on their suede cover.

As he started to wrap them, Helmi reached out a hand to stop him. "Don't, I have to ensorcel them first." She had regained some of her color.

His hackles raised, Rhys carefully moved the daggers across the floor, closer to her. "Do what you must."

She shook her head and rose to her knees. "You can't be here for this, Garret. These enchantments were taught to me by the goddess herself."

"Say no more," he pushed up off his knee and stood. "How long will this take?"

"Not long." She bent over the bloodied daggers and closed her eyes.

Rhys hurried out and shut the door behind him, happy to have nothing more to do with the matter.

The others had done as he had ordered, and everything was prepared for the climb back up the Ymr. The Ilban was crouched, topping off the lanterns and sharing words with Joren as the boy held his baby sister and fed her some cheese.

"Are you sure we shouldn't wait until dawn, Sergeant?" Grim asked, shifting his weight from one foot to the other, looking nervously over at the children. "It'll be more dangerous in the dark, especially with the little ones along. And are you really sure we should bring them at all?" His blond brows furrowed.

"You heard the Ilban, Grim," Rhys answered, glancing through the sack Holywell had filled with provisions that Grim now wore on his back. "It's his family. Who are we to stop the boy from going after them?"

"We're people who know better than to throw children into danger needlessly," the young soldier said with a scowl.

Rhys grunted. "I won't argue with you. But the alternatives are either leaving them here, with their murdered mother, or sending them alone down to the village. All things considered, I would rather have them with us."

"I suppose," Grim muttered bitterly.

"And as for waiting for daylight, as much as we would all adore a few hours of sleep, that only gives the creature more time to choose and lure another victim." He lowered his voice, even though they were speaking Carthan. "She seems to use those she enthralls as her mouthpiece; Blackhart said something about her not wanting any more soldiers. Which means —"

"She'd go after Joren next."

Rhys nodded. "That is my fear, yes."

"I don't think I could stand to see that, Sergeant," Grim confessed. "Not after everything else."

"Then we had best make haste." As he said it, the door to the hall opened and Helmi came out, the suede parcel under her arm. She handed it to Rhys, who tucked it into Grim's pack as the young soldier helped her into the big fur jacket.

Rhys beckoned to Aedric and Joren, and when they had come over, he rested his hand on the pommel of the dagger at his side. "Are we all prepared?" It was a rather ridiculous question, he realized, as nothing could truly prepare them for what they were about to attempt — especially the young ones. Regardless, his companions all assured him that they were. "Joren, we don't have the time now, but I want you to know that when we return, we will help you build a pyre for your mother." The boy gave him an impassive nod. "Alright, let's be off, then. Gods — and the Slain — be with us."

Holywell and Grim took a lantern and started off first, followed by Aedric and Joren, with Rhys and Helmi bringing up the rear.

The wind whipped up as they left the hall, and Rhys felt a hint of reinvigoration, despite his lack of rest. Blotting out nearly all of the northern stars, the towering silhouette of the Ymr rose imperiously before them, and Rhys knew that with every step, the shadow would grow only darker.

10

FINAL ASCENT

R hys hoisted his lantern again after having rested his arm for a bit. As before, the wind grew in strength the farther up the slope they climbed. Every now and again, the group would pass through the cleft between two hills or by shelves of standing rocks that would grant a brief reprieve from the gusty howling; each time, the temptation to stop and shelter for the night was harder to resist.

Joren valiantly carried his baby sister as far as he could, much farther than Rhys had thought he would be able to, but finally his struggle was impossible to ignore, so the Ilban scooped up the little girl in one arm and carried her from there.

Helmi made a point of staying close beside Rhys. He thought at first that she was frightened of the dark and wind, but each time he misstepped, she was quick to take his uninjured arm and help him keep his balance, and he realized she stayed close for his sake. Still, he allowed himself the release of cursing loudly whenever he stumbled over a rock, which, in his fatigued state, he did with an irritating regularity.

Rhys insisted on a number of rests throughout the trip to allow them to catch their breath, and it was then that the cold began to worry him. Each of them was forced to keep their waterskins inside their coats to prevent them from freezing through. Helmi and Joren were both grossly unaccustomed to the rigors of mountain climbing, and Aedric had to tuck the toddler inside his own coat to keep her from shivering.

All things considered, though, they were doing better than Rhys had anticipated. He was impressed by the boy's fortitude; not once had he complained on the hours-long journey. Recalling the unspoken understanding Joren had seemed to have with the Ilban, Rhys's curiosity finally got the better of him.

He gave Helmi his lantern and urged her to go ahead with the boy, then bid Aedric fall back with him for a while.

"Young Joren has quite the spirit," Rhys observed in Carthan, between breaths.

"Aye," the Ilban burred. The man's mood remained chilly toward him.

"He'd make a damned fine recruit in a few years, don't you think?"

"For your Knights, or my Dalbragh?"

"Either, I'd imagine."

Aedric nodded. "We'd be honored to have the likes of him." After a moment, he added, "The lad had questions about your order, you know. I answered them as fairly as I could."

"I appreciate that." Rhys looked at him sidelong, starting to feel guilty about the mistrust he had shown the man since the start of their journey. "What I said earlier," he began, unsure how to broach the subject. "Laying the blame on you, I mean —"

"Nothing needs to be said, Sergeant," the other growled. "I've lost brothers-in-arms before. I know what it does to a man."

Rhys could not think of a response to that, so he said nothing, and they walked in silence for a time. After a while, he decided to pose the question he had been meaning to ask in the first place.

"While I maintain that bringing Joren and his sister up this infernal mountain is probably a bad idea," he said, "I will admit I do see a bit of a change in the boy." Aedric nodded. "You were much quicker to want to bring him with us, though. Why?"

The Ilban sighed, his breath forming icicles on his beard. "The lad and I had words, while you and the rest were away. Told him about my people, our beliefs about the dead, trying to help him, give him something to hold on to. You understand, in case his brother didn't come back."

Rhys nodded his understanding but found himself surprised by the Ilban's concern for the boy; he did not seem the kind of man to involve himself in the problems of others.

"Anyway," Aedric continued, "we talked a bit about doing what one must in spite of anything else. I think — after what happened to his mother, and finding out Pedr was dead — he understands now. He wants to help save what family he's got left. And it's not right to stop someone from doing what he must."

"Whatever you said to him, it seems to have done the job."

Aedric shrugged and lifted the toddler a little higher, pulling his coat further up to shield her face. "I think his parents taught him well, and the Fjalr have a strong culture. He'll be alright, and he'll teach his little sister when she's old enough, about the ones they've lost." He took a deep breath and coughed on the icy air. "As for me, I'll just be glad to quit this damned mountain."

Soon, the climb was too steep and treacherous for talk and Helmi and Aedric switched places again. They kept an even pace, Holywell leading with his lantern, as sharp in his tracking abilities as ever. As they passed the snow line, he was gifted with fresh tracks to follow: heavy footsteps with the smooth trail of something being dragged alongside. Rhys could see no sign of a struggle from Vandra, and red stained the snow every few yards.

The wind tossed flurries of snowflakes into the air around them; Helmi pulled her fur jacket tighter until only her eyes were exposed. As the cold crept steadily deeper, their only relief came from constant movement.

By the time Rhys was sure his toes had thoroughly re-frozen, they came to a spot he remembered passing on the first journey. The towering boulder jutted from the mountain's flank and the shallow impressions of their original footsteps skirted around where they had passed it. They were nearly to the creature's lair.

As the sky paled in the east, Rhys called a halt and everyone huddled together next to the standing monolith. He had spent the majority of the climb devising a plan of attack and it was time to discuss the matter.

"Listen here," Rhys said over the wind, pointing in the general direction of the cave. "Around this bend, we'll soon come to a ridge which leads to the creature's lair. It's set on a high precipice — just be aware of that in case we have to take the fight there." He spoke in Fjalr so that Joren could understand. "If she still has Blackhart and Fergus under her control, we'll have three in total to contend with."

"Assuming she doesn't just sing her demon-song to one of us," Grim noted bitterly.

"Assuming that, yes. Even assuming she doesn't, and given that each one of them has the strength of a dozen men, I'd wager we won't be able to hold them for long, regardless. That means we need to clear a path quickly for the Ilban to get to her. He's the only one we know for certain is immune to her magic."

Grim shivered. "What about the pit with the monster-arm?"

"Just stay as far away from it as you can," Rhys instructed.

"What will we do about it, I mean, if we manage to kill the witch — er, creature?"

"You leave that to me," Helmi answered him.

Rhys had Grim shrug off his pack and retrieve the suede parcel; he handed it over and Rhys carefully laid it in the snow, unwrapping it with his useful hand. The blades were crusted and dark in the pale morning glow.

"Here," Rhys passed Aedric one of the daggers. "If you can, kill her with this."

The man frowned. "I prefer my hammer."

"As Helmi explained, these will have a better chance against a wider variety of creatures."

The Ilban nodded reluctantly and took the weapon from him.

"Strike for her heart," Helmi added, "or remove her head if you are able."

"Is that blood?" Joren asked, his voice sounding small on the wind.

"It's manticore blood," Rhys lied quickly. "Very powerful." He spoke again to Aedric. "You'll have to be quick, before we're overpowered. Grim, Holywell," he switched to Carthan, "I am hereby ordering you to do everything in your power to kill

Blackhart, Fergus, and the shepherd on sight, do you understand?"

"But what if killing the creature releases them from her spells?" Grim protested. His eyes were wet, and Rhys guessed it was not because of the wind.

"We have no proof that will happen and it's not worth the risk. And as I said earlier, our brothers are mortally wounded already. Even if they were to recover from her power, they would be dead soon thereafter. It is far more important that we clear the way for the Ilban. Tell me you understand my order, Grim."

The young man's lip trembled as he scowled at Rhys. Finally, though, he answered. "I understand, Sergeant."

"Good. When this is over, I swear to you, we'll send them on to the afterlife properly, and cut their patches off to bring back with us."

Grim swallowed hard and nodded.

"Joren." He turned to the boy and paused as his tired mind tried to change back to Fjalr. "As we travel along the ridge just ahead, you will see the mouth of a cave come into view. Just inside is a long tunnel that connects a cavern to the outside. I have only one instruction for you: you must remain in that tunnel no matter what. If it grows quiet, and none of us come to get you, you must flee at once, do you hear me?" The chances that they would actually be able to get away were slim at best, but they at least had to try, should it come to that.

The boy opened his mouth to speak, but hesitated as he seemed to think better of what he had been about to say. Instead, he simply nodded, a resentful expression settling over his face

"Right, then. Take a moment and prepare yourselves." Rhys took Helmi's arm and drew her aside, out of earshot of the others.

Pulling the other blooded dagger from its suede wrapping, he slipped the hilt into her hand.

"Why are you giving this to me?" she asked.

"I'm old, but not so old I don't realize that if this thing is truly related to the sirens, her song would not effect you, either. But I give you this with the instruction that you are not to go anywhere near the creature or the others unless Aedric fails and is killed. You are too valuable to the Order to risk unnecessarily." Helmi scoffed at that, but Rhys ignored it. "Have you ever had to attack something or someone before?"

She blinked. "No."

He looked down at the dagger gripped in her fist. "Turn it around." He demonstrated. "Hold it with the blade pointing to the ground and stab downward — it will help to keep your wrist from turning."

She nodded and arced the weapon down as he said.

"Just like that. Keep it at the ready, do you understand? If anyone or anything finds its way out to you, stab it as many times as you can; aim for the neck or the groin if possible."

She grimaced, but nodded. While she practiced a few more swings, Rhys took the dagger at his own belt and used it to cut away the sling on his injured arm.

"What are you doing?" she asked, reaching out and catching the triangle of cloth as it fell.

"I'm not going into a fight with one hand voluntarily tied," he said, gritting his teeth against the pain as he tried to work the mangled joint.

Helmi bit her lip. "You'll likely only injure it further, though."

Rhys knew she was right, but was struck by an overwhelming sense of indifference on the matter. "I'll deal with that afterwards, if I have to. Right now, only one thing is important."

She nodded, understanding.

"Are you ready?"

She paused before answering, turning her head to look in the direction of the dawn, and her face was bathed in its warm, rosy light. "Yes, Garret."

"Let's get this over with, then." They returned to the others and together, the party set off along the ridge toward the cavern.

11

THE BURNT LADY

The wind along the ridge was harsh, and Rhys had to steady himself against it once or twice as they went. They came to the spot where Blackhart had succumbed to the call and saw that the clifftop was barren — there was no sign of Blackhart, Fergus, or the shepherd, and the wind had even covered the marks of their earlier scuffle almost entirely.

As the group hurried for the cave opening, the muscles of Rhys's back bunched as he expected to start going mad any minute if the monster tried to influence him. Nothing happened, though, and they reached it unharmed.

Holywell stopped at the entrance and looked back at Rhys, the wind whipping his grey hair about wildly. Rhys gestured at him and Grim, and the two of them went in first, swords at the ready. After a moment, Holywell's lanky arm appeared, beckoning them inside.

The strange light of the crevasse flared more brilliantly than he remembered, rebounding down the tunnel and lighting their way adequately once their eyes had adjusted from the brightness of dawn outside. With still no sign of activity, Rhys stopped the group about halfway down the passage, where the noise from the wind had quieted and the warmth of the sickly fire could be felt on the air.

He took Joren gently but firmly by the arm and led him over

to a nook in the tunnel wall, sitting him down inside it. Aedric handed him the toddler and he placed her in the boy's lap as Grim and Holywell took up defensive positions between them and the large chamber.

"Do you remember the instructions I gave you?" Rhys asked.

Joren nodded. "Stay here no matter what, unless you don't come back for us, then run."

"Good man. If you have to run, be sure to follow our tracks back down, and go straight to your grandfather's — do not go back to your father's hall." Rhys laid his good hand on the boy's head for a moment. "Take care of your sister." He stood and the Ilban stooped to whisper something in Joren's ear that he could not make out. Then the rest of them continued down the tunnel.

Pausing yet again just before the opening of the big cavern, Rhys looked back and made eye contact with each of the others in the reflected firelight. They were haggard and frightened, but determined, so he took a breath to steady himself and rounded the corner, his companions following after him.

The pale, ghastly flames were indeed burning brighter; the deep shadows had retreated further, and only a small corner of the chamber remained blanketed in darkness. Flames were not the only thing rising from the infernal crevasse, however: the massive arm that had taken Felix was no longer there, but in its place, dozens more had risen. They were smaller, and some looked like human arms reaching up from the shoulder, while others appeared more bestial in form, with articulated paws and wicked talons. They were charred and cracked, like the Burnt Lady.

To the right of the crevasse, near the shadow, Blackhart sat against the wall and Fergus crouched on the ground, facing away from them and toward the darkness. Neither of the two reacted to their presence immediately. The shepherd was nowhere to be seen.

Grim dropped his pack and he and Holywell both kept their swords out in front of them. His dagger in hand, Rhys motioned at Helmi to stay back while the rest of them advanced slowly forward. After a few steps, Grim tugged at Rhys's shirt and gestured to their right.

There, unobtrusively, Vandra lay on the stone floor, her chestnut hair in a pool beneath her head. Her face was puffy and purple and there were dark bruises on her neck. The girl's eyes were open, bulging, and bloodshot; her lips were swollen and dark, parted slightly. Her father had dragged her by the neck, he guessed, and she had likely been dead within minutes of her abduction.

Sickened and appalled, Rhys instinctively took a step toward her; as he did, the shepherd stepped out from the pool of shadow, startling him.

Olen hobbled into the light and Rhys recoiled at the sight of him. Like Fergus, a chunk of flesh was missing from his neck and the wound bled heavily. Even more disturbing was the state of his leg — the twisted ankle had shattered entirely in his crazed dash up the mountain and his foot flopped to the side, hanging on by a sliver of muscle and sinew. The shepherd's weight rested on the splintered shin-bone that protruded from the ragged flesh of his leg.

"How many times has she warned you?" he asked, his rosy cheeks wet and his eyes red from tears. "She just wants to be left alone." The shepherd took a step forward and made a sickening click as his bone struck the stone floor. "She will give you one last chance to flee."

There was a long pause; Olen stared at him blankly, and Rhys finally realized the creature was waiting for a response.

He shifted his gaze from the shepherd to the ebbing shadows behind him, where he remembered the reflection off the monster's inhuman eyes. "By the blood of my fallen brothers," he promised, "you will not see the sun set this day."

Next to Rhys, Grim twitched.

Fergus looked over his shoulder and spat, his face pale and contorted in agony and rage. "You will not hurt her." He rose and turned to face them, drawing his sword, as Blackhart seemed to be lifted from the ground, independent of his own volition, and propped on his feet. His eyes and the flesh of his face were grey; the wounds inflicted by Holywell had drained him of nearly all life, and the creature's power, alone, moved him.

"No!" Grim cried and stumbled back, his sword falling to the ground with a clang. He clutched his ears and shook his head violently. "I can hear it!" he shrieked. "Gods save me, I can hear it!"

Rhys immediately searched the darkness again; still he could see nothing, though he knew the creature lurked somewhere within.

Grim clutched desperately at Rhys's sleeve with one hand, trying to block his ears between the other and his shoulder. "Help me, Sergeant," he begged, tears pouring from his eyes, already beginning to succumb to the mania. "Please!"

Rhys looked on him piteously, but was forced to turn away as all three of the creature's thralls charged into them.

As soon as the rest turned the corner, Joren stood from the hollow in which Sergeant Rhys had placed them. He waited a moment to see if any of them would come back and when no one did, he set Agata down on the floor. She whimpered and clutched the leg of his trousers as he quickly removed his heavy coat and laid it across the nook, making a soft, warm space. Picking up his baby sister and placing her down on it, he folded the jacket over her, trying to make it tight so that she could not undo it.

"I have to go help Papa and Van," he whispered to her, though he knew she could not understand. Joren had promised the sergeant he would stay put only because he knew making an argument would not help him. It was just as the Ilban had said: they were *his* family, and he had to make sure for himself that Van and his father were safe. Joren also wanted to see the Burnt Lady die for what she had forced his father to do to his mother, even if he could not kill her himself.

"Stay here. Everything will be alright." He tucked the fleece around her firmly and pulled it up to shield her face from the cold that clashed with the heat from the cavern. He leaned in and kissed her forehead and wiped a little tear from her chubby cheek. "We all love you so much, Aggy." If there was a chance she could remember that, he wanted her to, just in case things did not go as Sergeant Rhys had planned.

She cried softly as he left, struggling against her fleece prison, and it hurt him to leave her there, but Joren knew he must; he had to be a part of this. All of the Ilban's talk about rage had suddenly begun to make sense as he had lain down next to his mother's body, and even the exhausting climb and extreme cold of the Ymr had done nothing to cool the hatred he felt. Clutching the crook his father had made him, Joren advanced down the tunnel, careful to go as quietly as possible.

Before he had taken even a dozen steps, a deep voice reverberated out from the chamber. The echo confused the words, but he knew the voice. It was his father. Joren's pace quickened and he came to the opening, but he did not risk looking in and being discovered.

His father's voice fell away, and after a moment someone else spoke; it sounded like the sergeant. Then another voice, and someone shrieking. Finally, Joren poked his head around the corner to see what was happening.

A new kind of fear bloomed at the base of his spine when he saw what must have been the crevasse Sergeant Rhys had mentioned. At the sight of the pale flames and grasping, writhing, inhuman arms, only one thought cut through his terror: Nydheim. In that moment, he would have given anything to have Hala at his side again, even just to feel the comfort of her tail thumping against his leg.

Joren finally tore his gaze away from the crevasse and saw everyone else in the chamber. Grim wailed and grabbed at Sergeant Rhys just as one of the twins, bloody and ghastly-looking, leapt toward Helmi, swinging his sword wildly. Holywell danced between them and met him blow for blow, the clash of their blades singing in the small space. Brother Blackhart grabbed the sergeant by his heavy jacket, and Sergeant Rhys started stabbing the man's huge arms wildly in an effort to break his grip.

Another large man was grappling with Aedric, and Joren's heart started pounding desperately as he realized it was his father. Blood poured from a frightening wound in his neck and he wept and growled as he tried to subdue the Ilban. He looked like one of the rabid wolves they had seen from time to time on their slope: manic and wild and wholly not himself.

Grim staggered backward toward the wall to Joren's right, sinking to the ground, twitching and moaning. He could not understand what the young soldier said, but he looked much like Fergus had, that night he had heard the monster's song. Joren took a terrified step forward, wondering what he could do to help, but stopped short as he caught sight of a shape on the ground near Grim. It wore Vandra's dress.

She lay on the ground, her head turned toward him, and he could see the death in her face. He had never seen it before on a person, but he could tell. Without thinking, he dashed into the chamber past his father and slid painfully to his knees as he came up beside Vandra.

Laying down his crook, Joren put his hands on either side of her swollen face; she was cold. Her neck bore terrible marks, like a handprint, and he understood what had happened. He tried to turn her head up — he did not know why — but stopped when the bones ground against each other. His stomach turned and he removed his hands.

Joren looked behind him at the others. Brother Holywell and Fergus exchanged another blow and their well-used blades threw a spark into the air. Then Brother Holywell ducked to Fergus's side and swung an arc at his neck, chopping halfway through. He yanked the blade out and swung again as Fergus fell to his knees, this time sending his head tumbling. Brother Holywell stepped over the twitching corpse and came to Sergeant Rhys's aid, slicing down at Brother Blackhart's neck. Clutching her bloodied dagger tight at her breast, Helmi stood a few paces away, looking uncertain.

Grim suddenly shot to his feet as he tore his hair and screeched in what Joren guessed was Carthan. The young man dashed forward, barely able to keep his legs under him, straight for the wall of flames in the middle of the cavern. He ran into Helmi and knocked her down. Sprawling, she came dangerously close to the crevasse and the arms instantly all scrabbled toward her, as if they could sense her nearness.

Before any of them found her, however, Grim dove headlong into the flames and the arms rushed to receive him. Joren could not help but reach up and cover his ears to block the man's wretched screams as he burned, and the gnarled, clawed hands tore into him.

Brother Holywell had already hacked through Brother Black-hart's neck as well and kicked the body off of Sergeant Rhys. As he saw where Grim was headed, he dove to intercept him but was too late; once Grim hit the flames, he was gone so quickly that not even Brother Holywell had a chance at saving him.

Joren looked away from the slaughter, and his eyes fell on the deep shadow at the end of the cavern. With Grim's death came a bright flash as the fires grew and sickly light splashed throughout the chamber, for a moment abolishing even that deep darkness.

In that brief instant Joren saw her: the Burnt Lady.

She did not look as he remembered. Rather than haggard and emaciated, she was hale and youthful. Her body was no longer blackened by soot; the pale whiteness of her face ran down her naked body. The black hair remained, however, forming an ethereal cloud about her head, as did her gaping, shadowy eyes.

A familiar fear gripped him as he beheld the monster that had destroyed his family. It was impossible to tell if her glassy black eyes were looking at him, but he felt they were. Her lips moved rapidly as she sat, serene, while the Knights fought against their brothers and his father.

The flames shrank after Grim's passing and the deep shadows returned to envelop the Burnt Lady.

As Joren fumbled for his rough-hewn crook and gripped it tight in his hands, the fear began to give way to something else. Heat rose in his chest, his temples pounded, and he felt as though a scream was about to burst from his lips.

In a moment, he remembered when Pedr had smacked him in the mouth and ran away up the mountain — the last he would ever see of his little brother. He remembered watching Hala die and laying her to rest on a pyre he built himself. He remembered holding his mother's lifeless corpse, desperately praying for everything to be normal again. And now Vandra, too, was gone, and his father was bewitched, injured, and had murdered his own wife and daughter.

Joren also remembered what the Ilban had said, and he could almost feel the sorrow and the rage he had placed in his crook flowing back through his hands, into his heart. They overwhelmed him, and without having to convince himself to be brave, he leapt to his feet, hot tears streaming down his cheeks, and charged the creature in the shadows.

There was a choked cry from behind him, and just as the iron spike at the end of his crook pierced the darkness, he was jerked up and backwards, his wooden staff falling from his grasp and clattering to the ground.

Heavy hands turned him around and he looked into the face of his father. Only, it wasn't really his father, but a furious, desperate, weeping mask the Burnt Lady had forced on him. The creature that had been Olen Segurdsen squeezed hard and the air was crushed from Joren's lungs. "You will not touch her!" it bellowed. Then it threw him to the ground; Joren's head smacked against the stone and the thing poised its ragged, shattered leg over him.

Blackhart's heavy body rolled off of him, and Rhys climbed to his knees. His face was battered and swollen and it took a moment for him to right himself.

As he rallied, he heard Grim cry out, "No! No, I won't! Not me!" and charge forward blindly. He bowled Helmi over and — before Rhys could understand what was happening — dove into the flames. Rhys got shakily to his feet and made for him; Holywell was faster, but still not in time to save the young man. They watched as he burned and was taken by the arms and pulled, piece by piece, down into the abyss.

His head pounding, Rhys finally turned away and toward the Ilban, who was still wrestling the shepherd. Even Aedric's strength was no match for the frenzied power imbued by the creature's song, and he was getting thrashed as badly as Rhys had. He also noticed that Joren had sneaked into the cavern against his instructions, but there was nothing to be done about that right now.

Rhys took a step toward the Ilban to help, but whirled around at a cry from Helmi. She had fallen perilously close to the crevasse, and as Grim disappeared, one of the arms — longer than the others — had swung over and grabbed her by the ankle. It ripped her back to the ground, toward the abyss.

He and Holywell both leapt after her at once; Rhys stabbed at the spidery appendage with his dagger and Holywell let the captain's sword whistle through the air and cut deep into the arm, shattering bone and spattering dark blood across the ground. Another hand was able to grab her, then another. They pulled her closer and Rhys leapt atop her, sawing desperately at the wicked limbs that threatened to pull her down to whatever misery awaited below.

Another throaty cry rang out and Rhys looked up to see the shepherd had abandoned his assault on Aedric and had Joren in his hands. As Olen slammed the boy to the ground and brought down the splintered bone of his leg upon him, Rhys looked away, ashamed but unwilling to leave Helmi to help him. He cut through another limb and looked back to watch the Ilban tackle Olen, his great hammer in hand. He smashed the shepherd's head with his heavy weapon, then again, and Olen fell still beneath him.

More and more of the evil hands grabbed onto Helmi, digging themselves into her dress, and she inched closer to the crevasse. She looked up at Rhys fearfully as she used her own dagger to tear at her attackers and he redoubled his efforts. Perhaps if the Ilban killed the creature, this heinous pit would disappear. The flames were licking closer to them, and sweat poured from Rhys's brow.

Even as he cut through the arms with his dagger, he looked back to Aedric and his heart leapt into his throat. Anguish on his face, the Ilban fell to his knees next to Joren and took the boy in his arms, ignoring the creature completely.

"Kill it!" Rhys yelled, waving him toward the shadows. The

Ilban did not move. "Aedric," Rhys bellowed, "kill the damned thing!" The man ripped off his coat and then his linen shirt and pressed it against the wounds in Joren's chest. Still he ignored Rhys.

Holywell was swinging wildly and severed arms littered the floor until others grabbed them and dragged them back down. Rhys hacked through another and Helmi was almost free. She reached up and took Rhys by his shirt so that he looked at her. "Go," she said urgently, "kill it," and traded her silver dagger for his steel one.

Rhys looked back to Holywell, who clove another arm and nodded. Reluctantly, he rose and made for the shadows. He knew he must be quick, quicker than her song, or he would have no chance.

Crossing the cavern as swiftly as he could, Rhys kept a firm grip on the dagger hilt in his left hand while trying to ignore the agony in his right arm. The shadows before him swelled and shrunk menacingly with the flickering of the flames, and as he flew toward them, he saw the reflection in her eyes again. The creature was relaxed as she had been before, staring disinterestedly at him, whispering her silent enchantments.

As his feet fell one in front of the other, he suddenly felt as though he was slowing, and something began to itch in the back of his mind. His legs moved as though stepping through mud and the dagger in his hand grew heavier, until his fingers could no longer grasp it. The blooded blade fell from his hand, and he watched it float gently to the ground.

A sweet, innocent little voice called out in his mind: a lament in a language he had never heard, tragic and beautiful, piercing his heart with its purity. Tears welled in his eyes and instantly spilled over, down through his beard, and he took shuddering breaths as the notes of the girl's song told him her story, even though he did not understand the words she spoke.

The cavern before him all but disappeared and Rhys fell to his knees, grasping his head as he felt her pain, her sorrow, her longing, all swirling in a vicious tempest in his mind. The depth of her emotions was utterly devastating, shredding him of all thought of his own and filling him up with hers.

Suddenly, the storm came to an abrupt end, and his mind was thrown back into the cavern. Rhys's head felt as though it had been split in two, and a brilliant white light was all he could see for a moment. Someone put their arms around him and he tried to fight them off before Helmi's voice cut through the haze.

As his vision returned, Rhys looked toward the shadow and saw Aedric standing there, bare-chested in his kilt, one arm extended into the darkness. There was a snarl on his bearded face as he withdrew his arm, pulling the creature out into the ghastly light. He had her by the throat in an iron grip. Rhys watched as her lips sung her muted song to him, but the Ilban remained unaffected, and he dragged her toward the crevasse.

As her magic failed to take any effect, the creature's eyes widened even further, and she started flailing wildly, kicking and swiping, clawing red ribbons across his chest and shoulders. He came to a halt just outside the reach of the havoc of thrashing arms and in a fury, he hurled her down into the flames. A dozen monstrous hands folded over her, their fingers and claws sinking into her supple flesh, and ripped her down through the narrow crack in the stone. Her face twisted in agony, but she passed into the abyss without a sound.

"Are you alright, Garret?" Helmi asked, placing her hands on his face and forcing him to look at her. Holywell stood above them, the captain's sword ready in his hand and a pained expression across his weathered face.

"Yes, I think so." Rhys squeezed his eyes shut against the sudden absence of the creature's song. A wave of nausea and dread rolled over him, like waking from his nightmares, and it took a moment to remember exactly where he was and what was happening.

He wiped the tears from his cheeks and, with Helmi's help, got to his feet. Holywell relaxed, allowing the sword to hang at his side, and embraced Rhys for a quick moment, his relief palpable.

Aedric was already back beside Joren, listening for a breath or heartbeat. "He's alive," he announced, and looked desperately to Helmi. "Can you help him?"

Rhys's feet still were not quite under him, so he leaned on Holywell as they went to join the man at Joren's side.

"You're learned," the Ilban said as Helmi knelt down and placed a hand on the boy's forehead, "you can help him, can't you?"

Helmi carefully pulled back the shirt covering Joren's wounds and sucked in her breath. "Oh, no...." Two large puncture wounds from Olen's broken leg bone gaped on one side of his chest and made a sputtering sound with each shallow breath. His already pale skin had developed a deathly pallor, and Helmi blanched, too, as she inspected the injuries.

A little whimper came from behind them, and Rhys turned to see Agata had found her way into the cavern. The child sat next to Vandra, clutching desperately at her sister's corpse and turning her little face away from the carnage.

Holywell saw her, too, and crossed quickly over to her. The girl squirmed as he neared and when he squatted down and reached for her, she shrieked, tears spilling from her weary eyes. Holywell took her up under the arms, and she wailed and clung to Vandra's dress. Gently prying her tiny fingers from it, he lifted her up and away, resting her on his shoulder and rubbing her back as she cried.

Rhys looked over the death around them before turning back to the others. The exhaustion returned, the same he had felt after their first encounter with the creature.

"What can we do for him?" the Ilban asked again.

Helmi looked up at him uncertainly. "I... I don't know. I've never had formal training in the healing arts, and wounds like these are far beyond even what I've read."

"If Blackhart were here," Rhys sighed, "he would tell us to make the boy comfortable; wounds like those don't heal, Ilban, not even with a hospitaler's help."

The Ilban shook his head. "No, there must be something." He worked his arms delicately underneath Joren and lifted the boy up. "I'll take him down to Kaninholm if I have to, but I'll not let him die without trying to—" He stopped abruptly and narrowed his eyes. Rhys followed his gaze to Helmi, who remained kneeling on the floor.

Her face showed the bright sheen of a heavy sweat that had suddenly appeared and she twitched violently. Rhys watched in horror as her eyes rolled back so that only the whites showed and she went rigid.

"What's wrong with her?" Rhys asked as he approached her, his mouth dry. "Is this… is she communing with Othelia? You've seen it, is that what this is?"

"Aye." Aedric took a step forward, too, Joren still in his arms. "Othelia," he barked at Helmi, "I want a change of terms."

Helmi continued to twitch, sweat pouring from her brow, blank eyes gaping. Rhys went to his knees next to her, wanting to help somehow, but afraid to touch her.

"Do you hear me?" the Ilban cried again, an edge of desperation on his burr. "Save the lad, forget everything else."

The oracle still gave no answer.

"Damn you," he growled, "You spoke to me once, speak now! We've done what you wanted. Let the lad live."

Helmi lurched and drew a sharp breath, her eyes coming back around. Rhys took her in his arms as she doubled over and vomited. He pulled the damp hair away from her face and let her lean on him. "Are you alright?" he asked as she coughed and gradually regained a bit of strength.

She looked around at the cavern. "We're still here." Her voice was tremulous, and she clutched him to remain upright.

"Yes," Rhys answered, confused. "What happened, did Othelia speak to you?"

She turned in his arms to look at him. Little tears appeared in her hazel eyes and she pressed her hand to his cheek. Biting her lip to keep it from quivering, she gently extricated herself and faced the Ilban.

"Aedric," she said, struggling to catch her breath, "The goddess is thankful for your help."

"I want new terms," he demanded, hoisting Joren higher for a better grip.

"Othelia heard you." Helmi replied gravely. "But she cannot help him. She told me what you wanted to know from her."

"Stop," the Ilban commanded, his voice wavering. "I don't want that anymore, I'll get it from some other god. She needs to save Joren."

Helmi swallowed hard, her eyes glistening. "The deal has been made, Aedric."

"Forget the damned the deal!" he bellowed, holding Joren out to her in desperation. "He's dying!"

"There's nothing I can do!" Her shoulders quaked, and a tear broke free and rolled down her cheek. "The gods don't change their terms, nor does Othelia heal the sick." She implored him with her eyes to understand.

Aedric's gaze hardened as he realized she would not — could not — give him what he wanted. "Then damn the gods," he said, fury in his eyes. "And damn you." The broken boy suspended between his arms, he turned and made for the passage out of the cavern.

As he disappeared, Helmi put her head in her hands and shook violently as she wept. Rhys reached out a tentative hand to her shoulder, but she flinched at his touch and turned, wiping her nose. "You have to go with him," she said shakily, moving past him toward the crevasse.

Rhys looked at Holywell. "I don't think we have any objections to leaving this foul place." The mute shook his head in agreement. "But we can't leave our fallen brothers here. Holywell and I can move them outside for burial, if you want to wait with Agata."

"No," she stepped uncomfortably close to the heinous arms. "There isn't any time for that. You have to leave this place, Garret. All three of you. Now."

Her melancholy brought an unwelcome flush to his neck. "What are you talking about?"

"I have one more task to complete, and you can't be here when I do it."

"Well, I'm not leaving you — it's *my* task to keep you safe."

She shook her head. "The goddess has released you from your charge, Sergeant." He winced at the title — she had not used it since they had left the Eldric Citadel. "I know you don't trust him," she continued before he could interrupt, "but I need you to relay a message to the Ilban. When he spoke to Othelia in the sanctum, in exchange for coming with us, he asked after his wife and children. They were all recently killed, and he wanted to know where they had gone after death. Please tell him that his family is safe and at peace in Eirna."

"Fine." Rhys nodded impatiently. "But what's going on, Helmi? What does Othelia want from you?"

"Please, I can't tell you," she said, wringing her hands. "You just have to trust me and go."

"She told you what this is, didn't she?" he asked, gesturing at the crevasse. The fear in her eyes filled him with trepidation. "What does she want you to do?"

All she could manage was to shake her head again, shutting her eyes tight, and he understood.

"Tell her I'm volunteering myself in your place," he said, "Whatever it is, I'll do it."

"No, you can't, Garret."

"Why not?" he demanded, reaching for her hand.

"I can't tell you!" she cried, and pulled away from him. "If either of you learns any more of this place, she won't let you leave! So you have to go, please." She trembled, but whether from fear or anger, Rhys could not tell.

He sighed, understanding. "I can't replace you because she won't let you go either. Because she's already told you."

She wiped indignantly at her eyes. "Yes."

Rhys nodded. He was still for a moment, considering his options. As he tried to think, he became acutely aware of the aches and pains in his limbs and down his aging spine. He looked over at Fergus and Blackhart, both lying headless on the ground, then at the flaming crack that had taken Grim and Felix. As the rush of the fight faded, the horror of all that had happened began to crash into him, and Rhys felt the familiar exhaustion swell up again.

It was not a physical exhaustion — though there was plenty of that as well — but something else: a fatigue in the back of his mind that had been growing for the last few years. Now on the Ymr, after losing so much so quickly, he could no longer deny what that fatigue was. He was tired of living.

As the words consciously formed in Rhys's mind, he let out a heavy sigh that was almost a sob. It was the truth. What awaited him at the bottom of the mountain? In Carthannas? Only the next assignment with a new detachment, who were only new brothers to be mourned at some point. No, he could not do that again. He could bury no one else. It was *his* turn to be mourned.

Holywell stood there, the toddler on his shoulder and the captain's decorated sword at his hip, and gave him a strange look. Rhys beheld his old friend for a moment as the weight of a long, tired, and sorrowful life pressed down on his shoulders.

In the time it took to draw a deep breath and let it go, he allowed the memories of a life well spent, of friends made and lost, of wounds given and received, to wash over him. In that moment, he made his choice.

"Holywell," he said, making for the tunnel entrance, "with me."

"Won't you at least say goodbye?" Helmi called after them sadly.

Rhys ignored her and led Holywell over to the opening of the narrow passage. He turned around to face his comrade, the toddler still sniffling on the man's shoulder. Rhys regarded his friend, at a loss for how to say what he must.

"I don't know how you do it, old man," he finally admitted. "I'm too tired for this, anymore, I think."

Holywell blinked but did not respond.

"I've known you longer than anyone else in my life," Rhys continued, an uncomfortable tension growing behind his eyes. "You're the bravest and the best the Order has to offer, I've always thought so."

Holywell's eyes glistened in the low light, and he shrugged and made a firm gesture with his free hand, asking why Rhys was saying any of this now.

"I can't go with you, Leo," he explained, looking down at the ground, unable to face his friend as he said it. "I can't leave Helmi here by herself."

Holywell gestured again, then took the girl in his hands and held her insistently out to Rhys.

Rhys took a step back and shook his head. "No, you're not staying here in my stead. It must be me."

The scout brought the girl back to his shoulder and shrugged again, angrily this time, demanding an explanation.

Rhys met his friend's gaze and forced himself not to look away even as the tears welled and he felt himself begin to shake. He clenched his jaw as he tried to say the word that would make Holywell understand. "Fielding," he finally managed, and the tears broke free and fell down his rough cheeks.

Holywell looked at him for a long moment, grinding his teeth to fight off tears of his own. He finally shook his head and threw an arm up in frustration. Then he glanced over to where Helmi stood, and Rhys saw the guilt and anguish pass over his face. Looking back at Rhys, he grabbed the sergeant's good hand in his and squeezed it hard, his face racked with emotion, and then they embraced one final time as brothers.

"I'll see you again in green fields someday, old friend," Rhys said. His most beloved brother-in-arms gave an involuntary sob and nodded, then let go of Rhys, a tear sliding down his chiseled cheek. Turning to hide his shame, he stooped, grabbed up Grim's pack from the ground nearby, and hefted it over his shoulder. He was finally able to look at Rhys one last time, and then he left brusquely, carrying the child out of that evil place and back out into the sunlight.

Rhys felt a pang of sorrow and regret watching Holywell go, knowing he would never see him again, and he had to take a shuddering breath to calm himself. There would be more than enough time to deal with it all in the afterlife.

Helmi took a cautious step toward him as he returned to her. "What are you doing?"

"I'm staying here with you," he said, and the proclamation seemed to lift some of the burden from him. "I won't let you do… whatever it is… alone."

"Are you mad?" she asked. "The gods have brought me here to die, Garret; they won't spare you if you stay!"

Rhys shook his head. "I don't want them to."

"What on earth are you talking about?"

He tried to gather his thoughts, to turn them into something that would make sense to her. "Do you remember what I told you about Fielding?" he asked.

At the mention of his name, Helmi looked at him suspiciously. "Yes."

"I've been afraid for the last few years that someday soon, I would share his fate." She made to protest again but he held up his hand to stop her. "I know this probably doesn't make any sense to you, and I don't think I could explain it even if we had the time." He sighed. "Helmi, I'm ready for this. I'm ready to meet my fate, whatever it might be. But I don't want to go the way Fielding did, gods bless him. I've been hoping to die on assignment, but —"

"Garret!" she cried. "Don't say such things!"

"But for whatever reason, perhaps out of cruelty, the gods seem to conspire against me, and each day the strength to rise and fight grows fainter in me. I'm just a tired old man now, broken in spirit and in body. But if I can help you somehow, even just to be here with you, it will be a far better end than otherwise awaits me. A worthy end, one I can bear proudly. Please, Helmi," he reached for her hand, "Please just trust me, and let me stay."

Rhys stared into her eyes as she searched his soul with hers. For some reason, it was easier to say the things that were racing through his mind to Helmi than even to Holywell. The horror on her face slowly faded and was replaced by compassion and pity. The corners of her mouth tugged down as she put her arms around him. "Oh, Garret," she said, sniffling, "I don't know what to say."

"Just let me stay here with you."

She pressed her head against his chest and hugged him close. "Thank you," she whispered.

He held her for a long moment, until he felt the tightness in his throat again.

"Now," he said, letting her go and clearing his throat. "I think that's quite enough emotion for one day." She gave a sad laugh. "Tell me, what is it exactly that we're dying for?"

Helmi wiped a tear from each cheek and composed herself, following his example. "A good cause, Garret," she answered. "Truly." She sniffed and turned around to face the crevasse.

He waited until her back was turned to wipe his own cheeks and winced as he felt the damage Blackhart's fists had done. "What did your goddess tell you?"

She took a deep breath and released it. "Many things."

"Does she know what the creature was?" he asked, carefully prodding his face. "Did she know it from the start?"

"No," Helmi answered sharply. "I told you, she would not have sent us into a trap. She knew Aedric had a part to play in this, but not any of the details."

Rhys still was not sure whether he believed that or not. "How is that possible? For the goddess of wisdom not to know such things?"

"I don't know what they taught you when you were coming up in the Order, but the gods are not omniscient. Othelia is not only the matron of wisdom, but also of prophesy. She sees things in her dreams, bits and pieces of truth. She uses her oracles to gather more information when necessary."

"Goddesses dream?" he asked, brow cocked.

She gave a rueful smirk. "I hope this knowledge is worth the price you've paid, Garret."

"So far, I find it all quite fascinating," he assured her, glad to see even a ghost of that smile. "We were right, though, weren't we? She was related to the sirens."

"Yes." Helmi skirted the grasping hands, examining them more closely. They moved erratically, striking out, slapping the stone, always grabbing. "That the Ilban remained unaffected by her song proves it."

Rhys grimaced and glanced down, away from the crevasse. "She was human once," he said, remembering the creature's heartbreaking song. "Or at least, that's what she would have had us believe. A girl who turned into a monster. But this," he gestured to the flames and the cavern around them. "By all that is holy, Helmi, what is this place?"

Helmi looked up at him and held his gaze, then shivered and said, "The gods don't know what this place is, Garret."

"What do you mean?"

She frowned. "Exactly that — the gods don't have any knowledge of this crevasse or what lies within."

"No," Rhys furrowed his brow. "The gods carved out the world with their hands, gave it life, created everything in it. How can something exist that they don't know about?"

She shook her head. "I don't know. When Othelia spoke to me, I could hear the voices of the other gods, as well. They don't have any idea what this is. It shouldn't be here." Her lip trembled. "And they're frightened, Garret. The *gods* are frightened."

Rhys stared into the unholy flames that emanated from the crevasse with newfound discomfort. "A portal to an abyss unknown even to the gods." He shook his head in disbelief. "You sent the others away because the gods don't want anyone knowing something exists that they themselves do not understand."

"Yes. Mortal-kind is not prepared for that."

"'You don't want to be fodder for the abyss'," Rhys mused, "that's what Blackhart said. Fodder for what, though, exactly?" The arms slapped the stone and scratched and clawed for purchase, trying in vain to pull themselves out.

"Othelia has had… other visions," Helmi said quietly. "I saw fragments, when she spoke to me." Her eyes darted up to meet his. "There are worse things in there than the Burnt Lady, Garret, or these infernal arms. That's why I'm willing to stay, to give my life. It would be utterly ruinous for these things to escape."

"I'm well convinced of that," Rhys answered firmly. He took a deep breath, preparing to ask the question to which he did not want an answer. "And… how are we to prevent anything else from escaping?"

"It requires a sacrifice," she said, refusing to meet his eyes.

"Of course it does." He sighed and massaged his brow.

"The Ilban's purpose here became clear almost too late; mine was arranged by Othelia from the beginning, it would seem, but hidden from me. Virgin's blood is one of the most powerful arcane catalysts," she said sadly. "I think my sacrifice was always intended, even if the specific purpose was not known."

"Gods-damned blood magic," Rhys spat. The thought made him ill. "That's not right, Helmi. I know we can't leave, but it's not right for her to use you like that."

"'Tools in the hands of the gods'," she recited slowly, "isn't that what you said?"

"Us. Not you. You're too clever for that, too good. You deserve a better goddess."

Helmi laughed in spite of herself. "Careful, Garret. We'll be seeing her shortly."

Rhys flexed his fist. It broke his heart to think that so eager and intelligent a young woman must die on the side of a lonely mountain with only a tired old soldier for company. Helmi was a brave soul; he had known it the moment he met her in the courtyard of the Eldric Citadel. And here she was, prepared to give her life on the gods' whim. He wanted to tell her how proud he was of her, how he admired her, how — in a way — he loved her.

Now was not the time to say any of that out loud, though. Perhaps in the next life.

"What will happen when you…?" He did not know how to ask it.

"To be honest," Helmi said slowly, "we don't know. Othelia gave me the knowledge of a very powerful ritual, using my blood, that will channel the might of the gods and hopefully seal this unholy chasm. If it works, the force of the deed will likely collapse the cavern, perhaps cause an avalanche down the Ymr."

Rhys straightened. "But Holywell and the children —"

"We'll give them time to get away," she assured him. "It's why I wanted you all to leave as quickly as possible."

"I see. Thank you." He nodded, jarred by the idea of the mountain collapsing on top of them, but at the same time relieved that Holywell, at least, might make it away from there. "What if the ritual doesn't work?"

"Someone else will have to try something, I suppose. But that is for the gods to worry about."

"They had better have a damned fine seat at the table for you," Rhys said, unable to keep the emotion out of his voice.

She smiled at that. "And you had better come and find me. You and all the rest of our little road family."

"We will," he promised. "And we'll all drink and eat and be merry while we wait for old Leo to finally show up."

A little tremor thrummed up from below them. Helmi's eyes widened.

"What is that?" Rhys asked as the earth shifted slightly under his feet. "Is that the 'worse things'?"

"I'm afraid it might be. I hope we haven't dallied too long." She went quickly and grabbed up the bloodied silver dagger from the spot Rhys had dropped it. "Do we have any water left? I need to wash Runa's blood from the blade, quickly." Rhys took off his heavy jacket and unslung the two skins he had over his shoulders. He brought them to her at the edge of the crevasse, just out of reach of the diabolical arms.

Helmi knelt and started wetting the blade, scrubbing at the caked blood with her fingernails.

"Are you starting this ritual now?" he asked. "What about Holywell and the others?"

"We can't delay any longer, Garret. Just pray they've gotten far enough away."

Rhys did not like that answer, but knew arguing would be pointless. "What can I do to help?"

"Allow me to concentrate." She said firmly. Then she closed her eyes and began whispering strange words under her breath.

Discontent with doing nothing and simply waiting to die, Rhys decided to use the opportunity to prepare his brothers for their unconventional burial. Taking Blackhart's sword from the scabbard at his belt, he wrapped the man's stiff fingers around it and arrayed it on his chest. Then he lay Fergus next to him in the same manner, and — as reverently as he could — made sure to place their severed heads close by as well.

After a little searching, Rhys found what remained of his own sword lying near the shadows. Only a short length of splintered blade remained, but he held onto it for sentiment's sake. Tucking it into his belt, he went back to his fallen companions and rested beside them on one knee for a moment. He recited a few old prayers for them, and for Felix, Grim, and Thorne, asking the gods to shepherd them home safely.

Once he was done, he returned to Helmi, who remained kneeling on the ground, whispering mystic and sacred words, which men the likes of Rhys were never meant to hear. He shivered as she slit her palm with the dagger and squeezed her fist so that it wept heavy scarlet drops. The sight of it rankled him, but he kept his silence. Helmi stood and started walking around the crevasse with her wounded hand held out, leaving an uninterrupted trail of blood behind her.

Another tremor shook the ground beneath them, so strong Rhys had to steady himself to avoid falling over. He took a step toward her, but she held her other hand up, signaling him not to approach. Gritting his teeth, he remained where he was, fidgeting absently with the broken sword at his side.

The familiar hilt felt odd in his left hand, but he imagined he could have grown used to it if he had had the chance. Perhaps he could have even still been a Knight, in spite of his destroyed shoulder. But what he had told Helmi was true — he did not think his life would not have lasted much longer anyhow, and he was at peace with his decision to stay.

When Helmi had completed her lap around the abyss, she knelt again at her starting point and resumed the prayer or chant or whatever it was. The ground shook again and pebbles came loose from crevices and cascaded down the walls. Another quake rattled Rhys's teeth again after only a few moments, and then they came with a frightening regularity, growing a little in intensity each time. They sounded almost like....

"Footsteps," Rhys muttered. He had witnessed a giant walk

through a forest once, but even its titanic stride had not made the earth shake so. Tightening his grip on the sword hilt, he took a step closer to Helmi.

As he was about to say something in warning, the most powerful tremor to that point ripped through the cavern, knocking Rhys to his knees. A loud crack split the air and he looked up to watch the flailing arms disappear back into the crevasse. Two remained but were sheared off at the shoulder as four massive fingers shot violently upward to replace them all, only the tips able to squeeze through the tight space.

"Helmi," Rhys called out to her over the roar of fracturing stone.

She ignored him, speaking the mystic words louder and faster. As he crawled over to her, the monstrous, uncannily human fingers strained against the edges of the crevasse, sending a shower of sand down from the ceiling. The ends of the dark abyss spread a little further, inching toward the ring of blood. He wondered what would happen if the thing was able to widen the gap enough to break the circle, and he did not need Helmi to tell him it would be utterly catastrophic.

Climbing shakily to his feet, he moved carefully toward the crevasse, his shattered sword in hand. Helmi's chanting continued and — as bold as he had ever been — Rhys stepped carefully over the circle and up to the invading fingers, lined the tip of his blade up under the edge of a gigantic fingernail, and threw all his weight down on the hilt. It sunk deep enough to elicit an angry, sonorous cry from below and the hand jerked back down, taking his sword with it.

Rhys threw himself back, barely avoiding a fall into the pit himself. He looked over to Helmi and saw her drawing the blade across her other palm. Her eyes opened and found his, and she gave him a little nod. Going on all fours, Rhys started toward her, only to be bowled over as the fingers punched back through the crevasse, up to the second knuckle, and folded down, nearly crushing him. His sword still jutted from under the behemoth's nail.

Unwilling to die without his blade in hand, Rhys climbed to

his feet, gritted his teeth against the pain, and used both hands to rip it free. Sword of the Seraphin in hand, he crossed over the blood ring and sat down heavily next to Helmi. He looked at her, a little out of breath. She held her bleeding palm aloft, ready for the end. Placing the hilt in his injured hand, he secured it tight against his chest, and held out his good hand to Helmi. She took it.

Rhys took a deep breath and brought her hand to his bloodied lips. Helmi's eyes held a profound sadness as she met the sergeant's tired gaze and let her hand fall. The ensorcelled blood on her palm struck the ring around the crevasse and exploded.

The force of it tore them apart from each other. Rhys was thrown against the wall and fell in a heap to the floor. He was able to look up after a moment and watch as the circle — now a fiery blue ring — shrunk, forcing the crevasse closed. He cast desperately about, trying to find where Helmi had landed, and in the bright light, he spotted her amidst the rubble. As the cavern trembled and came apart, he scrambled over to her and pulled her back, away from the abyss and toward the wall. Helmi's flaming circle continued to shrink, and the titanic hand was unable to pull its fingers out in time; they were crushed and severed as the ground closed up as though it had never been split.

Darkness fell. The mountain shuddered again and a large rock crashed down just a yard or so away from them, then another. Just as Helmi had said, the cavern was collapsing. She did not move in his arms. He called out her name, but he could not even hear his own voice over the groaning of the Ymr.

Cursing Othelia for asking so much from such a selfless young woman, he held her close and leaned back against the slope of the wall. As he waited for the ceiling to come down, he realized his broken blade was still clutched tight in his hand, and for that he was thankful.

The rocks rained down around them and Rhys closed his eyes. He tried desperately to call up his most important memories: his family, his brothers in the Order, the battles he had fought, the people he had helped. Nothing came, though, and he started to panic. Taking a deep breath, he decided if he could not count on memories to ease his passing, then he might as well face it head on, so he opened his eyes, even though there was nothing to see.

The cavern roared around him as stones fell and shattered. Finally, one memory fought its way through the pain, the dread, and the darkness: their little road-family, sitting around the campfire in a green valley. Grim made grand gestures as he told them all a story, and the twins handed out the evening's supper. He saw Helmi sitting on the ground and laughing, while Thorne ran a hand through his blond hair, and Blackhart sat with folded arms and his typical dour expression.

But it could not have been a memory, because others were there as well: Fielding and countless other men he had not seen in years, friends long ago fallen in the service of the gods. They were joyful and at peace after a hard life. Rhys did not know if it was a vision of what was soon to come for him, but he smiled, and he hoped.

RAGE

H olywell hugged the little girl close as he flew down the slope, navigating the icy rocks with a practiced step. Another distant tremor, the largest yet, traveled up his boots and momentarily blurred his vision. Ahead of him, Aedric plodded through the shallow, crusty snow, Joren still cradled in his arms. Frozen breaths plumed from his open mouth. If he felt the mountain trembling, he gave no sign of it, continuing his tireless march down the rocky slope undaunted.

Holywell tried not to wonder what was happening back in the cavern. Leaving Rhys there was perhaps the hardest thing he had ever done, and there was no time yet to mourn. Instead, he focused on keeping Agata pressed against him so that the rough travel was not too jarring on her poor, exhausted frame. She squirmed and whimpered, but he could not risk stopping to comfort her.

A deafening crack cut through the wind and Holywell whirled around to look back. The precipice in front of the cave loomed high above to the west, quivering as the sound echoed down toward the valley, rolling like thunder. He watched as the cliff face came apart from the mountain and slid away in a sheet of snow and ice and rock.

They had followed their earlier route, taking the gentler eastern slope, and the little avalanche slid past them down the steeper face of the Ymr. Huge clouds of snow billowed in its wake, rising up high enough to blot out the sun. Heart in his throat, Holywell realized that if anything broke off further up the mountain, they could very well be in its path.

He let out a sharp whistle and bolted down to Aedric. The Ilban was in a trance, paying no heed to anything around him, his sole focus on making it down to the village. Holywell finally caught up and passed him, turning around to get the man's attention. He waved his hand and Aedric reluctantly came to a halt.

"What?" he barked, adjusting his hold on Joren.

Holywell pointed back toward the collapsed precipice and did his best to mime an avalanche. Then he pointed east.

Aedric seemed to understand, but shook his head. "That's further from the village, I've no time for that." The boy was limp and terrifyingly pale in his arms. Tiny puffs of mist still came from his nostrils, but too infrequently. The Ilban shoved past him and continued down toward the valley. Frustrated, but not knowing how to convince him of the danger, Holywell followed, throwing an apprehensive look back over his shoulder at the mountain.

Their path naturally wound further east along the slope, just enough to give him some peace of mind, but even as they crossed the snow line, Holywell fancied he could hear the deep knocking of shifting ice high above.

Aedric pushed the pace, and they made the descent faster than Holywell and Rhys had previously. The lower they went, the warmer it became, until sweat beaded on his forehead and dripped occasionally into his eyes. By the time the sun had passed its zenith, they were within sight of the shepherd's hall. Holywell was spry for his age, but even so, the multiple journeys up and down the mountain were starting to wear on him. There was fire in his knees and even the tiny child on his shoulder was becoming a heavy burden. A little longer, though, over easier terrain, and they could be at the village.

Aedric followed the little stream down and around, stopping briefly near the hall. He lowered Joren onto the soft grasses on the bank, cupped his hands, and tried to get the boy to drink. Holywell stooped and drank as well, having given Agata the last of his waterskin earlier. As he dipped the neck into the stream to refill it, Aedric muttered, "Oh no...."

The Knight looked over at him, fearing the boy had finally passed, but found the Ilban staring past him, back toward the mountain. Holywell turned to look and did not understand at first what he was seeing. It looked like the mountain was bending over toward them, but after a heartbeat, he realized what had actually happened: the explosion that had shattered the precipice had also weakened the entire peak and half of it was now plummeting down in a plume of snow and a hail of stones. It fell silently for a long moment before the thunder of its fracturing crashed down upon them, a trumpeting harbinger of disaster.

"Run!" the Ilban bellowed, lifting Joren and bounding away in the same motion. The waterskin forgotten, Holywell chased after him, holding Agata close as Aedric headed for the hall, perhaps instinctively.

Holywell spun around at the door, trying to see the path the majority of the debris would take. In an instant, he knew a dismal truth: they could not outrun it, no matter which way they went. The titanic chunk of mountain that slowly tumbled down the slope looked to Holywell like it would miss them, but even so, the force of the accompanying avalanche would likely tear the shepherd's hall apart. Still, they had little choice.

He ducked into the dark hall and followed Aedric past the corpse of the shepherd's wife and into the far corner. They set the children down and together flipped the table and dragged it over to set a barrier. The roar grew steadily louder as Holywell gathered the scattered fleeces as fast as he could and threw them to Aedric, who piled them up behind the table as a cushion against the impending impact. The two men hunkered down and threw some fleeces over themselves for good measure, then bent to shield the children with their bodies and braced for the destruction.

Prayers from his youth racing through his mind, every tired muscle in Holywell's body tensed as the cacophony of rent earth built until it was almost a silence. He could see from beneath the fleeces as light suddenly flooded the hall. Something hit him in the back and he was pressed forward by a great weight and pinned, nearly crushing Agata beneath him, as the light disappeared again. He pushed back as hard as he could to protect the girl and the strain in his back nearly broke him.

The ground shook violently underfoot and Holywell thought back to what Helmi had said: the gods would not let her leave because she already knew too much. Perhaps the Pantheon had decided he and Aedric knew too much as well.

After what seemed like a very long time, the roar finally diminished until all that was left was the ringing in his ears. More light spilled over them as Aedric threw off his fleece, revealing the heavy snow pressing against them. He used his arms to shovel away enough of it so that he could lift Joren out and lay him down on top of the drift. After taking Agata next, he helped Holywell pull himself from under the massive weight. Agata's cries slowly came into hearing.

Once free, Holywell uncurled himself, and pain shot through his spine. Powdery snow hung in the air and nipped his skin. As it cleared, he saw that their corner was all that remained of the shepherd's hall. The roof and most of the walls had been ripped away and a great fir tree was impaled like an arrow in the spot where the fire pit had been.

They clambered onto the snow drift and took the children back up. Holywell absently patted the girl's back in an effort to calm her as he surveyed the cataclysmic scene. Boulders large and small littered the plateau on which the hall had stood; the forest they had searched days prior for Pedr was all but gone, flattened or uprooted by the avalanche; all was covered in snow.

Aedric immediately started on again, stepping around the ruined wall, sinking knee-deep with each step. Holywell made after him. Reaching the lip of the little plateau, they looked down into the valley, where the devastation was utterly complete. The monstrous slab of mountaintop had carved a deep scar in the land as it raked down the slope, finally coming to a halt in the lowest part of the valley. The snow and rockfall and abducted trees filled the space all around it, drowning the crops and pastures in their tumult. The village had been annihilated, crushed beneath the

Ymr's fractured peak, and there was no sign of life anywhere to be seen.

"No," the Ilban groaned. Holywell came up beside him. "It's gone. They destroyed the whole damned valley." He turned to Holywell. "Are there any other villages nearby, do you know? We have to help him, what can I do?" His voice trembled in desperation and exhaustion.

Holywell did know of a few relatively close villages, but they were still leagues away, and he did not need a hospitaler's training to see that Joren would not make it half the distance. He simply shook his head.

"Ach!" the Ilban cried, falling to his knees in the deep snow. His arms shook as the truth finally struck him: Joren was going to die. "Othelia," he growled, his face red with fury. "Othelia, you owe me." Holywell took a step back from him. "You didn't fulfill our bargain. You owe me a debt. One boy's life, it's all I ask." He fell silent, perhaps awaiting a response, but none came. "Do you hear me?" he roared, and his voice echoed out over the desolate valley.

Joren shuddered in his arms. The Ilban laid him gently in the snow and took his hand. The boy's breath came quicker and stronger. His chest heaved, the gruesome wounds gaping, and his lips parted, sucking in air. His eyes fluttered open and found Aedric's; he stared emptily at the Ilban before taking another gasping breath.

"Joren," Aedric said gently, "you're alright, lad." The boy's breath came faster, but more shallow. Finally, his head fell back and the air hissed out of his parted lips as the life slipped out of him. "Joren." He gave the boy a gentle shake; he did not move.

"No!" the Ilban cried, understanding. "Oh, no. No, no, no!" He cast his eyes up to the clouds floating serene in the summer sky. "Othelia!" he shouted again, desperate; still, only his echoes answered him.

Aedric bellowed wordlessly, his voice ragged, realizing there would be no answer from the gods. Taking Joren back in his arms, he slumped forward as his rage faded to sorrow. "Not again," he sobbed, holding the broken boy close. His shoulders quaked as he wept unashamed, the tears rolling down his ruddy cheeks into his beard. He clasped the medallion at his neck tight in one hand as the grief racked him.

Holywell felt a tear leave a cold trail down his own cheek. Agata began to whimper, too, and he hugged her close, pulling the little fleece tighter around her. Remembering what Helmi had said about Aedric's family, he could only wonder at the battle raging in the man's heart. After a moment, Holywell took the girl back toward what remained of the hall, allowing the Ilban the time he needed to mourn.

The fire crackled inside the big ring it had melted in the snow. Dawn was only a few hours off, but Holywell remained wide awake. Agata dozed in a bundle of fleeces as the Ilban prepared to place her brother on the pyre. He had spent all night digging wood out of the snow or hacking it from ruined trees, then agonizing over creating a tiny ember and finally lighting the fire. Holywell had offered him food from Grim's pack, but he had refused it each time, keeping his silence. The man had, however, finally accepted a fleece to drape over his bare, bloody shoulders.

Holywell had also helped him dig out the children's mother from under the snow. The cold had stifled the smell of decay, but as she lay in the open air, it was starting to return. Holywell was glad they could put them to rest in the manner their culture prescribed. He assumed the shepherd and his daughter remained in the cavern with Holywell's own brothers, a fate any proud Fjalr would abhor, but he trusted the Slain would see to their souls all the same. Pedr, too, though the gods only knew what had become of him; Holywell did not want even to imagine.

Finally, Aedric lifted the shepherd's wife and placed her on the pyre, heedless of the flames that licked hungrily at the offering. He laid Joren beside her and murmured something before coming to sit heavily on a recovered bench next to Holywell. Together they stared into the fire for a long time, until the bodies were shriveled and dry and black.

"The sergeant and Helmi," Aedric said slowly. "They stayed behind, didn't they? To take care of that... whatever it was, the pit?" Holywell nodded and the Ilban sighed. "I shouldn't have spoken so harshly to her. It wasn't her fault." The hand on his knee curled into a fist. "Was it your gods that brought the mountain down on us?"

Holywell had wondered the same and was disturbed that he could not deny the possibility. He shook his head and shrugged.

"They killed Joren twice," Aedric muttered darkly. "Othelia wouldn't help him, and then they destroyed his grandfather's village."

Another long pause followed, and then he asked, "Will you take the lass back to Carthannas with you?"

Holywell nodded again.

"That's good. The Sisters will take good care of her." He sounded hopeful rather than confident, but he was right. The Sisters of the Order had raised Holywell after his rescue, and he knew them to be kind, though scrupulous. Agata would be safe there.

"I'm sorry about the others," Aedric said after a while. "They were good men, all of them." Holywell nodded, struggling to keep his own grief locked away for the present. "The Dalbragh have a belief," he continued, eyes lost in the flames, "that conflict comes as the spirit of War moves between neighbors and nations, sowing hostility and bloodshed.

"And there's a story told about a man who met the War spirit itself, once. War said to the man, 'Come and fight, and earn a soldier's wages'. 'How much does warfare earn a man?' he asked. And the answer came, 'So much you could hardly carry it'. So the man took up the sword and went off to battle. When all was said and done, he came back and sought out War for his recompense, but it had already moved on to the next land. The man was left with naught but rage and anguish, and it was then that he realized War was right: a soldier's wages truly are too much to carry.

"It's all we get for our efforts, in the end, isn't it? When the war is over and we're left with that dreadful quiet. The rage... it seems never to end. Does it for you, Brother?" The Ilban looked at him with hollow eyes.

Holywell slowly shook his head. His own experiences were different than this man's, but he understood what the Ilban meant all too well.

"I thought not. And now we've even more reason to mourn." He clutched his pendant tight.

The moon came out from behind the clouds and washed the snowy expanse in silver swaths. Holywell looked up at the crippled peak of the Ymr and his thoughts went to Rhys, Helmi, and all the others. Then he remembered Othelia's message to Aedric. In the midst of all the carnage, at least the Ilban should have a bit of peace if he could.

Laying a hand on Aedric's shoulder, he tried to think of a way to explain without the man knowing his signs. He could not, but he spied one of Helmi's massive tomes peeking from under the snow, so he rose and retrieved it. The pages were mostly soaked through, but in the center, he found a few that were dry, so he ripped them from their binding. Taking up a bit of charred wood from the fire pit, he started scribbling down the message. He blew off the excess charcoal and judged it legible enough, so he handed it to Aedric.

The Ilban took it with a weary expression and looked it over dispassionately. "I'm sorry, Brother — I cannot read."

Holywell sighed, frustrated. He could think of no other way to convey Helmi's message. Instead, he took the page back and folded it carefully to preserve the hasty writing. Then he pressed it to Aedric's chest, stressing its importance.

The Ilban understood that, at least. "Alright, I'll keep it until I find someone who can read it for me." Holywell nodded emphatically and Aedric tucked the folded paper under his belt, opposite the heavy hammer.

They resumed their silence after that, sitting and staring at the fire, each wrestling with his own thoughts until the sky had lightened and the blazing tip of the sun climbed over the horizon.

Aedric stood abruptly and cleared his throat. "I suppose it's time to move on, then," he said, and held out his hand. Holywell took it. "Safe travels, Brother Holywell. Perhaps we'll cross paths again someday."

Without another word, the Ilban leaned over and rested his hand on Agata's back for a moment, then rose and took up his big shield from where it jutted out of the snow. He nodded once more at Holywell and cast a long look at the pyre before climbing up the large drift and making east toward the rising sun.

Holywell turned back to the dying fire and bowed his head to recite prayers of safe carriage for the souls of the fallen. Once he was finished, he wept quietly for a bit as Agata rested, allowing the sorrow to take its course as the terrible absence of his brothers consumed him. After a time, he calmed. Then he lifted himself to his feet, dried his eyes, and stretched his weary form. If nothing else, he would be glad to be done climbing mountains for a while.

Finally, he hoisted Agata up and secured her tiny fleece jacket around her. Turning to look one last time at the Ymr, its fresh scar glaring in the hazy light of dawn, he lifted his arm in a final salute to his brothers forever entombed in that evil cavern. Then, Agata Olendottir on his hip, Holywell tossed the paltry food sack and a few waterskins over his shoulder and started on the long walk back home to Carthannas.

The End

AUTHOR'S NOTE

I want to offer you my heartfelt thanks for reading this book. *The Rage That Follows* is a prelude: an introduction to much greater things to come. Of course, for me personally, it's also much more than that. It's the expression of a lifetime of lessons hard-learned, a memory of friends lost, and a tribute to those who have given far more than I ever could. It is the deepest and most humbling honor for me to be able to share this story with you. I hope you enjoyed it.